Alvin Torry, William Hosmer

Autobiography of Rev. Alvin Torry

First Missionary to the Six Nations and the Northwestern Tribes....

Alvin Torry, William Hosmer

Autobiography of Rev. Alvin Torry
First Missionary to the Six Nations and the Northwestern Tribes....

ISBN/EAN: 9783337123505

Printed in Europe, USA, Canada, Australia, Japan

Cover: Foto ©Raphael Reischuk / pixelio.de

More available books at **www.hansebooks.com**

AUTOBIOGRAPHY

OF

REV. ALVIN TORRY,

FIRST MISSIONARY

TO

THE SIX NATIONS AND THE NORTHWESTERN TRIBES
OF BRITISH NORTH AMERICA.

EDITED BY REV. WM. HOSMER.

AUBURN ;
WILLIAM J. MOSES.
1861.

INTRODUCTORY NOTE.

The reader of the following pages will be struck with the clearness and vigor which pervade them. The writer leaves nothing obscure, expresses nothing feebly, and in short gives us a well-sustained, interesting narrative throughout. We have not elsewhere met with so connected and intelligible an account of Methodist Missions among the Aborigines of Canada. In the rapid work here sketched, the careful observer will see much bearing a very close resemblance to the recorded successes of the earliest christian preachers — the seventy disciples and the twelve apostles. Nor were these effects confined to mission fields. The same, or nearly the same, proofs of our author's call to the ministry, appeared on every circuit which he travelled.

A correspondence in instruments, as well as in results, is also to to be noticed. The apostles went not from the schools, but from their secular pursuits, to the ministry, and so did the subject of this work. In this, however, his case was not different from that of the great body of our early preachers. Those who love to trace the onward march of Christ's kingdom, will greet this volume with a cordial welcome; they will see at a glance that it reveals, with artless simplicity, the only way in which true religion has been, or can be propagated in the earth.

PREFACE.

For several years my numerous friends have been urging me to write out the particulars of my labors among the "Six Nations," and north-western tribes of Indians in Canada, together with other incidents of my itinerant life. Inasmuch as I was the first christian missionary sent among the tribes, and as I saw the commencement of that great work of God now going on under the supervision of the Wesleyan Canadian Methodists, I have endeavored to notice the special providences of God which led me into the work; and of his wonder-working power in saving the lost and wandering from ruin and eternal death, through the Gospel of his Son.

I have borrowed somewhat largely from different sources, all, however, intimately connected with my subject, and calculated to make this work interesting and profitable to the reader. If what I here present shall have a tendency to wake up a deeper concern in the hearts of our ministry and membership, for the salvation of the millions of heathen now groping in pagan darkness, and shall cause a more earnest seeking for that apostolic faith and power necessary for success in the great enterprise, I shall consider my labor not in vain.

THE AUTHOR.

CONTENTS.

CHAPTER I.

CHAPTER II.

CHAPTER III.

CHAPTER IV.

CHAPTER V.

CHAPTER VI.

CHAPTER VII.

CHAPTER VIII.

CHAPTER IX.

CHAPTER X.

CHAPTER XI.

CHAPTER XII.

CHAPTER XIII.

CHAPTER XIV.

CHAPTER XV.

CHAPTER XVI.

CHAPTER XVII.

CHAPTER XVIII.

CHAPTER I.

I was born July 27, 1797, in the town of Stafford, county of Tolland, State of Connecticut.

My parents were both natives of this State. They both became members of the Presbyterian Church in early life. As yet, Methodism had no existence in that part of the State, but no sooner did one of the Methodist itinerants visit the town of my father's residence, and publish an appointment for preaching, than he became one of his first hearers ; and so well pleased was he with this first sermon, that he invited him to preach at his own house in another part of the town. The minister accepted the invitation, and this was the beginning of Methodism in old Stafford, Conn.

A reformation soon followed ; a society was organized ; my parents became members, and three of my mother's brothers (of the Dimmick family) became ministers. My parents became members about the time I was born. They emigrated to New York State in the year 1801, and settled on the Butternut Creek, Otsego Co. Here the country was new ; no Methodists, nor Methodist preaching near.

This same year the Tioga circuit embraced Unadilla. The preachers were Gideon C. Knowlton and Moses Morgan. These heralds of the cross soon planted Methodism along the Unadilla River, which was only four miles from my father's residence. They established preaching at his house ; a society was organized, and a glorious reformation followed. The Chenango circuit was formed soon after, embracing both the town of Unadilla and the Butternuts. John P. Newman, David Dunham, Matthew VanHousen, John Husselkus, Benoni Harris, Benj. Bidlack, Wm. Heyer, Sylvester Hill, Ebenezer White,* and Chas. Giles, were some of the itinerants who visited and preached

"*Ebenezer White—O, that man of God! Truly his memory is blessed—he was my spiritual father. I must be allowed here to speak the language of one who knew him well, and who wrote his obituary notice.

"The term, 'Father White' was used—though only forty-three years of age when he died—out of deep reverence for his piety and usefulness ; and it may be said of him, as was said of Job of old times, 'When the ear heard him,' whether in social converse or in the public assembly, it blessed him ; and 'when the eye saw him,' in all at my father's house, and under whose ministry I received my first religious impressions.

All these have gone to their final reward in heaven, excepting the last mentioned. He still lingers upon our earthly shores ; but, doubtless, will soon be released, to join that holy band of martyrs who worship around the throne of God in heaven.

When I was seven or eight years old, I remember

---

the relations he sustained to his fellow beings, it bore witness he was truly a man of God.

"He had, naturally, a rohust constitution, but in consequenee of a fractured limb, his future life was marked with afflictions. This stroke of Divine providence, which fell upon him while questioning his call to travel and preaeh the Gospel, he received as an admonition from heaven.

"His daily sufferings taught him the bitter consequences of disobedience, and proved a spur to him in his religious course. He was devoted to the work of the Lord; he denied himself; he left all; even the ties of affection toward his dear family, though strong, did not draw him from the duties of his charge. He made it the business of his life to point sinners to the eross, and to build up the Church of Christ, in which his soul delighted, in holiness and truth. He counted not his own life dear, so that he might please God, who called him to the ministry, and be instrumental in doing good to his fellow men. He labored—travelling through heat and cold—when his infirmities indicated dissolution near. Many, in his condition, would have pleaded exemption from such laborious duties, but his ardent soul, burning with an immortal flame, could not rest; and when he was not able to preach standing upon his *feet*, he stood upon his *knees*, and thus, in that humble posture, declared the whole counsel of God. In his ministerial character, he was deservedly esteemed as a father and a pattern. He was plain, artless, and solemn, in his style and address. He never studied to ring the ear with pleasant sounds, or dazzle the eye with shining things. His aim was at the heart, and the heart he won. Conscience seldom slept where he preached. He loved the souls of men, and would not be denied. He went deep, and swam far being powerfully operated upon in a great meeting at my father's house. A pentecostal shower fell upon the people. All seemed to be overwhelmed with the power and love of God ; and I shared with the rest, and was happy. From this time until I was soundly converted to God, which occurred when about seventeen, I was inclined to read my Bible—for as soon as

in the Gospel sea. From his golden treasures, through the vehicle of his heart, he brought forth things new and old. He was a faithful shepherd; he never carried sand instead of salt to the flock, nor fed them with flowers instead of fruit; but he fed them after the great Shepherd's example, *with the words of eternal life.*

"He was not only a preacher in the pulpit, but out of it; he was instant in season and out of season, reproving and exhorting. One essential trait in his ministerial character, and which distinguished him as eminently useful, was his unwearied labors in catechising and instructing children. His toil was crowned with marvellous success, and his happy soul has often been transported by hearing children from eight years and upward, praising God in the temple, and singing hosannas to his name.

"He was a lover of order in the Church, and under his administration of discipline, which was strict and mild, the Church always flourished like a garden of lilies.

"Thus was our beloved brother White eminent as a minister, yet not less so as a Christian. He ascended high in the kingdom of grace —possessed great faith, humility, zeal, and love; and in the elevation of his soul in spiritual things, he learned to count all things below as dross.

"He was a good counsellor, a consoling friend, prudent in judgment, reserved in conversation, discreet in behavior, and patient in suffering. He was a great blessing, not only to his family but also to the Church of Christ. He entered the itinerant ranks in 1802. He filled eleven stations in the old Genesee Conference. He was attacked by the prevailing epidemic, which in about three days terminated his useful life, in the town of Hartwick, Otsego Co., N. Y. About half an hour before he died, he raised the window of his room to reprove some children who were playing in the street, it being the Sabbath day. Soon after, he laid down upon his bed, and calmly expired."

I became old enough to read, one was given me ; and I remember how much better I understood it after reading it through by course, than when reading it promiscuously ; and I believe I shall bless God to all eternity, that I was favored with religious training in the Methodist Episcopal Church fifty years ago ; and that I learned in the Methodist school, to distinguish between the power of religion and its form.

From the time I received my first religious impressions, which was at the meeting at my father's house, of which I have spoken, until I became a member of the M. E. Church, at sixteen, my love for Christians, and a relish for the means of grace increased, until I received the evidence that the Lord accepted of me as his adopted son. This was about six months after I joined the Church on trial. When brought into the full light and liberty of the Gospel of Christ, I soon found I was in my greatest element when engaged in the Lord's work of persuading men to be Christians, and in preparing myself to be useful in the Church and to the world.

I had strong impressions of mind, from the time I began to give my heart to God, that I must preach ; but I kept these impressions to myself until interrogated by Rev. Loring Grant, preacher in charge of the Lebanon circuit on which I resided.

I had been called upon to pray and exhort in the public assemblies, and the Quarterly Conference had voted me a license to exhort, without my asking for it. I was conscious I should have to preach, but how I could ever start out as a travelling preacher, under my embarrassed circumstances, was something I could not then know. My father had died suddenly, and through the dishonesty of one he had confided in as an old friend, had lost all his property. My mother, with four children who were too young to support themselves, was thus left to the care of myself and a younger brother. But he being from home, at school, during the winter, and working through the summer, the care of the family devolved upon me, until Br. Loring Grant, preacher in charge of the circuit on which I lived, called upon me on his way from Conference, and said, "Br. Alvin, are you ready to mount your horse and enter the itinerant field?" I said to him, "I *have* no horse." "Well," said he, "*I* have a horse, saddle, bridle, and portmanteau, which I will let you have, and you can pay me when you get able."

I laid the matter before my mother; she said she did not know how she could keep the children together, and get along without me; "but," said she, "I must not oppose nor discourage you in what seems to be your duty to God and to the Church. The Lord will provide.   Go, and my prayers shall ascend to heaven for your success."

Accordingly, having made every necessary preparation for leaving, I bade farewell to my weeping mother, sisters, and youngest brother—who was but four years of age—mounted my horse, and set my face for the west.   After getting fairly off, and alone on my horse, I gave vent to my feelings in tears.   I lifted up my heart in prayer to Him who I believed had called me to the work of the ministry, that he would help and bless me, and give me favor in the sight of the people with whom I was to labor.   After travelling sixty miles, I reached Cortlandville, where the first quarterly meeting was held for Cayuga circuit. I was warmly received by brother and sister Grant ; and George Harmon, the presiding elder for Cayuga district, greeted me with a fatherly tenderness.   I was directed to take the appointments of the circuit, and go to work as the junior preacher.   I had only received an exhorter's license, and, of course, the official board of the circuit, after some months trial, were to determine whether I was competent to be a travelling preacher or not.

None but God knew what trials and sore conflicts I had with the powers of darkness during my first year's labor ; but the Lord gave me favor in the sight of the people. Brother and sister Grant were like a tender father and mother to me during the whole year; and Br. Kimberlin, who was supernumerary on the circuit, also treated me with great kindness, and encouraged me to go on in the great work I had entered upon. During this Conference year, the Lord gave me the most satisfactory evidence that I was doing the work he had made me for. On one public occasion, while I was preaching, the power of God fell upon the people, and before we closed our exercises, several were powerfully converted to God. O, what sweet and heavenly seasons I enjoyed with the good people of old Cayuga circuit! The remembrance of those days revives me now in my declining years, amidst suffering and poverty. I like to survey those retreats in groves and barns, where the Lord revealed himself to me gloriously. I remained on the circuit until Br. Grant returned from the Conference, which held its session at Elizabethtown, U. C., where I was admitted on trial, and appointed to Scipio circuit, which lay directly north of the one I was now leaving.

At this time, Genesee Conference included all the territory now embraced in the Genesee, East Genesee, Oneida, Black River and Wyoming Conferences, and Upper and Lower Canada.

During the year, I had visited my mother, and

found that the Lord had, indeed, been providing for her, and in a way I had not expected. My brother, Daniel, with my oldest sister, Hannah, had embraced religion, and united with the M. E. Church ; so she now had three of the five that were with her, who could unite with her around the family altar in prayer and praise to God. Wealthy, one younger than the last mentioned, had experienced religion at a camp-meeting which I attended. When she emerged into the light and life of the Son of God, her bodily strength gave way, and she had no use of any of her bodily powers excepting her voice ; with that she cried, "Glory, glory, glory," for three hours, while the multitude gathered around, gazing upon her, for her face shone like the face of an angel. She was, at this time, but ten years old, and has long since taken her place by the side of her sainted mother, fast by the throne of God in heaven.

During this Conference year, I had an impression of mind that I must visit a certain village of people from house to house, and talk and pray with them. I followed out the impression, and when about half through my work, visiting and praying with the people, a gentleman of the village said to me, "will you preach to us this evening ?" I said, "yes, if you have a house the people can be convened in." He said he would open their new school-house.   He did so, and when evening came, the people came rallying to the place, to see who the crazy fellow was who had been crying, "Repent and believe on the Lord Jesus Christ, and be saved."   I gave out my text, "Escape for thy life ; tarry not in all the plain ; escape to the mountain, lest thou be consumed."   The word took effect ; salvation came to the people ; and in a few months a good society was raised up, which has remained to this day.   The above mentioned village is Dryden, Cortland county.

This year (1817) I found I was to be associated with Br. Zenas Jones for my colleague.   He was a good man, and a spiritual preacher.   After having an interview with him, and receiving a plan of the circuit, I found it was as large as the one I had just left.   It embraced Scipio, Cayuga, Mentz, Elbridge, Jordan, Manlius,. Onondaga, Owasco, Otisco, Auburn, Skaneateles and Spafford.

Through all these towns we travelled, and preached in every neighborhood and village where the people would give attention.   It was a four weeks' circuit, and all we could do in the preaching line, was to give each congregation one sermon once in two weeks ; and this required us to preach almost every day in the week, twice or thrice on the Sabbath, and long rides between. Thus we had plenty of work in preaching, visiting and praying with the people, and in attending to revival meetings, which were very common in those days of Methodism.

In the town of Spafford, we had several week-day appointments in private houses, school-houses and barns. At one of these appointments, in a barn, on what was called Spafford Side-Hill, was a small congregation, for as yet we had not got the attention of the people turned much to the great interest of the soul.

I had preached to them but two or three times in my turn round the circuit, before the Lord favored us with a glorious revival. It commenced one afternoon while I was trying to preach to the people assembled in the barn. I gave out my text, and when about half through with my discourse, there appeared at the door a young woman of some seventeen years. As she was entering the barn, to take her seat with the people who were now listening to the word preached, she stopped suddenly and began to weep. The word of truth had taken fast hold of her heart, and in a moment or two, while she was yet standing in the door, the Lord converted her soul. She shouted aloud, and passed from the south door, through the congregation, to the north door, to lay hold of her father, who was sitting near the door. When he saw her coming towards him with a quick step, and shouting "glory," his first thoughts were to run, for he made no profession of religion, but before he had time to leave his seat she had fast hold of him, and was exhorting him to give his heart to Christ.

This was like the shock of an earthquake among the people, and the power of God was manifested to save lost and perishing sinners.

The father and mother of this young woman, and several of her brothers and sisters, were converted to God; and this was the beginning of Methodism in Spafford.

Another glorious revival began in the town of Marcellus, in the vicinity of David Holmes'. David Holmes was a local preacher in our Church; his wife was a woman of a powerful mind, and a devoted Christian. They have given to the Methodist Church two or three strong and able ministers of the New Testament. From this revival was raised up one of the most noble bands of young men and women that I have ever known; and who can tell the amount of good, that, during the past forty years, has grown out of this revival! When I beat up for volunteers at the commencement of the reformation in brother Holmes' barn, brother Stephen Cobb was the first to give in his name for membership. He has not only been a successful minister for many years, but two of his sons are able and successful itinerants in our Church.

During this year I was invited to preach at Skaneateles village. I was obliged to preach on a week-day evening. The word of truth took effect, and we soon organized a society. This, on the whole, was a good year. I labored in harmony with my colleague to the close of the Conference year. I attended the Conference, which held its session on the banks of Cayuga Lake. At the close of this Conference, I was read off for Long Point circuit, U. C. After receiving my appointment, I visited my mother, divided my hundred with her, and prepared for my journey to the then far off regions of the dominions of George the Third.

CHAPTER II.

The war of 1812 had spread desolation through the provinces, but the English, in order to repair the damages done the inhabitants, and to induce immigration, offered one hundred acres of land to every settler who would clear a small place, build a log house, and live in it. These inducements brought thousands from the European kingdoms, and new townships were filled up with families from England, Ireland, Scotland, Wales, and the United States.

Hundreds, throughout the length and breadth of these newly settled towns, were without the Gospel and holy sacraments, except when the Methodist itinerants occasionally visited them.

At this time, there were only two Presiding Elders in the Canadas, and they took the supervision of the whole work. They were William Case and Henry Ryan, and to them constant applications were made, from the people of the new settlements, for preachers. The fields were all whitening to the harvest. The Genesee Conference was under obligations to supply these perishing thousands with the Word of Life, by sending them the men of their own body who were prepared to make sacrifices, endure hardships and suffering for Christ's sake, and the salvation of souls, and who counted not their own lives dear, if they could but please God and win souls to Christ. This year, 1818, Br's Case and Ryan attended the Conference above named, and requested the Presiding Bishop to select from the Conference, a troop of young men for the Canadas.

It was done, and as soon as the Conference closed its session, they mounted their horses and started. I was among the number whose fields of labor were assigned them in the British provinces. Our equipage for the battle field, was a port-manteau and valise ; in them we stowed our wearing apparel, Bible, hymn-book, and what other books we were able to get ; and but a few dollars in our pockets. Our outward dress and appearance, when mounted, gave us the name of "The Methodist Cavalry."

A single man's salary, in those days, was from seventy to a hundred dollars, if he could get it from the people among whom he labored. With this he had to equip himself with a horse, saddle, bridle, port-manteau, valise, and a small library of books.

After travelling one hundred miles, our company was reinforced by the addition of *one* to our number, Br. Z. Paddock, now of Wyoming Conference, and who has since become D. D. He was on his way to his field of labor, assigned him by the Bishop. His pleasant and enlivening conversation, mingled with a deep, devotional spirit, added greatly to our social and religious enjoyment, and cheered us on our march to our distant fields of labor. We were privileged with his company only three days, as he had then reached his destination, on the east side of the Niagara river. We parted in tears, wishing and praying for each other's success in cultivating Immanuel's land, and in bringing souls to Christ.

Often, while far away among strangers, did my mind revert to those pleasant hours which were passed with such congenial spirits ; and often while toiling and laboring in the dominions of King George, did memory revert to those pleasant communings, and thus cheer me on my way.

We now pursued our journey till we reached the

waters of Niagara, having travelled already two hundred miles. Crossing over, we entered the Canadas at Queenstown, a little below where the great battle was fought during the war of 1812, in which the brave and noble Gen. Brock and his aid-de-camp, Col. McDonald, were shot from their horses within a few moments of each other, by American riflemen ; and whose remains are interred beneath a monument of marble, near the spot where the last named officer fell dead from his horse. We stopped to survey the battle ground where so many brave men lost their lives, through the mismanagement of their commanding officer.

Here I took leave of my brethren, they going to the north and I bearing off to the west. I still had over sixty miles to travel before reaching my circuit, and among entire strangers ; but I found them very kind, and as hospitable as those of my native State.

When within about twelve miles of Long Point, the oldest settled place in that part of the Canadas, and which gave its name to the circuit which I was to travel, I entered a small valley where was a little village, called Lodersville—it had received its name from a wealthy merchant of the place, who owned a large distillery there, and who had in his employ and under his control, a large number of men. Neither the merchant nor his men professed religion, and I found, on inquiry, that it had been given over and abandoned by both Presbyterians and Methodists ; the former of whom had commenced building a church, but when half finished, had left it to the moles and bats.

I turned my eyes towards it as I passed through the village, and said to myself, "I must make an effort to save this people, as soon as circumstances will permit." I went on to my field of labor—found the class-leader of a small society at Long Point, who received me kindly, and directed me to the dwelling of a local preacher in our Church, Dan Freeman, who I found had been an itinerant in the early days of Methodism in the United States, but had taken up his residence here. I found him a good brother, in good circumstances, and with a most amiable family. They bade me welcome to all that was calculated to make myself and horse comfortable.

One night, while at Br. Freeman's, I dreamed a great fire broke out on Long Point plains, and seemed to light up the whole country around. When I awoke, I said, we shall have a reformation through this country. When the family called me to breakfast, I told them my dream and said, we shall have a reformation soon through this country.

I found I was to be associated with an aged brother

for my colleague, David Yeoman ; but he did not remain long on the circuit, as the Presiding Elder removed him to another part of the province, and sent on a Br. Jackson, who was not what I wanted for a colleague.   He, after several years travelling under the direction of the Genesee Conference, left our Church, and showed by his works that his heart was not right with God.

My experience in the work of the ministry was small, for I was not yet twenty-one, but my Presiding Elder said I must consider myself in charge of the field of labor in which I was at work.   My first appointment was at a small, unfinished meeting house, on Long Point plains.   Before entering upon my Sabbath labors, I retired to the grove to ask the Lord to bless and prosper me in my work of winning souls to Christ.   I took for my text, "And now if you will deal kindly and truly with my Master, tell me ; and if not, tell me ; that I may turn to the right hand or to the left."

The Lord helped me and gave me tokens for good ; and before I had gone one round on my circuit, the Lord began to convert sinners and reclaim backsliders.

Our circuit extended into many of the new settlements which were difficult of access, by reason

of the badness of the roads and the large, un-
bridged streams of water, we were obliged to pass in
getting to them ; and after reaching them, the ac-
commodations, for both man and beast, were very
poor, the people living mostly in small shanties ; but
so hungry were they for the Word of Life, that when
we entered their dwellings, they would greet us with
tearful eyes, and express a desire to make us as comfortable as possible.

I had not gone once around my extensive circuit,
when the work of reformation began ; and in one
round, I admitted into the Church sixty on probation.
The most of these were new converts.

At Long Point, Br. Ephraim Tisdale, who was one
of the first Methodists in Canada, and the leader of
the society there, had fitted up a large room in one
part of his house for meeting, and in which he had
preaching once in two weeks, and regular service every
Sabbath. He had a numerous family, and several of
his sons and daughters, with his pious companion,
were members of our Church ; and several of his sons
and grandsons are now ministers in the M. E. Church.
The father and mother of this noble and pious family years since joined the Church triumphant, and are
receiving their reward for their kindness and liberality
to the servants of Christ.

At an evening meeting at this brother's house, while trying to dispense the Word of Life to the people, the mighty power of God came down upon the congregation, and two stout, able-bodied young men were brought trembling upon the floor, crying for mercy. They were brothers ; and one of them seemed in such agony of mind that he stretched himself upon the floor, crying, "The Lord charges me with his death." Others, all around the room, were crying for mercy, or praising God for his redeeming and saving power. This meeting lasted all night, and the young man whose agony was so great, continued in this death-like struggle until the morning light appeared. Just as the king of day rolled up the eastern horizon, and threw his first beams aslant the earth, the sun of righteousness shone into his heart, and he sprang to his feet, with his soul filled unutterably full of glory and of God. His face shone with a heavenly smile, and his tongue was loosed to tell the wonders of redeeming grace and dying love.

The other brother had found peace to his soul, but was differently exercised ; they both became faithful members of our Church, and one of them a zealous and successful minister of the Canada Conference.

The number converted during this night I am not now able to give ; but this mighty flame spread rapidly, and we soon commenced a camp-meeting within the bounds of our charge, and God was with us in great power. A company of rowdies from a distance came on to the ground during the meeting, with the intention of disturbing us. They had chosen one of their number as leader, but soon after entering the encampment, he was arrested by the mighty power of God. He tried to leave the ground, but suddenly fell, and lay all night as stiff and cold as a dead man. In the morning animal life returned, and he was able to walk around; and his countenance showed that a great change had taken place in his mind. His jaws were set, and he could neither open his mouth nor speak, until towards noon, when he said he had seen heaven and hell; he was remarkably solemn and devotional. Our camp-meeting closed up gloriously, and the Lord was with us in great power, to save lost sinners from death.

I now resolved to visit the people of Lodersville, who had been on my mind from the time I first passed through the village, on my entrance into the province. By my orders, an appointment for preaching at the old, unfinished church, had been given out, and when I entered, I found a respectable and intelligent congregation assembled. I stepped upon a platform which elevated me above the people, knelt down and

prayed, and then sung some appropriate verses.
While singing, I perceived I had gained their attention ; and during my sermon, I saw the truth had
taken fast hold of the hearts of many in the congregation, and I knew the Lord would save this people.
As soon as I closed, I was obliged to mount my horse
and start for my afternoon appointment ; but before leaving, I told the people that in four weeks, the
Lord willing, I would preach to them again.   So extensive was my circuit, and so · great the work
already on my hands, I found I could not preach to
them sooner.   When the day arrived for the next
meeting with them, I was enabled to reach their village at the hour appointed.   As I was making for the
old church, I was met by a man who told me that the
people were assembled in a large, unfinished house, in
the Centre, and said he would take care of my horse.
All this was by the order of Mr. and Mrs. Loder.   I
entered the house, and found a fine congregation, well
seated, waiting for the minister. I immediately commenced our religious exercises, and the Lord was with
us in great power. The people melted down like wax
before the fire.   Weeping, and cries of, "What shall
I do to be saved," were heard from every part of the
congregation ; and before I closed the meeting, I read
the "General Rules" of our Societies, as found in the

Discipline, and said, "All who are willing to be governed by these Bible rules, and wish to be joined together in Church fellowship, will rise up." Over twenty rose and gave in their names. Among these were Mrs. Loder, her only child, a very amiable daughter of sixteen, a sister, who was an inmate of her family, and a young gentleman who was clerk in Mr. Loder's store.

After closing our meeting, which was lengthy, Mr. Loder invited me to his house, saying that he had ordered my horse taken care of. I went. After seating ourselves in his parlor, he said, "Mr. Torry, I am glad you have succeeded so well in organizing a Church among us to-day; and I am pleased that my family have become members of the same, and when I shall become fit, I intend to be one among you. And now we want a decent house to worship in, and I am determined to build one. I can do it without asking for a cent from any one."

The Lord wrought gloriously for this people. Mr. Loder built a neat, good sized house, finished it to the turn of the key, and I was called upon to preach one of the dedication sermons.

About this time, I was requested to preach the funeral sermon of an aged Presbyterian minister, who lived within the bounds of our circuit. This aged man had been preaching about forty years. He was one of the first settlers of Upper Canada, and had a numerous family of children and grand-children. He was properly a Calvinist of the Old School, and was not inclined to let Methodist ministers preach within the bounds of his parish; but when he died, I was sent for, though twenty miles away, to preach his funeral sermon. The services were held in the same house that he had preached in forty years. A large circle of relatives, with his Church and the citizens of the surrounding country, had come to pay their last respects to this aged and respected citizen.   .

I felt that I needed special help from above on this occasion. My desire and prayer was, that I might be the means of doing this people some good. The Lord did assist me to preach, and to go through with the services, to the satisfaction of the friends of the deceased, and I was invited to preach to them again. I did so, and in a short time organized a society, with which nearly all of the members of the Presbyterian Church united, and in less than six months we had built a respectable house for worship, and Methodism took fast hold of the hearts of the people in that place.

We were constantly enlarging our circuit, by penetrating newly settled neighborhoods, and the word of truth took immediate effect upon the hearts of the people to whom it was dispensed. At one of these new settlements, on the west part of our circuit, called Talbert-street, the spirit of awakening began. In the same place lived two men, who professed to be Presbyterian ministers, and who seemed to think it was their privilege to say just what they pleased about Methodism and Methodist ministers. They had told the people that I was as well calculated to deceive as the devil, and that Methodism was a system of error. They came to one of my meetings, and I gave out for my text, "We are journeying unto the place of which the Lord said, I will give it you; come thou with us, and we will do thee good, for the Lord hath spoken good concerning Israel." When about half through my discourse, a woman who had not professed religion, nor appeared serious before this meeting, seemed to be deeply affected, and springing from her seat, began to shout, "Glory, glory to God." When she had given vent to her full soul, she wheeled around, and facing those persecuting ministers, began exhorting them to repentance before God, "for," said she, "you have been persecuting this minister of Christ, and speaking against this blessed religion enjoyed by these Methodists, and which now makes my soul so happy." During her exhortation, I of course paused, and blessed God for his wonder-working power upon the hearts of these people. The ministers turned pale, and were glad to retreat from the house of God. O, what a victory was achieved at this meeting! That woman, with her family, became a member of our Church, and they were good soldiers of the cross. The word of life here was like fire in a dry stubble.

From Long Point circuit went forth some of the most able and successful preachers the Canadas have been favored with. From one family at Long Point, Col. Ryerson's, five sons became itinerants, and members of the Canada Conference, and several of them are now efficient and successful preachers in the provinces. Toward the close of this Conference year, Bishop George visited the Canadas, and appointments for him were published through Upper Canada, as far north as Kingston. He commenced his labors upon Long Point charge, and preached at our last quarterly meeting for the year, and his visit and preaching were a great blessing to us all. The Bishop, in those days, rode horseback, as did all other Methodist itinerants; he therefore requested the Presiding Elder of Upper Canada district, Henry Ryan, to furnish him with one of his preachers, that he might accompany him through the province. Br. Ryan told him to choose for himself, from a number who were attending quarterly meeting, and he would have his place supplied during his absence. He accordingly chose me. This pleased me right well, for I thought I should now have an opportunity of profiting by his preaching, praying, and able counsels. Accordingly, we mounted our horses and set off. I found he was in the habit of making remarks on almost everything that appeared beautiful and lovely in nature. Occasionally he would relate some facts connected with his history, and which were calculated to instruct and benefit myself, yet he always appeared solemn and devotional. When he entered a house to put up for the night, he, after speaking with the family in a very familiar and fatherly manner, would ask for a room to which he might retire ; or if he perceived there were no conveniences of this kind, which often happened, he would take his Bible and retire to some grove, where he might read, pray and meditate undisturbed. During the day on which he preached, it was seldom any one could have access to him until the public services were over.

He was very reserved in conversation, and seemed deeply afflicted with any one, whether of the ministry or laity, who evinced a spirit of levity. I said to him one day, "Bishop, since entering the ministry, I have become fully satisfied that I cannot do as some of our ministers do ; some of them even, who are called great ministers. If I allow myself to spend hours in light and trifling conversation, or in relating some funny anecdote which will set the company in a roar of laughter, dissipation of mind immediately follows, and the sweet and heavenly influences of Christ are grieved away from my heart, and I am left like Samson, when shorn of his locks. And I have spent days in darkness, regretting and repenting, and not until I had resolved to be more guarded in future, could I regain the favor of God. To carry out my plan more fully, when I am in such company, or visiting families that think a minister should spend most of his time in common chit-chat, I immediately abscond, and spend my leisure time in prayer, or reading my Bible, and such other books as I have. For this the people complain of me, and say I would be more popular if I would be more like themselves, and not so reserved and melancholy."

After hearing me through, he said : "You are right. When I first entered the ministry, I found I could not spend my time even as older ministers did, and make that advancement in holiness which the Lord requires of all, both preachers and people. When we are happy in the love of God we will be cheerful, yet grave and solemn, and such a spirit becomes all people who are so soon to close their probationary existence, and try the realities of an unending eternity.

> " 'No time for mirth or trifling here,
> If time so soon is gone.'

"Well," said he, "after struggling along for two or three years, I fell in company with an aged minister who set me on the right track, and I have followed his advice ever since, and have been *saved ;* and brother, I advise you to move steadily on in the way the Spirit of the Lord is leading you, and you will be guided into all truth."   He said moreover, "How ministers can pursue a different course, a course popular with many of our people, and preach in the demonstration of the Spirit, and with power, is more than I can tell.   Indeed, their effort is not preaching, but talking, and this is why our people are not more holy ; why Zion languishes and sinners are not saved." The Bishop said further to me, "brother, if the people persecute you for your serious, devotional, retired course, glory in it, but never yield to friend or foe, and God will bless you."

After the Bishop had performed his mission in the Canadas, we put aboard a sloop at Kingston, crossed over Lake Ontario, and landed at Ogdensburg.   From thence we went to Watertown, where I left the Bishop, and steered a direct course for home, at my mother's.

My youngest sister, Lydia, had passed over the river death during my absence, but my mother said she believed she had made safe the haven of eternal rest. After spending a few days with my mother, and leaving a part of what the people whom I served had given me, for her support, I went on to our Conference, and again received an appointment for Canada.

CHAPTER III.

On reaching the Westminster circuit, I found a field of labor more extensive and laborious than the one I had left. I was placed alone on this circuit, and as I passed around to the appointments left me by my predecessor, I found there were continued calls, from the newly settled parts of the country for preaching, and truly could we say, "The harvest is great, but the laborers are few." I had but little time for rest. While preaching at a place called Mount Pleasant, from the text, "Quench not the Spirit," a young man was awakened and soon converted, who afterward became a member of the Canada Conference, and, I believe, is still in active service, and an efficient preacher.

We had formed a small society in one of the new settlements, where was but one house convenient for preaching, and this was owned by a brother, who, before experiencing religion and joining our Church, was inclined to Quakerism.   His father, who lived near him, was what some term a "Hickory Quaker."   He was opposed to his son's remaining in the Church, partly because he wished to break up the Methodist society in that place, and partly because his son had to feed the minister and his horse.   So the old man went to work at his son to convince him that the Old Testament, the Sabbath, baptism, and the sacraments, were of no particular use under the present dispensation; and this doctrine which he called Quakerism, he finally made his son believe to be true.   On arriving at the settlement, I found this brother had been at work with his team on the Sabbath.   As I had an appointment for the evening at his house, I called upon him as usual, and perceiving he received me coolly, I sat down and said to him, "brother, I understand you, with your team, work on the Sabbath as on other days."   "Yes," he said, he "thought the Sabbath no better than any other day."   As I cast my eye around the room I saw the family Bible was gone, and the New Testament had taken its place. "Well," I said, "then you have really embraced Quakerism?"   "Yes, and I wish to withdraw from the M. E. Church."   "You should have asked for dismission from our Church," said I, "before you violated, not only the laws of the Church, but of God and man, in working on the holy Sabbath. My duty will require me to call you to an account before the society, and if you do not repent of your sins, and make confession, I shall have to expel you."

As I closed, he looked at his wife, whose countenance expressed deep trouble, for she was a member of our society, and had remained unshaken in her faith in the doctrines of Methodism, and after a pause of a few moments said to me, "If you will prove the Old Testament to be the Word of God, the Sabbath a divine institution, and baptism and the sacraments obligatory under the present dispensation, and meet the objections the Quakers raise to them, I will give up my faith in Quakerism and acknowledge my wrong; but now, I believe it to be right."

After reflection, I concluded to advertise the people that evening, that at my next visit to them I would prove the authenticity and divinity of the Old Testament, show that the Sabbath, baptism by water, and the sacraments, were as sacred and binding on us now as when first instituted, and meet all other objections the Quakers raised. I therefore set myself at work examining Fox and Barclay, and making myself thoroughly acquainted with Quaker doctrines.

My advertisement spread like wild-fire among the people, and when the evening arrived for me to preach, the house was crowded with people, some of them from a great distance.

The Quakers had employed a female speaker to meet me—their great champion, Peter Lawson, it was said, not being able to be present. I gave for my text, "All Scripture is given by inspiration of God, and is profitable for doctrine, for reproof, for correction, for instruction in righteousness; that the man of God may be perfect, thoroughly furnished unto all good works." I had liberty in speaking, and felt strengthened mightily to explain and enforce the truth of the Bible upon the hearts of the people, and show the sophistry and error of Quakerism.

When I had finished, the female speaker took the floor, but the Spirit did not "move" long enough for her to make a proper defence of her creed. She soon took her seat. Then rose up the brother who had been led astray from the path of right, and who had sinned against God, by believing in Quakerism, and said, "I am satisfied the Methodists are right, and that I have greatly sinned, and I hope the brethren will forgive me." His tears showed his sincerity and deep sorrow of heart, for having broken the holy commandments of God.

But the Quakers were not willing to give up this matter in this way. So they appointed a meeting in the same neighborhood, and brought on their great champion and defender of their faith, Peter Lawson. I told our brother to be present and hear all that was said, for Mr. Lawson would say all that could be said in defence of his doctrine. He did so, and afterward said to me, "I am now more than ever convinced that we are right in reference to the Bible, Sabbath and sacraments, and that the Quakers are wrong." After this skirmish, Quakerism took leave of this part of the country, and was never heard of more while I remained there, except what was left with "old Hickory."

But the Quakers, though they do not believe in war or fighting, resolved on giving me battle, if I should ever again attempt to preach in their principal settlement, which was about thirty miles from the one in which they had made their first attack, and they had noised around that they should rally and make an attack upon me, and they seemed to think they would force me to retreat, and be glad to leave that part of the country. Accordingly, before I had time to reach their settlement, they had made bitter complaints of me to the only family we had to call on in that part of the country. Happily, I received timely notice of this, so, going directly to their settlement, I engaged

an old building for a short time, fitted it up as a kind
of fort to use during our campaign, for I saw we must
have a regular fight with them ; gave out that I would
have a two-days' meeting, embracing the Sabbath, and
during which time the sacraments would be administered ; invited some of my brethren to meet me there
and see what the Lord would do for Quakers, and
others of their neighbors who had not embraced their
doctrine.

When our meeting began, there was a great rally
of Quakers, and others, who had come to see how the
battle would go. On Saturday, we began leveling our
artillery at error and the devil's strongholds, and in
about twenty-eight hours we had broken the enemy's
ranks, and nearly twenty persons, embracing some of
the most influential in the settlement, were completely
subdued, and fell upon their knees crying aloud for
mercy, and it was not long before the shout of victory
rolled up and over the battle field.

The Lord, in his own way, showed these deluded
Quakers that there was power in his Gospel to save
from error, sin and death ; and that his method of
saving men was by sanctification of the Spirit, and belief in the whole Bible truth. We organized a society
and erected a good sized church, nearly in the centre
of their settlement, and in sight of their own ; and

when I left that circuit we had one of the best societies there was in that country; and these *peaceable*
Quakers found, by sad experience, that it was bad
policy for them to wage war with Methodism.

This was a year of great toil and sacrifice, and yet
it was a good year, for the Lord blessed us, and many
souls were saved through the blood of the atonement.
At the close of this year I attended the session of
our Conference, and again received an appointment
for Canada. After visiting my mother, and spending
a few days with her, I again mounted my horse, and
after three hundred miles travel, reached Ancaster
circuit, of which I was 'in charge. Here I found a
comfortable resting place at Father Bowman's, one
of the stewards of my circuit. I had placed my horse
in his pasture, intending to give him several days in
which to recruit, but going out soon after, I found
him dead.

I was now without a horse, or means to buy one,
as I had but a few shillings in my pocket, having
given my mother about half the one hundred dollars
I received as my salary from the people among whom
I had labored during the past year. The rest I had
to lay out for clothing, and in increasing my small
library. My colleague, Br. Furguson, a poor man
with a family, soon after met with a like loss, and

thus we were left without horses to travel an extensive circuit. I borrowed a horse to begin with, and as I passed around the circuit, I found the brethren sympathised with us in our misfortune. It was not long before a brother let me have a horse on credit, and as my colleague was successful in getting one also, we went to work. But it was not long before my health became poor, and I found much of the time I was not able to do the work assigned me, still I kept on attending the appointments. The Lord gave us refreshing showers, and manifested his power to save souls from sin and death.

In closing up this year, I requested my Presiding Elder, Br. Wm. Case, to use his influence with the Bishop, to give me a field of labor in the States. He said he could not promise me a discharge from the Canadas. I said, "you know we entered these mission fields with the understanding that after two or three years' labor in these provinces, we should be released, and others of our age in the Conference should take our places, and share in the toils and sacrifices necessary to be made in serving a people in a new country." Br. Case replied, "Br. Alvin, there is a hereafter, and we shall see who will have the most stars in his crown, by and by." So I saw I must calculate on staying longer in Canada.

I attended the Conference, received my appointment back again, on Lyon's Creek circuit, and after visiting my mother, and dividing my pittance with her, bid adieu to home, and again started for my distant field of labor. My health remained poor, and the fatigues of a journey of three or four hundred miles on horseback were too much for me. However, I entered upon the duties of my charge with as much courage as I could command. I was alone, and I found a large field to explore, which required the greater part of my time. At all of our appointments the Lord gave us evidence of his power and willingness to save perishing sinners, and we had some very signal manifestations of his divine mercy and love.

Toward the close of this year, I felt an impression of mind that I must visit the Six Nations of Indians, whose Reservation lay to the west of my circuit. During the whole time I had been in Canada, I was accustomed to cross the Grand River within a few miles of the Mohawk tribe, and frequently met with groups of them here and there, and not unfrequently saw them lying drunk around huckster's shops, kept by white people for the purpose of getting the Indians drunk, and then robbing them of all that was of use to them. But it had never occurred to me that the Gospel of Christ could be the power of God to the salvation of Indians.

Now, however, my mind was impressed with a desire to visit these Six Nations, though for what, I really could not tell. From the west end of my circuit to the Indian Reservation, was twenty or thirty miles ; and now, at the closing up of the year, while on the west part of my charge, I put off for their settlement. As I struck the Grand River, and passed along up through the several tribes, I stopped and talked with them, and questioned them as to their views of our holy religion ; and my mind began to be impressed with the propriety of making an effort to instruct them in the first principles of the Gospel of Christ. After spending a part of a day among them, I returned to my charge, and now began to prepare to take a final leave of the Canadas, for I had received encouragement that my next appointment would be in the States.

My Presiding Elder, Br. Case, had appointed a meeting on his district, at which I was to meet him and then go directly on to Conference. But before the time for the meeting arrived, I thought I would make the Indians another visit. So off I went, and after further conversation with them in respect to their views of our Bible religion—for they had a religion of their own, which they supposed pleased the Great Spirit, but which gave them no proper knowledge of salvation from sin, by faith in our Lord Jesus Christ —I became interested in their behalf and felt a desire to instruct them in the way of salvation.

After leaving them, I hastened on to meet Br. Case, and the next day fell in company with him. As soon as opportunity offered, I told him of my visiting the Six Nations, and expressed my belief in the probability of Christianizing them. While I was speaking, he listened with his sharp, penetrating eyes fixed upon me, and then bringing his hands together he said, in a raised tone of voice, "Br. Alvin, prepare to go a missionary to those Indians after Conference." I asked him to explain himself. "Well," said he, "my mind, recently, has been impressed with the importance of our trying to better their condition, and I have spoken to several of our brethren about this matter, and one said he would give ten dollars and another said he would give five, towards supporting a man among them. Now," said he, "the Lord is in this, and you must prepare to enter upon the work of teaching and preaching to those nations."

We now made preparations and started for our Conference, which held its session at Vienna, N. Y. On our way, and after we had reached the seat of Conference, the subject of a mission among the Indians was the all-absorbing topic of conversation with Br. Case and myself. At the close of the Conference, I was read off for "Grand River Mission."

Duty required that I should spend a few days with my mother, for I had to see to her, which, with what my brother Daniel could do, kept her and her younger children comfortable.

When my mother first received the intelligence of my appointment among the Indians, she seemed somewhat alarmed for my safety, for she had been accustomed to hear frightful stories of their cruelty to the whites; but when she heard from me the circumstances which led to my appointment among them, she became calm, and her mind seemed to take strong hold of the promise of the Savior, "Lo! I am with you alway, even unto the end of the world."

I took leave of my weeping friends, and started for Grand River, which I struck near its mouth. This river is one hundred miles long, and empties into Lake Erie about forty miles from Buffalo. It is navigable for twelve miles.

During the war of 1812, the British ran a number of sloops up this river, which, with a body of troops, remained after the war, and during my stay in Canada.

CHAPTER IV.

Although the Indian tribes which have been scattered over the entire continent were very numerous, they have been all found to belong to eight or ten distinct groups or families. Four of these at present are of Canada, viz: 1. The Esquimaux, who, in their *physique*, but still more in their manners, belief and superstitious customs, resembled the natives of Lapland and Greenland. 2. The Chippewayans, (who should not be confounded with the Chippewas, or Ojibwas,) including the following tribes: (1.) The Dog-ribs; (2.) The Hares; (3.) The Yellow-knives; (4.) The Slaves; (5.) The Deer-eaters; and (6.) The Beaver. 3. The Algonquin; and 4. The Huron-Iroquois.

Each of these four groups, or families, spoke a distinct language, having no affinity to the other. The four groups were sub-divided into various tribes, each speaking a separate dialect of their original tongue, yet among all the tribes a remarkable similarity in customs and institutions prevailed. In color, form, temperament, religious belief and pursuits, all were alike. The men engaged in war, hunting and fishing, while the women performed all other kinds of labor.

The SACHEM, or head of a tribe, was frequently a hereditary monarch, and sometimes owed his elevation to his prowess or to his oratorical powers. He could be deposed; but while in power he was supreme. In council composed of the elders, he presided as umpire, and to his decision all bowed with submission. A chief was subordinate to a Sachem, and was the leader of a war-party. A war-party generally consisted of forty braves, or warriors, but sometimes six or nine would venture out upon the "war-path" alone.

The principal groups of Indians which occupied the area of Canada at the time of its discovery, were the Adirondacks, (the Algonquins proper,) and the Huron-Iroquois. The Algonquins, with the Huron-Iroquois, are said to have descended from the north, by the Ottawa (or Uttawas) river at the close of the fifteenth century, and to have occupied the left bank

of the St. Lawrence.   They were called Adirondacks,
*(or bark-eaters,) in derision, by the Iroquois.   They
received the generic name of Algonquins from the
French.   In Indian they were called *Odis qua gume*,
"People at the end of the water."   In arts and other
attainments they excelled the Iroquois.   They are
supposed to have been at the head of a great northern confederacy, similar to that of the Six Nation
Indians.   In later times they were allies of the French
and Wyandots, in their wars against the Nodawas or
Iroquois.

The principal tribes of the Algonquin group were,
(1.) The Sangenay Mountaineers; (2.) The Bull-
heads of St. Maurice; (3.) The Ottawas; (4.) The
Ojibwas, or Chippewas of Lake Superior and river
Winnepeg; (5.) The Maskegons of the river Nelson
and the Crees (les cris) of the river Saskatchewan.
No tribe of this group has been found west of the
Rocky Mountains, nor have any of the Chippewayan
group been found east of Hudson's Bay.

The O-jib-wa, or Od, jib-way, (plural Odjibwäig)
occupied the shores of Lake Superior, and included
the Mes-sas-saques (or Mis-se-saugas,) who occupied
the area at the mouth of a river called by their name,
lying between Point Tessalon and La Cloche, on the
north shore of Lake Huron.   The Ojibwas and Mis-

sesaugas are both called by different writers, Chippeways. (The Chippewayans are a Rocky Mountain tribe.) The Chippewa, like the Algonquin of old, is now the common business language of the Indians, and is as necessary among them as French is among Europeans. The Huron-Iroquois group, or family, included, (1.) The Six Nation Indians ; and, (2.) The Hurons (Wyandots) as well as the following tribes ; (3.) The Sioux ; (4.) The Assineboins, (Sioux of the rock, or Little Iroquois,) and the Blackfeet.

The history of the Indians of the Six Nations, although chiefly identified with the history of the State of New York, is also intimately connected with that of Canada. As a confederacy, they were faithful allies of the British crown from the earliest colonial times, until the close of the American Revolution.

At the close of the revolutionary war, the Mohawks, Cayugas, Onondagas, and others, removed to Canada and settled ; 1st, at Brantford, on the Grand River, (so called from Brant, the celebrated Mohawk chief,) where they received a grant from the crown along both sides of the river to its mouth. 2d, at Tyindinaga on the Bay of Quinté, (so called also after Brant's Indian name,) and 3d, on the river Thames. In 1671, a party of Mohawks settled at Sault Ste. Louis, near Montreal.

The origin of the Iroquois is very obscure. Their own tradition is that they originally descended the river Ottawa, and resided as a small tribe at Hochelaga, or Montreal. They were subject to the Adirondacks, and from them learned the arts of husbandry and war. Becoming numerous, they sought to secure their independence, but being vanquished, they were compelled to fly. Having ascended the St. Lawrence, and coasted the southern shore of Lake Ontario, they entered the Oswego river, and scattered themselves in separate bands through various parts of the State of New York. Afterwards, for mutual protection, and at the desire of the Onondagas, they formed a league, under the title of Hodenosaunee, or "people of the long-house."

This house extended from the river Hudson to the great lakes of Canada. The Mohawks guarded the eastern end, and the Senecas the western. The structure of this league suggested the union of the thirteen colonies in the revolutionary war—a union which was afterwards developed into the political compact of the present United States. The confederacy is supposed to have been formed in 1540. It was successfully maintained for upwards of 200 years; indeed, it has never been formally dissolved. Originally, it only included five cantons or nations, but in 1712 the Tuscaroras, a southern tribe, were admitted and became the sixth nation.

The Necariceges, a remnant of the Hurons at Michilimacinac, (the "Great Turtle," abbreviated to Mecinaw) was nominally admitted in 1723 as a seventh nation. By the Adirondacks, the Indians of this celebrated league, were known as the Min-goes ; Vodowas, or Adder Enemy, by the Ojibwas and Hurons ; Iroquois, by the French ; and Six Nations, by the English. The French term "Iroquois," is founded on the Indian approbatory exclamations, "Yoe ! Haugh !"

The Ottawas have a tradition that many, many years ago, they, with the Adirondacks and Hurons, belonged to a great confederacy of the North, similar to that of the Six Nation Indians, and that about the close of the 15th century they emigrated, descending the Ottawa river and stretching themselves along the banks of the St. Lawrence, occupied what is now Canada and through to Lake Superior.

At this time, the nations now known as the Iroquois, were a small tribe who had descended the river Ottawa, and were living at Hochelaga or Montreal. They were subject to the Adirondacks, and from them learned the arts of husbandry and war. In the course of time they had increased in numbers to such an extent, that liberty was talked of by the boldest of them, and not many moons passed ere they had risen in arms to assert their rights. But their masters, not willing to allow them more freedom than they already enjoyed, declared war upon them, for the purpose of subduing them, and bringing them back to their allegiance.

The Adirondacks succeeded in defeating them, and destroyed many of them; but now that they had tasted liberty, they would not yield to enslavement again, so they fled from their native land. They passed up the St. Lawrence till they reached lake Ontario. They coasted along the eastern and southern shore, till they came to the Oswego river. Up this river they paddled, till, becoming satisfied with the face of the country, they landed and scattered themselves throughout what is now the State of New York.

Some years afterward, at the suggestion of the Onondagas, they formed that celebrated league by which they became so formidable to their enemies. This combination was first formed for protection against their former masters, the Adirondacks, or, as they were known by the French, the Algonquins. The Hurons, of Canada, claim to have been at the head of this league, but afterwards making peace with the Adirondacks, war was declared by their former allies, the Five Nations, and they were defeated and chased from their country, until they came among the Ojibwas, who were a tribe of the Algonquins. The Ojibwas joining with their fleeing allies, gave battle to the Iroquois and defeated them at Pt. Iroquois, or place of the Iroquois bones. The Iroquois afterwards overcame the Algonquins, defeating the Ottawas and utterly routing the Hurons. They then established colonies along the shores of Lake Ontario.

The Tuscaroras, a nation from the south, emigrated in 1712, and taking up their abode in this State, were admitted as another nation. The Six Nations were in possession of Canada, besides owning all the State of New York, the right of the great lakes, &c. About 1740, they reached the zenith of their greatness, and after the Revolutionary war, began to decline in power.

The Iroquois have always been firm friends of the English, while the Algonquins were allies of the French. In the treaty of Paris, in 1763, France ceded to Great Britain all her northern settlements in America, thus withdrawing herself from all intercourse with the Indians, after which the Algonquins formed a treaty of peace, besides selling their right to their lands in Canada, reserving only some portions in different parts of the provinces, along the course of rivers or near some fisheries on the lakes. The treaty provided for the annual payment of the interest in blankets, guns, ammunition, jewelry, &c., which they were to receive at their Reservations.

At the commencement of the Revolutionary war, there was a division among the Six Nations regarding the justice of the course pursued by Washington and his co-patriots; many, under Brant, continuing their allegiance to Great Britain, while others were firm supporters of Washington and his principles. Accordingly, at the end of the war, many emigrated to Canada, where lands were granted them for their services. Here they had a government and laws of their own, and lived in every respect as free and independent as their fore-fathers. In their treaty with Great Britain, they were to arrest and try any of their number who should commit depredations on the whites, and if not brought to justice, Britain claimed the right of doing so herself.

Joseph Brant, (Thayendanega) a pure Mohawk by birth, was a prominent ally of the English. He influenced several cantons, or tribes, of the Iroquois, to fight under the British standard during the Revolution. At the close of the war, he removed, with the Mohawks, to Canada, settling on the Grand river, a grant three miles wide, and extending the length of the river. The town of Brantford, or Brant's ford, on the river, was named after him; as was also the county of Brant, in the same locality, and the township of Thayendanega on the Bay of Quinté, where a number of the Mohawks had settled.

In 1783 he visited England, and was received and treated by Britons as a prince, and such he really was.   He, in many ways, exerted himself to promote the temporal and spiritual welfare of his people.   He was employed by the Church of England to translate into Mohawk portions of the Holy Scriptures, some part of their prayer-book, and also the ten commandments—the latter were written upon two boards in large gold letters.   The Church of England built them a meeting-house, the Queen gave them a bell for their new church, and the ten commandments were placed in the altar.

The Brant family, with a few of the Mohawk nation, renounced paganism and were baptized and admitted into the English Church.   The holy sacraments were administered to them by their missionary, who lived thirty or forty miles from them.   He only visited them once or twice in a year, and after the Sabbath exercises closed in the church, it was his custom to go with the Indians to their horse-racing and card-playing, where they had plenty of the fire-water to drink, and I have been informed upon good authority, that he has often become so intoxicated as to be unable to leave the ground. This was the condition of these Indians, when, in the year 1822, I commenced my labors among them.

How to commence with these Indians so as to arrest their attention and draw them from their pagan customs and worship to the true worship of the living God, I had yet to learn. I had received no particular instructions as to the manner of commencing or proceeding with my labor, and I doubt if there was a man in Genesee Conference, excepting Br. Case, that believed that the Indians, in their pagan state, as we now found them, could be christianized, and I am sure my brethren in Canada did not believe I would succeed in this work. Their theory was, "First civilize, then christianize." In order that the mission might not be an entire failure, I had embraced in my mission two townships, Reignham and Walpole. These lay bordering on Lake Erie, and had been settled many years ; but the people all through these were as destitute of the gospel and Bible, as the Indians themselves—some of them had not heard a gospel sermon in ten years.

Part of my time was devoted to them, and in almost every settlement that I visited and preached, the Lord was present to bless and save. In one of these settlements, a very wicked man opened his house for preaching, and seemed to have much care for me and my horse. The Lord converted his wife, a very amiable woman, who joined our Church, and remained a devoted member till she joined the Church triumphant. By her will she left, at her decease, a hundred dollars for me to dispose of as I thought best. This was some years after I left the province, and not until five years after her death did I receive information of the fact.

I then gave Br. Case a written order for the money, with instructions to use it for the benefit of the Indians with whom he was then laboring, which he did. This woman's husband became powerfully awakened under my preaching, and seemed resolved on being a Christian, but his instability of mind was such, that though truth found a lodgement in his heart, yet it was like the seed which fell upon stony places. He died before his wife, and after I left the country, so that I am not able to say what his end was, but his wife is among the blood-washed company in heaven.

But to return to the Indians. It will be perceived by those who are familiar with the history of christian churches in America, that no apostolic reformation had made its appearance among the North American Indians since the days of Brainard, except what had appeared among the Wyandots in Upper Sandusky.

Brainard, it seems, was employed by a Missionary Society of Scotland. He was a remarkable young man, and had his work greatly at heart. He had not been preaching long to one of the tribes of this country, before a glorious revival followed ; but, in the midst of his labors of love, and when it seemed his little flock needed him most, the Lord called him to join the ransomed above, and wear the martyr's crown. Before his death, he committed his little flock to a younger brother, with a solemn charge to care for them as he had done. But his brother being so unlike himself, the work in a little time withered in his hands, and nothing like an apostolic revival appeared among the Indians until the work commenced in Upper Sandusky, through the instrumentality of a colored man, John Steward.*

*John Steward, a colored man, but born free, was raised in the State of Virginia, Powhattan county, having been brought to the knowledge of salvation by the remission of sins, and become a member of the M. E. Church at Marietta, Ohio, being divinely impressed, as he supposed, the latter end of the year 1815, went among these people, with a view to impart to them the knowledge of the true God.

Unauthorized by any body of Christians, he went of his own accord, under, however, a persuasion that the Holy Spirit had moved him to it; nor did he stop, except for rest and refreshment, until he arrived at Upper Sandusky, where dwelt the Indians to whom he believed God had sent him. He was first directed to Jonathan Pointer, a colored man, who had been taken a prisoner when young, and adopted by them as one of their nation. After making known his mind to this man, he prevailed on him to become his interpreter, and he accordingly introduced Steward to the Indians as their friend. They were at that time amusing themselves in dancing, and they seemed at first very indifferent

In different parts of these United States efforts had been made by several religious denominations to christianize tribes of Indians on our continent ; but it had never occurred to any one of these, that these pagan nations could be converted and made humble Christians without first civilizing them. No one, it seems, had thought, since the days of Brainard down to the time of the reformation among the Wyandots, that the gospel of Christ could march directly up to the · wild, drunken, degraded Indian's heart, and make a successful attack upon the evil of his moral nature, and prove itself to be the very same power which anciently arrested the wild man among the tombs, who,

---

in respect to the message of their strange visitor. He, however, requested as many as were willing, to come together and hear the word of the Lord. To this they all consented, by giving him their hands.

Accordingly, the next day was appointed for the meeting, at the house of the interpreter; but instead of a numerous assembly, which might have been expected, only one old woman attended. Not disconraged at this, Steward preached—as Jesus had done before him to the woman of Samaria—the gospel to her as faithfully as if there had been hundreds. He appointed to preach again the next day at the same place, when his congregation was increased by the addition of one old man. To these two he preached, and it resulted in their conversion to God.

Next day being Sabbath, preaching was appointed in the council-house. Eight or ten attended this time, some of whom appeared deeply affected. From this time the work of God broke out rapidly, and meetings were held every day in the several cabins, and on the Sabbath days in the council-house. The consequence was, that crowds flocked to hear the Word and to learn to sing, and a glorious reformation was the result. Br. Finley was sent to take charge of these, as his history shows.

presently, was found sitting at the feet of Jesus, clothed, and in his right mind.

I commenced attending their councils.   I found that
each tribe or nation had a council-house, and that at
the Mohawk Castle was a grand council-house, where
the head chiefs of the Six Nations met to consult and
deliberate, to sanction or veto any matter that related
to their general interest.   In general council, while attending to national affairs, they appeared in their best
dress, their heads adorned with large feathers, jewels
often hanging in their ears or noses, or in both, and
silver brooches fastened on their garments ; and from
their appearance and actions they felt their independence and consequence.

Independence of thought and action is one great
characteristic of the Indian ; they would sooner see
their children tomahawked than enslaved, and though
they have been wasting away, and decreasing in numbers and power ever since the English began to people
this continent, yet their brave, free, and independent
cast of mind is not subdued.   They most certainly are
the descendants of some great and powerful nation.
Each tribe or nation speaks a different dialect ; but
the Mohawk language is spoken exclusively at their
general councils.   If a speaker cannot speak that language, which, however, rarely happens, he must speak

through a Mohawk interpreter. I found some of their speakers in council, perfect orators ; though all do not make a practice of speaking on the council floor, yet such as do, speak with as much ease and fluency, if not as eloquently, as any orators the world can point to. Perfect order is observed in their councils, and no one is allowed to speak above a whisper while a speaker has the floor.

When any new subject is introduced, or any difficult matter is brought before them, they deliberate upon it with great moderation, often spending days upon one topic before giving a final decision. They seem not to be embarrassed at the presence of white men, though of distinguished reputation and high rank. When they noticed me seated in their council-house, and listening to their deliberations, they seemed to be in a great quandary as to what could be my object in spending my time among them. They knew I professed to be a minister ; but they had formed a very unfavorable opinion of ministers, from what they had seen of the minister who officiated, occasionally, at the Mohawk church. When they would speak of me to wicked white men, especially those who were dealing out fire-water to them, they would tell them to look out for me, for I might be after their squaws, or devising some plan to cheat or injure them. This put them on their guard to look out for me, and though I would use every available opportunity to address them on the great interest of their souls, yet they had no confidence in my professions of friendship. They believed that before I left them I would do them some injury. Whenever I wanted food for myself or horse, I would pay them their own price for what I received. When calling upon them to make pastoral visits, if it happened to be their mealtime they would sometimes ask me to eat with them.

I have been with the pagan Indians for days and weeks, and left my portmanteau in some one of their houses, or wigwams, and sometimes unlocked, and yet I never had the value of a penny stolen from me by any Indian, but I have had fifty dollars stolen from me at a time by white men. They are not given to thieving, even in their pagan state, and in this they excel almost any other nation on earth. All these tribes were given to intemperance except the Cayugas, who had renounced all spirituous liquors. The subject of intemperance had come up in their councils, and they had deliberately considered the evils of the fire-water among them, and they had said, "It destroys our young men and women; we will put it away; and when liquor dealers come among us to deal out their poison in exchange for our money or furs, we will drive them from our nation." If any one of the tribe became intoxicated while abroad, as was sometimes the case, they would call a council to deal with him, and if the offender was stubborn, and refused to promise reformation, they would continue their labor with him for days, until he promised not to drink any more of the white man's poison. When I conversed with them upon the good of our Bible religion, they said to me, "We not like your Bible religion ; it says 'Drink whisky.'" I said, "No, that is a mistake." "Well," they said, "Look at the Mohawks ; they have Bible religion, and they all get drunk ; we not want it." I said, "Their Bible and my Bible says, 'No drink of the fire-water ;' but they don't do as the Bible says. They not good, very wicked, and the Great Spirit very angry with them. They all go to the bad place if they don't put away the white man's poison."

It was easy to see what the Church of England had done, and was doing in the way of religious instruction. Instead of reforming and bettering their condition, they were likely to prove their ruin, both soul and body. We found the so called "Mohawk Christians" were persuaded that the Methodist religion was not good, for it prohibited their drinking rum, and playing cards, and horse-racing. So they said, "We won't have Methodist religion." These were some of

the difficulties we had to grapple with when we entered upon our work of christianizing the Indians of Canada.

I had now been three months on Grand River,
and during that time I had tried to make myself acquainted with the history of the Six Nations, by attending their councils, and visiting them from house
to house, and when opportunity offered, singing and
praying with them. But as yet, no one among them
seemed inclined to renounce paganism. But among
the people of those isolated settlements, bordering on
the Indian Reservation, the Lord was at work gloriously. My visits to them, and labors with them, served
to keep me from desponding.

Winter began to close in upon us, and the fall rains
had filled up the swamps, and raised the Grand River
so as to make it difficult to cross. The streams running from the swamps to the river were, at this time,
bridgeless, so that myself and horse were often in danger during the winter, and I found very few places in
my travels among the Indians where I and my horse
could be comfortable.

Br. Case had made me one visit, and said and done
what he could to help me in my work. He thought
with myself, that the time was not far distant when
many of the poor, dark, pagan Indians on Grand Riv-

er, would know and feel the power of redeeming grace. Many days and nights I spent in the woods on my knees, supplicating a throne of grace for the blessing of God upon these nations. Some of my brethren in the ministry thought it was cruel to keep me toiling and suffering among the Indians, when they could see no prospects of saving them.

As the spring opened upon us, I found my roads through the swamps were at times impassable with a horse, and I was under the necessity of footing it. At one time, I left the Indians for a white settlement lying east of Grand River.

I not unfrequently, while among the Indians, would have to pass whole days and nights without food, or but very little, for the Indians themselves, at times, seemed to be without enough to satisfy hunger. I was in this situation at the time of starting. I had ten or twelve miles to travel, and an almost empty stomach to begin with. But I commenced my journey. When a little over half way through the wilderness, I began to feel faint, and extremely hungry. I looked along in the woods, hoping to find some roots, or something which would satisfy the gnawings of hunger, but I could find nothing. As I approached the settlement, my faintness increased, and my strength began to fail. But still I dragged myself wearily along.

The road, as it wound around through the trees and brush, or over logs, and through the swamps, now turning out of my course to find a crossing place, as I came to a stream that took its way to the river, seemed to be without end ; and when, at last, I came in sight of the settlement, I could go no farther. My strength was entirely gone. I sunk down upon a log, and as I gazed wistfully on before me, I saw a single house not far off. O, how I longed for a crust of bread even, for then would I have strength to reach that house. But nothing could I get. To proceed, seemed impossible—to stay there and starve to death, in sight of friends and plenty, was a thought not to be endured, and I strove to press on, but I sunk back exhausted. I had not ceased to pray to God for help, and as I sat there, with my eyes fixed upon that house, from which, as yet, I had seen no one come, I began to feel a little rested, and I said to myself, "I *must* reach that house," and then with what remaining strength I had, I pressed on. Every few rods I had to stop, but the sight of that house, and the fearful gnawings of the hunger pain within, made me strain every nerve to reach the house. At last I reached it. As I entered, a decent looking woman made her appearance, and I said, "Can you give me something to eat, for I am *very* faint." She saw from my appearance and manner of speaking, that I was suffering greatly for want of food ; and in a few moments she had placed before me the very best her house afforded. As soon as I had eaten, my life and strength returned ; and when this good woman found that she had been feeding one of God's ministers, she seemed highly gratified, and I now had an opportunity of asking the blessing of the Lord upon this kind and benevolent woman, the blessing which he had promised, "That to him who should give to one of his servants a cup of cold water, even he should not lose his reward."

On another occasion I had to pass through an extensive swamp, in order to reach the Indians on the river. I entered the swamp with my horse. The spring of the year was just opening upon us, and the roads were breaking up. Soon after entering the swamp, it began raining very fast. I had many small streams to cross which were bridgeless. As the rain continued pouring down, the streams began to rise and overflow their banks, and soon the swamp looked in many places like one great river or lake. I could tell by the current when I came to a stream, and at such times I would take my saddle and port-manteau from my horse, and telling her to swim across, would wander up or down till I could find some log or tree by which to cross. Then returning to where my horse waited for me, I would proceed till we came to another stream, and thus we passed the whole day, while the rain was pouring down in torrents.

Towards sundown, we came in sight of the river, which had risen to high water-mark. Near the river, and entering into it, was a deep, wide gorge, or gulf; and over this gorge was a bridge of poles, which, at most seasons of the year, was safe enough to cross upon. But now the water had risen and filled the gulf full. The poles, wonderful as it may seem, still lay where the bridge used to be, though they were all afloat.

The waters of the river went roaring and surging past me ; the bridge was afloat ; night was coming on ; neither myself nor horse had tasted food since morning, and upon examination, I found I had left my tinder-box and flint behind me, so that it was impossible for me to kindle a fire ; and whether to go on over the bridge or wait till the waters subsided, was a question which I debated for a few moments. If I should venture across, a single misstep might plunge either of us into the dark, deep, boiling waters below, and no chance for escape, for the sides of the gorge were nearly perpendicular.

On the other hand, if I staid, I must spend the night without fire, without food, and wet through.

My horse seemed to understand my difficulty, and stood with her head close to mine, as if conscious that I would help ourselves out of this difficulty. At last, with a prayer to God for safety, I said : "Well, Fancy, we must at least make an effort." So, stepping up to the bridge, I put one of my feet on the first pole. It settled down till it rested upon the cross pieces, which were still solid. Fancy was by my side, and when she saw me step on the pole, she carefully put out her foot upon the same, and finding it solid, she proceeded without fear to step when I did, keeping close to me all the time, and we soon reached the other side. We shortly came to an Indian wigwam, where we stopped for the night. After seeing that Fancy had the best the place afforded, I laid myself down beside the roaring fire, and thus passed the night.

We now began to make preparations for a camp-meeting, within a few miles of the Indian Reservation. In the appointment of this meeting, we had the Indians in view, hoping they might be inclined to attend a wood-meeting ; but in this we were disappointed. They were always on the lookout for white men, expecting injury from them. I did not arrive at the camp-ground until the last day but one. I reached the ground at the time of intermission. Br. Case was holding a quarterly conference with the official board of Ancaster circuit.

From what I could learn, the meeting had not been as good as on former occasions, and in a few moments I passed from the encampment, and retiring into the woods some two hundred yards, I knelt down and lifted up my heart in prayer to God ; in a few moments I felt the sweet, melting influences of Jesus' love filling my heart, and I could weep freely. With this blessing came a text of Scripture, and I felt the Spirit of the Lord God upon me, like a fire shut up in my bones.

I arose, returned to the camp-ground, found Br. Case, who was still engaged with the official board, and whispering to him said, "Are you going to have more preaching to-day?" "Yes," said he, "if you will preach." "Very well; if you say so," said I. He closed his business, and we repaired to the preacher's stand. The horn was sounded, and from the tents came the people to hear the Word.

As the people flocked around, I commenced the public exercises. I gave out my text and began to preach. The power of the Lord was upon me, and I felt his mighty influence in my soul. As I proceeded, a deep feeling of solemnity came over the people. They swayed to and fro, and as the mighty power of God came sweeping down from heaven upon us, saint and sinner fell before it, and the slain of the Lord were in the camp. The groan of the sinner, the cry of the penitent, 'mingling with the shout of triumph, and the song of the victor, rolled up from that encampment like a mighty cloud of incense, and angels looked on and shouted for joy.

Away on the outskirts of the congregation, and leaning against a tree, stood a poor, benighted son of the forest, who, during the day, had been wandering about among the tents and over the ground, and now, drawn by the sound of the minister's voice, he had approached nearer and nearer, till he stood gazing at me. As he listened, the word of truth sunk deep in his heart, and conviction seized upon his soul. The tears streamed from his eyes, and when the call was given for all who wanted religion to come forward and kneel at the altar, he hastened forward and cried aloud for mercy.

Attracted by the same heavenly influence, a sister of this poor red man, came weeping and crying for mercy to the altar. How our hearts thrilled with joy and thanksgiving to God, as we beheld these benighted youths bowing before the God of the white man.

Here, at last, were the fruits of all our toil and labor ; for this had we suffered cold and hunger, privation and want ; for this had we given up the comforts of home and friends, and gone forth among strangers ;

to this end had we breasted wind and storm, snow and hail, and made our couch upon the damp earth, with nothing but the sky and stars above us, and the dark, dim woods, like watchful sentinels, around us ; and now, as we saw that youthful couple before us, all our toils were forgotten, and we kneeled around and wrestled earnestly in their behalf.

The sister was the first to be converted. When the first beams of the sun of righteousness shone in upon the darkness of her mind, she sprang to her feet, and shouting forth the praises of her Redeemer, she then hastened to her brother, saying, "The Lord will bless you, Peter, for he has had mercy on me and blessed me." It was not long before his soul was brought into the full liberty of the gospel of Christ. When the victory was proclaimed to the anxious, praying friends of the poor Indian, a shout of triumph rolled up and swelled out upon the air, till the sounding aisles of the dim, old woods echoed back the joyful cry. We had now unlocked the door of the red man's heart, and thrown back the bolts and bars that superstition and suspicion had placed there ; and as we looked forward into the future, we could see crowds of Indians coming from their distant homes from the far West, and bowing down to the gospel of Christ.

As we advance in our history of facts concerning

the great work of God among the Six Nations, and the North-Western tribes, we shall discover the infinite love of the Son of God, as manifested towards the most degraded of our fallen race, and his willingness to raise them up, and bring them back to his favor.

Our camp-meeting closed up gloriously. The Indians above named, Polly and Peter Jones, returned to their home in the north part of the Mohawk tribe, and began to talk with, and pray for those with whom they associated. The blessing of God attended their labors, and the result was, when I reached the settlement, a number of Indians were awakened to see their lost and ruined state, and were seeking salvation through Jesus Christ.

On the following Sabbath we had a meeting appointed at the house of Thomas Davis, a Mohawk chief. He and his wife had renounced paganism, and been baptized by the English missionary who officiated at the Mohawk church. When asked for the use of his house to worship in, he said, "You can have it, but I not change my religion. If you can reform my people, I be glad." He had renounced spirituous liquors, read the prayer-book in his family, and they considered themselves Christians.

This Indian was no common person. In stature he was tall, well formed, and as straight as one of his own forest pines. Born to command, he had the air and mein of one who knew his power. His forehead, like his spirit, was high ; his eye as piercing as the eagle's. His mind corresponded with his person ; it was like those vast solitudes of the American wilderness, which civilization has not yet reached. Though its spontaneous productions were luxuriant, and often-times gigantic, yet, had the ploughshare of civilization, and the refining process of art passed through, and over the virgin soil, mankind would have been astonished at the result.

As an orator, he would have graced any of our legislative halls ; and he far exceeded many who hold themselves up as patterns in the art. Bishop Hedding said of him, after listening to him, as he gave his experience in his own tongue, and seeing the grace and artless simplicity of his gestures, "I have seen many who professed to understand the rules of elocution, and those who carried those principles out in practice, but never before did I see a perfect orator." He was grave and dignified in his manner and address, and prided himself on his stoical indifference in all minor matters, which moved the mass around him. He was respected by his nation, and his counsel was sought in all matters of public interest. His influence over his people was great, and in all matters of legislation he moulded them to his will. He was in the habit of calling his people together at the church every Sunday, and reading parts of the prayer-book and scriptures to them, after which, they were accustomed to finish the day in card-playing, horse-racing, and drinking fire-water, as taught or allowed by the missionary of the Established Church. But Thomas could see the inconsistency of such conduct, and he never allowed himself in any of these things. He knew me to be a Methodist, and as he had been taught by his minister that Methodism was an error, he had not been disposed to look upon me with much favor. But when he heard Polly and Peter talk about leaving off their bad practices, he thought there might be something more than he at first believed, and though he believed his religion was *the* religion, yet he was willing to countenance anything which promised reform among his people.

At the time appointed, we commenced our meeting. The house was crowded, and many gathered around the windows and doors. There were several there who had been awakened to a sense of their lost and ruined condition, by the efforts of Peter and Polly. I commenced the exercises, it was not long before sobs and cries broke from every part of the house; men and women, old and young, crying out, "O, my sorry, wicked heart! O, my sorry, wicked heart! I shall go to the bad place!" The scene was solemn and impressive. Scattered all over the room, were eighteen or twenty, who were wringing their hands, and crying as though their hearts were breaking under some great grief; while others, crowding up to see what was the matter, looked on in wonder and awe. Their sorrowful faces showed, as they peered through the windows and doors, their heartfelt sympathy; while a feeling of wonder, as to what all this might be, mingled with their sympathy—caused them to stand silent and attentive. We found it necessary to point them directly to the Lamb of God. We said to them, "Jesus Christ, the Son of the Great Spirit, and who lives with the Great Spirit above, will save you. He can cast the bad spirit out of your hearts, and make your sorry, wicked hearts good and glad, like Polly's and Peter's. If you will say in your hearts, to the Great Spirit, and his son Jesus Christ, that you will put away the fire-water, the white man's poison, and drink no more of it; that you will not be wicked any more; that you will do all this Bible tells you to do—for this Bible contains his will; he will help you, and bless you. You must believe he will help you, and his blessed Bible says he will, if you ask him; and you must believe that Jesus Christ can drive the bad spirit out of your hearts, and make them glad and happy, by entering in himself."

They seemed at once to believe these gospel truths, as thus simply expounded to them, through an interpreter, and simultaneously with their believing, they fell from their seats either to the floor, or into the arms of some one near by, and to all appearance were dead persons. The Indians at the doors and windows, and those in the house, were very much frightened at this, and ran for water.

One little girl, who was sitting by the side of her mother when she fell under the power of God, thinking she was dying or dead, ran home to tell her father. He immediately came, but before water could be brought by Indians without, they had begun to drink of the waters of salvation. In a few moments the shout of victory was heard from those who, a few moments before, seemed plunged in hopeless despair. The father, who came expecting to find his wife dead, found her shouting and praising God. His soul was awakened, and he was soon rejoicing with his wife. Jesus Christ had now taken possession of them ; their souls were filled with light and love ; their tongues were loosed, and from all parts of the house was heard the cry, "O Jesus, he make me happy ! O Jesus, how I love thee ! Glory ! O glory !"

During all this time, Thomas Davis had remained a silent, and to all appearance, an indifferent spectator ; but now he arose, and wrapping his blanket around him, went out of the house. Taking his prayer-book with him, he went into the field, and seated himself under an oak. He had seen the deep grief manifested by the others, and had seen that grief changed to joy almost unspeakable. He had never felt anything like this, though he had long been a Christian. He began to reason on the subject, and enquire what made this difference. He began to feel bad at heart, and remembering what he had heard the missionary say, he thought he would pray. So, kneeling down, he began to say over the words, as he had heard them. Soon the love of God filled his heart, when he arose and came to the house. During his absence, his wife, who had remained during the whole service, was awakened, and following the example of the others, soon was made happy. She said when she gave up her heart to the Great Spirit, the power of God came down upon her, as she expressed it, "All over, hoo, hoo."

Both Thomas and his wife were converted, and at about the same time of day. Thomas immediately began to exhort those about him, who still remained sinners, to turn to the Great Spirit, and partake with him of the blessed peace and joy which he felt. This meeting lasted all day. We immediately proceeded to organize a class ; we read and explained the "general rules," and received between twenty and thirty as the fruits of that day's labor.

We now started the building of a house which should serve the double purpose of church and school-house. The Indians turned out with their axes, cut down trees, hewed them on two sides, drew them to the building spot, which was in the north part of the Mohawk tribe, and we soon had a good sized house erected. I went to the white settlements, procured boards and shingles for the roof, and we soon had the building finished. Just at this time, Seth Crawford, a young man, and a licensed exhorter of the M. E. Church, living at Saratoga, feeling a desire to visit, and if possible be of benefit to the Indians of the Canadas, came among us. We immediately employed him as our school teacher, and leader of our Indian society. When we dedicated our house, it was filled with Indians, who seemed to be friendly to our cause. We established a day and also a Sabbath-school, where the children were taught English. When we called the children together, we used a tin horn, but when we wanted the Indians to assemble for worship, we blew a shell, which could be heard from two to three miles. Whenever this was sounded, the Indians dropped all their work and repaired immediately to the church. This house we had cleaned out very often, in order that it might be perfectly neat and decent. Whenever they met here for worship, they would kneel before taking their seats, and ask the blessing of God upon them ; and often in so doing, they would receive such direct answers to their prayers, that they would be unable to take their seats for some time.

As soon as they were brought under religious influence, they became as docile and as tractable as little children. We taught them to observe one day in seven as fast day ; we appointed Sunday for such a day. Accordingly, they abstained from all food until after the morning service and class-meeting, which generally closed about one o'clock in the afternoon. About three, they would take their dinner, and at five, or evening, they assembled for prayer-meeting, and if there were any who were seeking religion, they would all unite in prayer for them, and seldom closed until all were made happy.

Morning and evening devotions were established in their families as soon as they gave evidence of renewed hearts. Baptism was administered by sprinkling at the altar. The parents all seemed anxious to have their children baptized, for we told them, "the promise is to you and your children." The sacrament was administered to them quarterly, and these seasons were always of great interest. We endeavored to present to their minds the blessed Jesus as he appeared upon the cross, "pouring out his blood unto death," and to explain to them the object and utility of eating the bread and wine consecrated before them, and so great was their faith in Jesus Christ and his blood shed out for their redemption, that they did truly feed upon him in their hearts with thanksgiving and praise. At such times, the love of God would so fill their hearts with its overwhelming power, that their animal strength would be suspended, and they would sink to the floor.   O, we all could say,

"Even now we mournfully enjoy,
  Communion with our Lord,
As though we every one,
  Beneath his cross had stood,
And seen him heave and heard him groan,
  And felt his gushing blood."

It seemed, on such occasions, as though we could all soar to higher regions of light and love than at other times.   On one occasion, while the altar was crowded with communicants, the power of God came down upon them, and they sunk to the ground as though a mighty wind had passed over them.   Tears streamed down their faces, as the windows of heaven were opened upon them, and the fountains of their hearts seemed broken up, while amid shouts of praise and tears of joy, they lay perfectly helpless upon the floor.

O why is it that some of the professors of religion, at the present day, living as they do in the broad, mid-day sunlight of science and christianity, and at a time when the gospel of Christ, spreading its wings of light, and sweeping over mountain and plain, over river and sea, has pierced the blackness of darkness that has so long hung, brooding like a pall, over the nations of the earth, and has sent its loud, joyful trumpet tones, thrilling through the hearts of millions who sat in the valley of the shadow of death, and now poising its bright pinions, hovers over our own fair land—why is it, I say, that professed Christians, knowing all this, will point the finger of scorn and derision at those who, by faith, drink of the waters of salvation as they flow from under the throne of God, and yield to the glorious influences of joy unspeakable which, with every draught of love that they receive from the fountain of light and life, fills their souls, till they are constrained to cry aloud, and with uplifted voice, proclaim to those about them, the wonders of redeeming grace and dying love?

What wonder is it, O ye of little faith, that under the mighty influences of such love, they fall to the ground? Is the arm of the Almighty shortened, that

he cannot save ?   Is not his power the same that it was
in olden days, when on the plains of Bethlehem there
appeared an unnumbered host of shining ones sweeping through the air, and with voice of melody, pro-
claiming to the astonished and awe-struck shepherds,
the joyful tidings which they bore ?

Is not the love which thrilled the hearts of angel
and archangel, of cherubim and of seraphim, and that
caused them to tune their harps anew, and swell the
mighty anthem of praise, till heaven's high arches
echoed back the joyful strains, mighty enough to
overcome the strength of puny man ?   Is not that
power which sent, from beyond the vast realms of
space, the chariot of fire to escort Elijah safely to his
home above ; or, which set at defiance all nature's
laws, when the Savior, standing on the Mount of
Ascension, rose silently, slowly, and majestically, up
into the bright blue of heaven's dome, till he was lost
from sight in immensity ; or, which on the day of
Pentecost, came with the sound of a mighty rushing
wind, and sat in tongues of flame upon the heads of all
present, endowing them with power to speak in all
languages of the earth ; or, which struck Saul to the
earth, blinding him with the brightness of its glory ;
and which opened the prison doors and loosed the chains
which bound the apostle Peter, the same now as
then ?

Is not that power which darkened the sun in mid-heaven, which rolled back the door of the tomb, and filled the hearts of those brave old soldiers with such fear that they "became as dead men," able to fell to the earth the proudest, the mightiest of earth's nobility, now ?

If so, then why, when you look upon the prostrate form of some fallen son or daughter of Adam, why say it is all delusion, and that though you wish to enjoy all that can be measured out to you, yet you can never be willing to "lose your strength?" Where is the propriety of such reasoning ?* Where is the philosophy that countenances such unreasonable desires ? and what is the foundation on which you build your argument ?

CHAPTER V.

The Indian children showed great aptitude in learning to read English, and were very devout when in the sanctuary. They always came neat and clean, and whenever the rest kneeled they kneeled also, invariably preserving a serious deportment while in church.

We endeavored to inculcate habits of industry among them; for in their pagan state they were brought up to think it was degrading for an Indian to work. His business was to sit in the council, smoke the pipe, hunt and fish, while the women had to plant the corn, beans, and potatoes, hoe and gather in the harvest, chop the wood, and in fact do all the drudgery. But we told them, "Indian man plant potatoes, corn and beans, he hoe and gather in the harvest, cut the wood, and help carry the children when travelling, while the women must stay in the house, bake the bread, cook the victuals, wash, and make the clothes,

and keep the children neat and clean." Our instructions were generally well received, and as a consequence, those Indians who followed the Savior were
temperate and industrious, provided well for their
families, and proved the truth of the apostle's doctrine, "Godliness is profitable unto all things."

We now found it necessary to prepare for Conference, which held its session in Westmoreland, Oneida
Co., N. Y.   This journey, going and coming, could
not be less than from six to eight hundred miles,. to
be performed entirely on horseback ; and no one who
has never performed such a journey can form a correct opinion of the fatigue consequent upon it, especially when encumbered with the baggage we were
obliged to carry. It was in the heat of summer, and
many long and weary days we travelled over the dusty
roads, the sky seeming like brass above us, while the
parched and thirsty earth reflected back the intense
heat of the sun, that rolled through the heavens like
some avenging angel, whose mission was to punish, by
thirst and heat, the nations of the earth. Often would
I have to dismount and walk by the side of my Fancy,
for such weather was unendurable by any horse, with
the load she carried.

I reached the Conference the morning it commenced.
Here I found an agent for Dr. Clarke's Commentaries,

Rev. Charles Giles. These works had but just found their way into this country, and of course were prized very highly, but Br. Giles let ministers have them at reduced rates, sixty dollars being the price as reduced. They were in pamphlet form, unbound, and about the thickness of a spelling-book. I had never seen these volumes, and of course they were a treasure to me. But as I only had one hundred dollars a year, and half of that went to support my mother, I could only pay him fifteen or twenty dollars at a time, which I did every year until they were paid for. I had them packed and sent on to Canada, for I had received my appointment back to Grand River Mission, and at the close of Conference, paid my mother a visit before returning.

My mother had heard from me during the year by letter, in which I spoke of the commencement of the work of God among the Indians, but yet she seemed not fully to conceive how wonderful it was, till I gave her a full account of it. She rejoiced greatly that the war-whoop had been changed to shouts of joy and praise ; that the drunken revel, and midnight orgies, had been superceded by the earnest tones of midnight prayer, or the joyful song of peace and love ; and she said if she had a dozen sons, and every one should be called of God to preach his gospel to the heathen, she would willingly say, "Go, my son, and may God bless you."

I now took leave of home and friends, and again started for my mission. But with a somewhat different feeling did I start, than when, one year before I bade adieu to all my early associations, and started on an enterprise which promised much of danger and suffering, if no more. Then I started, like a mariner on an unknown sea, with nothing but God and my own judgment to guide me ; now, I was going to a church of Christians, whose hearts were all aglow with the love of Christ ; where I would be welcomed as a brother ; where I expected to meet many old friends. Then, I started with the good *wishes* of all, to be sure, but with the expectation from every one, that my attempt would be a failure. Now, I was returning to a field of labor which, through the blessing of God, began to blossom as the rose.

After a long and fatiguing journey for both man and beast, I reached the Niagara waters. Here I found my box, containing my Commentaries, which I took across with me at an expense of four dollars as duties. I carried them to the house of an old friend, near my field of labor, where I left them, only taking one at a time with me. I had a tin box made in the form of a cylinder, with a cover fitting so closely that no water could find its way in. I then rolled up one of my pamphlets, and slipping it in there, packed it away in my valise. The cover to this box served the purpose of drinking cup, when alone in the wilderness. By improving every leisure hour, I could read òne through by the time I came round to my starting point, when I would take another, and in this way I first read Clarke's Commentaries. During the first year of my itinerancy, I had found Dr. Coke's Works. I read them what I could, but this work was not common in those days, among our brethren of Western New York. I had also read Mr. Wesley's Notes on the New Testament, which, with Dr. Clarke, seemed to put us right on all the most difficult parts of the Holy Scriptures.

I found our Indian brethren expressed much joy on my return. One Indian, on hearing that I was again stationed among them, said, "O, I so happy, I jump up !" In passing around my extensive mission, I found the spirit of awakening had got hold of Indians for thirty miles from our mission-house ; and the Indians here and there, on hearing what was going on among the Mohawks, were anxious I should preach to them.

The Mohawk chief, Thomas Davis, after joining our Church, had discontinued his attendance at the Mohawk Castle. Soon after, he was visited by an

English Bishop, who was on his annual tour through the Canadas, and their interview was rather amusing. The Bishop enquired of the old chief, why he had left their Church, and joined the Methodists. The old chief replied, "Bishop, you know your ministers preach to Indians forty years. No see at all; all dark—no feel any good. All drink fire-waters—get drunk—all bad. But the Methodist minister come preach to Indian; he feel sorry, then glad. He put away all the fire-waters; begin to pray—be sober—work—have plenty to eat—all very happy. What you think of the Methodist religion, Bishop?"

The Bishop sat listening attentively to him, till he finished, then with a shake of his head replied, "I don't know anything about this Methodist religion." The old chief quickly replied, "You not know anything about this Bible religion? I very sorry." And then warming up with the subject, he gave him such an exhortation that the Bishop was glad to bid him "good day," at the first chance he could get. The Bishop soon returned to England, and immediately dispatched a young minister to fill the church at the Castle. This gentleman took up his residence a few miles from the Indians, and preached to them one sermon every Sunday. He then returned to his boarding place; but the Indians, as on former occasions, spent the rest of the day in their old amusements, horse-racing, card-playing, and drinking. Mr. H——, their minister, hearing of this, resolved to give them a severe reproof on the following Sabbath. Accordingly he told them what he had heard about them, and said he should have no more such work on the Sabbath, if he preached to them. But the Indians, not liking his reproofs, put on cloudy faces, and said to him, "We not want you to preach to us—we not have you."

He called upon me, and wished to know how it was that we reformed the poor drunken Indians, and brought them under religious discipline. I said to him, "In order to get pagan Indians converted to God, we must go among them, visit them, eat with them, converse with them, pray with and for them, and look to God for his Spirit to accompany his truth to their hearts, then there is no difficulty in leading them to Jesus Christ, who saves them." He said he believed in being religious, and in attending to the means of grace, "but," said he, "the wonderful change of heart you speak of, I don't understand." He wished-ed me to give him the charge of the society of the converted Indians, while I should go among the wild ones again, "for you have such success," said he, "in converting Indians, you can soon establish another society equal to the first." This I declined doing, and he left me, and in a few months returned to England.

Peter Jones was a young man of about twenty years, and though connected with a Mohawk family living near our mission-house, was a Chippewa of the Mississaguas tribe. Not long after his conversion, he began to talk of trying to hunt up his mother, and of persuading her, and the tribe to which she belonged, to come up to Grand River, and share with the Mohawks in the blessings of the gospel.

At this time the Chippewas were not confined to any one place, but, like the Arabs, moved about from place to place, and wherever a white man had erected a huckstering shop, there would they be seen, rolling in the mud like swine. Their yells, when in their drunken frolics, were frightful, and often has my horse been frightened, when passing these haunts of vice. No one cared for these poor Indians, nor would any one give them shelter from the weather, unless to get their money, or their furs from them. When these were gone, they were turned into the open air, where they were obliged to stay during any and all the storms of the seasons. This constant exposure to the inclemency of the seasons, together with their habitual use of the "fire-water," caused a rapid diminution of numbers, and when I became acquainted with them, they were comparatively few in numbers.

Peter, after thinking over his mother's condition for months, and praying for her salvation, concluded to go and hunt her up. In this work, he was encouraged by us. Accordingly, one day, he put off for the river Credit, where he thought he would be most likely to find her. On reaching the river, he found the whole company, with the exception of their chief, Captain John, holding a drunken frolic.

When he beheld their condition, he turned away with disgust and sorrow of heart, thinking, "Surely these people are too far gone in sin and wickedness, to be saved ; I will return." So, turning about, he started for home, but he had not proceeded far, when he was met by Captain John. He told the old chief what had been done at Grand River, and his errand there. Captain John said, "You wait a little, till my people get sober, then you tell them your story." He concluded to wait.

After they had finished their frolic, and were again sober, Peter began a talk with them. He told them how the Son of the Great Spirit had saved, and blessed him, and other Indians at Grand River ; and how happy they were after putting away the fire-waters ; and concluded, by asking them to come to Grand River, and get this religion for themselves. Their answer was : "You say you no drink whisky there."

"Well," says Peter, "we something better than whisky ; come, get this religion, and you shall know for yourselves." They finally promised to come, and Peter bidding them "Good-bye," returned. When he related his story, we concluded they would soon forget their promise, and this would be the last they would think about it.

CHAPTER VI.

The Reservation of the Six Nations, as we have before remarked, lies on both sides of the Grand River. This valley, for miles on each side of the river, is hardly above "high-water mark," and in some places it is below, thus causing the many swamps which are found along this river, some of them being of great extent. Where the land comes above "high-water mark," the ground is dry and the soil fertile. In many places on these plains, the timber consisted entirely of oak, hence their name, "Oak Plains." These oaks were scattered thinly over the surface, forming beautiful groves, and as the ground was free from underbrush, objects could be seen at a great distance.

One day, while at the mission-house with several of our Indian brethren, we descried, away in the distance, a long line of persons in Indian file, winding in and out among the oaks of the plain, and making towards us. We called attention to them, and they were immediately pronounced by our brethren, as the Mississaguas. We at once concluded they must be Capt. John and his party. We accordingly blew the shell, or trumpet, and in a few moments the Mohawks were flocking in from all quarters, to make ready for the reception of their visitors. As they came up, there was a general shaking of hands by all present. We found Peter's mother among the number.

Before starting from their homes at the Credit, they had fixed themselves out in all their finery, and dressed in their best clothes ; they intended to present quite an imposing appearance, but they were obliged to pass several whisky shops, and at each, they thought they could stop and take "just one drink around." The consequence was, that long before reaching Grand River, they had parted with all their money, and much of their jewelry, besides getting their clothes stained with dirt and filth. We now invited them into our church, in order to gratify their desire of knowing more of the work of the Great Spirit, as related to them by Peter. They were seated at the back part of the house, the front seats being reserved for those who took part in the exercises. The Mohawks, on coming in, kneeled, as was their custom, and asked the blessing of the Great Spirit upon them-selves and their visitors.

For a few minutes all was still. Then rising, they commenced singing some verses in their own tongue. They were beautiful singers, and their music produced a visible impression upon these wild, untutored savages. After singing, we addressed them, told them of the Savior, and how they might be saved ; told them of the work the Great Spirit had performed among their brother Indians, and exhorted them to seek for the blessing. We now all kneeled down, and Peter led in prayer, in the Chippewa tongue. For this time had Peter long wished, and hoped, and prayed.

The conversion of his mother was to him an all-absorbing theme ; and for months he had waited and prayed ; for months he had plead with the Great Spirit, to influence the mind of his mother and her tribe to listen to the Gospel of Jesus ; and with his faith strong in the Lord, that he would work in his behalf, did he start on his visit to the "Credit." And now that his desires were gratified, his prayers answered, his faith in God waxed stronger, and as he knelt in that room, and saw his mother on her knees before God, his soul was moved, and he cried with a loud voice to the Lord of Sabaoth, that he would hear his cry, and answer his petition. His faith was strong, his plea an urgent one ; his soul was stirred within him, and as he poured out his heart before God, his words were like fire in a dry stubble.

While Peter was still praying, being joined by the others in an undertone, the poor Mississaguas were pricked in their hearts by what they heard, and began crying aloud, while sobs and tears almost choked their utterance,—"O, my sorry, wicked heart, O, my sorry, wicked heart, I shall go to the bad place." When this cry arose from those poor heathen, the effect was almost indescribable. Those who had before been praying, earnestly, to be sure, yet silently, now broke forth as with one accord, and with a loud voice cried unto the Lord of hosts to hear and deliver. When the Lord saw that they had drunk the bitter cup of repentance long enough, the sweet balm of heavenly consolation was sent to heal their wounded souls, and then came the joys of salvation.

Now, as on a former occasion, they sank to the floor under the mighty power of God, and arose with shouts of glory upon their tongues. Before many minutes had passed away, nearly every one of the thirty who had entered the house of God as poor benighted heathen, was basking in the sunlight of Christianity, and praising God for his goodness in bringing them to a knowledge of the Gospel of Christ, who for the first time in their lives had stepped foot inside of a christian church.

Soon all these Mississaguas gave evidence of a change of heart by the power of divine grace, and that they had received the spirit of adoption, whereby they might cry, "Abba, Father," and call Jesus Lord, by the Holy Ghost ; and as they had just emerged from pagan darkness into the glorious liberty of the Gospel of Christ, and were in the fullest sense, "babes in Christ," it became necessary for us to pay particular attention to them, that we might instruct them in the first principles of the doctrine of Christ, and explain to them the devices of Satan, when combined with wicked men, that they might fortify themselves against them.

These Mississaguas were now enjoying the hospitality of our Grand River brethren, but we knew they must soon leave. Our anxiety on their account was great, for we knew if they returned to the Credit, they would have to pass many whisky shops, where every art that could be brought to bear upon them, in order to get them to drink again of the "fire-water," would be used ; and also if they returned, they would remove their children from the English school, the advantages of which they now enjoyed. But we were soon relieved of our anxiety, by an offer by our Mohawk brethren, of as much land as they would wish to till, and on which they might build houses, and make comfortable homes for themselves and children. How much this seemed like the days spoken of in Acts ii. 44–47, "And all that believed were together, and had all things common, and sold their possessions and goods, and parted them to all men, as every man had need. And they, continuing daily with one accord in the temple, and breaking bread from house to house, did eat their meat with gladness and singleness of heart, praising God, and having favor with all the people. And the Lord added to the Church daily such as should be saved."

After reading and explaining our "General Rules," to which they all readily subscribed, we administered the ordinance of baptism, by sprinkling, at the altar.

It was customary among the pagan Indians to marry by taking a woman and living with her as long as they both could agree. But should any serious misunderstanding arise between them, they would part, each going their own way, and leaving either free to marry at pleasure. We explained to them the nature and extent of the marriage covenant, as laid down in our blessed Bible, and they readily agreed to its precepts. They all stood up around the altar, and we joined them together in the holy bands of matrimony. They builded themselves neat, though small houses, planted and sowed, and seemed anxious to receive instruction in all subjects relating to their temporal and spiritual welfare, always appearing at the house of God, as neat and as clean as any of our Mohawks. They occasionally went on hunting excursions, and sometimes were obliged to be out in the wilderness over the Sabbath. At such times they would spend the day in prayer and praise, observing it as strictly as though at home. They always returned loaded with game. Not unfrequently they met with some of their own nation, who were also hunting, and they always invited them to come to Grand River and get the "good religion" which they enjoyed. Many did so, and often were they converted under the first sermon they ever listened to. Our number constantly increased. Daily were they added to the Church, till the mission-house was filled with christian Indians.

All seemed anxious to have their children learn to read English, and the adults even, would put themselves under the instruction of Br. Crawford, and were as studious as any persons could be. Capt. John's wife entered our day school with a determination to learn English enough to read the blessed Bible, and in a few months she was able to read intelligently.

CHAPTER VII.

Sometime before this, I had received intelligence
that quite a body of Munceys, (Delawares) who spake
the Mississagua dialect, resided on the river Thames.
This river had its source in the wilderness which then
extended from Grand River to Lake Huron. It runs
a north-westerly course, emptying itself into Lake St.
Clair, forty miles east of Sandwich, thus affording
communication by boats with Lake Erie and the
northern lakes. There were several bodies of Indians
on this river. In one of these the Moravians had
established a mission, and a minister resided among
them. This Moravian town was about ninety miles
from Sandwich. The Munceys lived one hundred
miles from Sandwich and seventy from Grand River.
There were two bodies of these Munceys residing some

seven miles apart. Of these tribes, one was a remnant of the Delawares, the other the Chippewas. They were designated as the Upper and Lower town. I had received a letter from John Carey, a young man some twenty-four years old, who was teaching school in Westminster, Talbott's street, U. C. He was a pious youth, the son of religious parents residing in Schoharie, N. Y. He had visited the Munceys (Delawares) once or twice, and now expressed a desire to become the teacher of an English school among them, if we could succeed in obtaining the consent of the chiefs and counsellors. In his letter he says:

"MUNCEY TOWN, May 2d, 1825.

"*Dear Br. Torry:*—As you desire me to give you in writing the particulars of my undertaking among the Indians, I send you the following: While employed in my school in Westminster, I had seen these people pass, and they had encamped near my school. They were given to intoxication. Their poverty and ignorance excited a pity, and I felt my spirit stirred within me to endeavor to improve their state by instruction. Accordingly, in December last, in company with a friend, we travelled through the wood about seven miles, and found the dwelling of George Turkey, the principal chief. He was not at home, but his family was hospitable, and appeared capable of improvement, which encouraged me to make them another visit, which I did on the 3d of April—but now I found none at home. The night was cold, and I spent it in a poor wigwam, without fire and without food. On the 15th, I made another visit, and again their wigwams were empty; but on the fourth visit to their town, (April 25th,) I found the Indians at home.

"I now endeavored to learn their wishes about having their children learn to read, and offered to become their teacher. Some appeared friendly to the design; others were indifferent. A council of all the chiefs was called, and I was permitted to be present. When assembled, they stretched themselves on the green grass and commenced their deliberations in their native tongue. After about two hours' debate, chief Westbrook arose, and gave me in English the opinions of the chiefs, the substance of which was, that some were in favor of the school, others were opposed to any innovation in their established manners. He, and others of his brethren, wished their children taught to read. I concluded to make the trial, and appointed a time to commence the school.

"The system of morality and religion entertained by this people, is very dark and sensual. It comprises a mixture of catholicism, paganism, and some correct notions—remains of the labors of the devoted Brainard. Heaven they think to be a place for the good, where are plenty of clothes, food, and other good things. I have endeavored to show them the difference between their sensual notions and the pure and spiritual blessings of Christianity. They heard attentively, and appeared more thoughtful. In my critical situation, I need the help of grace. Pray that my endeavors to do this people good, may be accepted and blessed. I hope to see you soon, accompanied by Peter Jones. Till then, farewell.

"JOHN CAREY."

Having a little spare time, I now resolved to visit

these Indians, and make an effort to save them. Accordingly, I enlisted Peter Jones, and five of our most zealous and reliable Missionaries, and off we started for the Munceys. Taking a westerly course, we travelled on till we reached the last white settlement which stood bordering on the wilderness. Here we met Br. Carey, who accompanied us, and was a very good pilot to Muncey town. I was obliged to leave my horse at the settlement, and go in on foot. On arriving at their town, we found the Indians preparing for their annual religious feast. They brought to the council-house, a little of all they had raised during the summer, as an offering to the Great Spirit. Night was fast closing in, and as yet, Br. Carey and myself had found no lodging place. Our Indians had early found both food and shelter, but to us nothing had been offered, and we had tasted no food since early in the morning. We finally received an Indian cake, and some boiled corn, which was thankfully received, and as heartily eaten.

Their council-house was from thirty to forty feet long, and eighteen wide, with no windows, chimney or hole, for the smoke to escape, that I could perceive. It had a door at each end, with a broad alley running through the center, from one door to the other. A pole, about six inches in diameter, extended on either side the alley, the length of the house. They had collected large quantities of wild grass, dried it, and placed it inside the poles, for the Indians to sit or lie upon. A large post was placed about midway from the doors, and running to the roof. As soon as it became dark, one of the leading chiefs called for all the men and women to hasten in to the house. This they immediately did, the men taking one side of the house, and the women the other. Fires had been kindled within four feet of each door, which gave light enough to see the way through the house. I, with my company, was invited in, and we accepted the invitation. We took sides with the men, who by this time were all seated. At the center post was seated one of their most intelligent looking Indians, with his head ornamented with beautiful feathers, and with other marks of distinction upon him. He was called their Commissary, and he had, properly speaking, a secretary by his side. Back of these, were seated a number of Indians, who had before them a pile of dried deer skins. Each one held in his hand a stick similar to a drumstick.

After all were in their places, the doors were ordered to be shut, and the fires smothered with hemlock, in such a manner as to stop their blazing. This was done by two smart looking young Indians, and now,

nothing was to be seen or felt, but smoke, and it seemed for a time, as though I should suffocate. I put my
face into my hands, laid them upon my knees, as I
was sitting on the ground, and tried to keep my eyes
shut as closely as possible. In every part of the house
was heard coughing and sighing. In about six minutes
the doors were opened, and gradually the smoke disap-
peared. One of the chiefs now stepped out into the
alley. He had a turtle-shell in his hand ; this shell
contained wampum, and shining beads. He began
shaking it slowly at first, and dancing moderately.

Opposite him, sprang up a fine looking woman, with
wampum in her hands. She kept step with the chief,
who increased his speed, and his efforts to shake the
shell, until he was dancing with all his might, the
woman meanwhile keeping up with him. This they
continued for some time. Finally, the chief took his
seat, and the woman, walking up to the center-post,
laid down the wampum which she held in her hand,
and then took her seat.

During the whole of these exercises, the men with
their drumsticks kept beating upon the deer-skins,
which made considerable noise. Directly, another
chief made his appearance, with the shell of wampum,
and commenced shaking and dancing, as the other had
done. He also was accompanied by a woman, as

before ; and thus these exercises lasted all night. A little while before daylight appeared, several men and women were requested to leave the house, and set the kettles, which contained their meat, &c., over the fires. The young Indians, for the occasion, had brought in twelve yearling bucks. These were dressed, and cut in small pieces. But the heads of the twelve bucks were neither skinned nor dressed in any shape, but were thrown in with the rest of the meat, as they were first taken from the animals. With their meat they had boiled corn, potatoes, squashes, and beans ; and when it was all cooked, they brought it into the council-house, where one of the chiefs distributed it to those who were present. To each person he gave *one* piece of meat, but to me he gave *two*. Their succotash, which they seemed to enjoy so much, was more than I could eat. None of it was salted, for they were entirely "out of" the article. As near as I could determine, the twelve deer heads were given to those who had used the drum-sticks. After devouring the twelve deers, and eating up all their succotash, the leading chiefs marched out of, and around the house, with their eyes upraised, and in a loud tone of voice, crying, hoo ! hoo ! hoo ! and thus ended this night's feast.

I now supposed they were through with their pagan

worship for the present ; but I was soon informed that they were preparing for another night's worship, in which the devil, or "bad spirit" was to be invoked. In this, they put on false faces, which they called their "grandfather's faces." These made them look very frightful. I said to some nearest me, "that no good to worship the devil." This spread like wild-fire among the warriors, and in a few moments they put on cloudy faces, and showed by their actions and looks, that they were much displeased with me, for condemning their proceedings. However, the Cony chief, Turkey, informed them they must prepare to meet me in council in about two hours.

The dwellings of these Indians were scattered in the edge of the forest, and bordering a large clearing. In the centre of this clearing rose a small conical hill, or large mound. This was covered with grass, and around the top were placed seats. Here the chiefs and warriors often met in council. Their council-house stood to the south of this, and just in the edge of the forest, being surrounded by those stern old oaks that stood like grim sentinels, watching the "council fires" that burned within. As one stood upon the summit of the clearing, the little log dwellings of the Indians could be seen on every side, some standing boldly out from among the front ranks of those giant monarchs of the forest, who stood, with arms interlocked, towering high and majestically, as if conscious of their grandeur, frowning upon the pale-faced intruder, but pouring forth sweet strains of music for the red man, as the wind sighed mournfully through their Æolian-like branches, or waking again the far-off echos of the forest, swept howling and thundering by in maniac strength, while threading the labyrinthine passages of the dark, shadowy old woods.   Others of these cabins, set farther back, stood peering out, as if watching for some advancing enemy, while others yet were buried deep in the leafy recesses of the forest, their existence made known only by the curling smoke which rose gracefully above the trees, and was lost in the deep blue vault of heaven.

It was a beautiful place, away there in the wilderness, far from the haunts of civilized men ; and as I stood upon that little eminence, with the bright sun shining above my head, and the beautiful carpeting of grass and flowers spreading out at my feet, and away to the edge of the woods, I listened to the sweet carol of the birds as they flew from tree to tree, or, perched upon the topmost bough of some tall tree, poured forth, in strains both loud and long, their sweetest notes of melody ; and then I heard the murmuring music of the rushing river, as it wound in and out among the moss-covered trees of the olden forest, and its tones, borne upon the wings of a passing zephyr, fell upon my ear like the enchanting strains of melody that 'float through the halls, and fill the echoing corridors of the fairy-like palaces of the dreamy Orient. All else was still, save when the watchful dog was aroused by the rustle of the timid deer, as it bounded through the thicket, or was heard the triumphant chattering of the squirrel, that, perched upon some high limb, had escaped the jaws of the eager dog below. Now and then a solitary Indian, with his blanket closely wrapped about him, would glide quickly and stealthily from one cabin to another, as if in secret consultation with his fellows upon some momentous subject.

My friends had scattered themselves among the different cabins, and were watching with anxiety the course of events. All the Indians, with the exception of their Sachem, Turkey, and his friend, Westbrook, were jealous of me, and considered me, in common with all white men, their enemy. During the time allowed them to consult together before meeting me in council, some of the boldest had proposed killing me, in case I persuaded Turkey to change their customs and worship, for they knew he was friendly to my enterprise, though I did not. My friends, the

Mississaguas, were acquainted with their designs, and waited with much anxiety for the time appointed. When the hour arrived, several of the chiefs appeared at the edge of the clearing, and giving the war-whoop, started for the rendezvous. Hardly had the sound of their unearthly yell died out in the distance, before the woods again echoed with the same yell, and this time it seemed as though the woods might be full of savages, so loud were the sounds of those horrid yells, as they echoed and re-echoed through the woods. In a few moments over sixty warriors, painted and dressed in war costume, with tomahawk and scalping-knife, made their appearance. Turkey and Westbrook, dressed in their ordinary costume, took a seat apart from the rest, and commanding a view of them all. I took up my position with the speakers chosen for the occasion, while the others, with eyes flashing vengeance, gathered themselves together in a group a little way from us. Our Grand River brethren were gathered in a group by themselves, and sat trembling with fear for me. Knowing, as they did, the threats that had been made, they expected nothing less than to see me killed before the council broke up.

I now informed them that I was a Methodist minister, and was patronized by the Governor and their agent, and that my business was to get their consent to preach to them Jesus Christ, and teach their children the English language. I then asked them if they were willing we should do all this. One of them answered "no." I then asked him why. He said the white man had cheated them out of the lands the Great Spirit had given them to live on ; and that where their fathers and grandfathers, their mothers and children had been buried, there the white man now planted and sowed his grain. The white man had cheated them out of their hunting grounds, and were continually seeking their ruin. They would have nothing to do with him nor his religion.

In reply, I said to them, "not all white men so bad ; some good ; they not want to cheat and hunt the Indian, but do him good. Such believe in the religion of Jesus Christ, the Son of the Great Spirit. Of him I come to tell you." They said, "Indian has been murdered after he get white man's religion. Many years ago Moravian preach to Indian on the other side lake. He get good many to join him. Then he get them all together in a house, where he murdered them, and burned them up."

I said to them, "you are mistaken. It was not the Moravians that committed this barbarous act. It was a band of renegade fellows, who, under the cloak of friendship, possessed themselves of the arms of the

Indians, and then confined them to their houses, where they put them to death.   This wicked act has always been disapproved of by good men.   Besides, the Moravian missionary could have no hand in the affair, as he was at Sandusky, while those that were murdered were at Muskingum, having gone thither for provisions.*   The Moravian missionary had never intended to do them harm, but had labored much to make them wise and good."   "Well," they said, "they understood the French were coming to make war upon them, and they would wait and see what they would do."   I told them the French could not get to them, and besides, they never would try to harm them.

I now spoke of my authority from the Great Spirit, and told them he had authorized me to come and tell them the good and right way.   They said, "the Great Spirit send us prophets.   They tell us to live as our fathers lived, and keep up the ancient customs."   I told them the Great Spirit had given us a great book, and that this book told us that the Great Spirit made all men ; that we must all live in peace, and love one another as brothers, and do each other good.   The

---

*In March, 1792, a band of ruffians, 160 in number, near Fort Pitt, formed the design of cutting off the Moravian Indians at Muskingum. Colonel Gibson, at Pittsburg, having heard of the plot, sent messengers to Muskingum, to inform the Indians of their danger, but the messengers arrived too late.

same great book told us of the right way to worship, and of the Savior who died for sinners. "Now," said I, "the Great Spirit has not given you any such book, but he has given it to us, and told us to hand it to our red brethren ; and if you take this good book, and obey what it says, it will make you wise and happy in this life, and direct you most safely to a happier life to come. Now, brothers, we come to hand you this book, and to teach your children to read it, that they may be wise and good."

When we told them that the Great Spirit had given them no such good book, and that we had come to hand it to them, and to teach their children to read it, they paused; hung down their heads, and appeared deeply thoughtful. Turkey, with Westbrook, both of whom were favorable to our design from the first, had listened with deep anxiety, to see how the controversy would end, and now, seeing that I had overcome and silenced them by argument, he arose, and pointing to a house that stood near the woods, said : "Brother, yonder is my house. If you come there and preach, you be protected. If any my people want to hear, they can come to my house." Pointing to another that stood near his dwelling house, he said, "There is another house ; you have it for school-house."

As soon as Turkey had ended, the whole council,

who had before stood waiting only the signal to hurl their tomahawks at my head, or to take me prisoner, and dispose of me as they might determine, and thus get rid of all innovations on their ancient customs, now put on smiling faces, and instead of the dark scowl of suspicion that before had rested upon them, they greeted me with friendship, and shook hands with me, to prove their good intentions. I now prepared to depart, while Br. Carey should remain and commence a school.

I have only given a synopsis of the arguments that were brought up in this council, which lasted some two hours or more, during which time none of us sat down, but remained upon our feet. During this time, I do not know that one fear entered my heart, though I knew by their looks that they were intensely hostile. Truly the Lord did protect me, and saved me from out the power of mine enemies. Br. Carey immediately commenced teaching their children English, and we thus laid a permanent foundation for the salvation of this whole nation. I, with my Indian brethren, now took our leave and started back for Grand River. I will relate one incident which transpired the night before I reached Muncey town.

In common with most of the tribes of North American Indians, the Munceys believe in witchcraft.

Their method of curing a bewitched person was, to lay the person bewitched upon the ground in the evening, and choose twelve young men to dance around the person all night, and with shouting and yelling and frightful gestures, they would try to drive or frighten the witch away. At the time of my visit, there was a woman among them who had the consumption. The night before my arrival, they, thinking she was bewitched, concluded to perform their incantations over her and see if they could break the spell. They therefore brought her out, and laying her on the damp ground, engaged a dozen young Indians to dance all night for what whisky they would drink. Accordingly, soon after dark they commenced their dancing, accompanied with their hideous yells. The whisky they drank served to keep up their ambition to see which should yell the loudest and dance the hardest, and they thus made "night hideous" with their infernal incantations. As a matter of course, the poor woman was much worse the next morning, and this fact, which I brought up in my controversy with them, seemed to have considerable weight in undermining their belief in their old customs.

On my return, I passed through two of my old fields of labor, and was greeted by many of my old acquaintances in the Lord, with much warmth, and many encouraging words did they give me, which much strengthened me in my labors and sufferings.

At Long Point, we called upon George Ryerson, Esq., who was teaching a high school there. He had requested me to make him a visit, and bring some of the christian Indians with me. His wife was an English lady, a daughter of Judge Rollf, and not having been in the province long, had hardly been favored with the sight of a North American Indian, especially a christian Indian. They both wished an interview, that they might see and converse with them, and hear them sing and pray. We were all very kindly received. Br. Ryerson invited his father, Col. Ryerson, to spend the evening with us, which he did. Br. Ryerson had a very large garden of melons, which were of the finest quality. During the evening, a large table was spread, and piled with melons of various sizes, and all were invited to partake. And, truly, it was a feast, such as we never before had enjoyed. The next morning we took leave of this excellent family, and pushed on for home on the Grand River.

I found, on my return, that our mission house was very much crowded with christian Indians, for we now had over one hundred and fifty converted Chippewas, and we began to talk of taking them down to the Credit River, the place of their former residence.

The Chippewa Nation had a Reservation of land at the mouth of this river, but it had long been occupied by white men, for it was one of the best fisheries on Lake Ontario. Several chiefs of this tribe had been converted, and Peter was made chief, and now gave evidence of being called of God to preach the gospel to his countrymen. After consultation with these chiefs, it was thought proper to make application to the government authorities, through their agent, Col. Givens, to put them in possession of their lands, which were secured to the Chippewa Nation, at the treaty with Great Britain, years before.

The Indians had never enjoyed their Reservation longer than to receive their annuities, or to make an exchange of their furs and money, for whisky, which kept them drunk a greater part of their time. They now, therefore, petitioned for the right of possession, which was granted them, and they made preparations to leave. Their place of settlement was about twenty miles from Toronto. Taking an affectionate leave of the Grand River brethren, they started for their new homes. Here they made barracks or loose shanties for their protection against the weather, until they could build themselves more comfortable homes. How soon that would be, we could not tell, for as yet they possessed no means to procure better buildings.

As soon as their dwelling houses were up, they erected a large one, in which we could worship the Lord God. This was done by driving posts into the ground, and nailing boards, which I had procured from the whites, to them. The roof, also, was made of boards. This building answered every purpose, until the foul weather, in the Fall, came on. I now began to prepare for Conference.

CHAPTER VIII.

At the General Conference, in 1824, the British Provinces were set off from the Genesee Conference, under the title of Canada Conference. This year was the first in which we held a Conference under our new title. But as it seemed duty for me to visit my mother annually, I concluded to visit the Genesee Conference, which held its session in Tetertown, (now Lansingville,) Tompkins Co., which was embraced in the first circuit I ever travelled—which I could take in my route home, and then get back in time for our own Conference at Hallowell. This would make a journey of about one thousand miles, to be performed on horseback, and on foot.

The Genesee Conference commenced its session July 26th, 1824. I found my boarding place was at Father Tooker's, one of my stopping-places when I travelled old Cayuga circuit. I had anticipated much pleasure in once more seeing and visiting those old friends who had treated me as a son, and I was not disappointed. At the close of the Conference, I pushed on for my mother's, where I spent several days. Canada Conference was to commence August 25th, so that I soon had to start again for my far off field of labor. As usual, I had reserved half my salary for my mother, which she found a great help to her. Bidding her farewell, I once more mounted my horse, and departed.

Hallowell was two hundred miles north of Grand River circuit, and for that place I directed my footsteps. Bishops George and Hedding, and Dr. Bangs, of New York, attended this Conference. Bishop George embraced me, and putting his hand upon my head, said : "Well, I see the Indians have not got your scalp yet !" At this Conference, about seventy of our converted Chippewas, by invitation, came and pitched their tents within a short distance of the place where the Conference held its sessions. In doing this, our object was two-fold : First, that the Indians might be benefited by the meetings ; and, secondly, that the preachers might behold the wonders of "redeeming grace and dying love," as shown towards these poor red men of the forest, and thus be able to understand the necessity and utility of the missionary cause. During the time they were here, news came to them that a band of Chippewas, living far back in the western wilderness, were within two or three days journey of them. Two or three of our chiefs immediately started out to hunt them up, and invite them in. Two days after, they returned, bringing with them about thirty of their pagan brethren. They arrived on Sabbath morning, during the hours of preaching. A meeting had been appointed in the grove, near the encampment of Indians, and Bishop George and Dr. Bangs preached to the assembled multitudes. Bishop Hedding, being attacked by ague and fever, was not able to be present. At the close of preaching, it was given out that after an hour's intermission, there would be a general prayer-meeting at the altar, or preacher's stand, for the benefit of the thirty Indians, who had just arrived, and who had expressed a desire to embrace our holy religion. When the hour arrived, the strangers were placed in a half circle before the stand, the christian Indians near them, while in front, were a large number of ministers, who intended participating in the exercises.

The chief of the pagan band was a brave and noble man. He wore a large silver plate upon his breast, a wide band of the same material upon his arm, and his dress otherwise gave proof of high rank among his people.

We commenced our exercises by singing, after which, all were requested to kneel and pray. I had placed myself near the chief, of whom I have spoken, in order to watch the effects of the Spirit upon him. One of the Indians led in prayer, accompanied, in an undertone, by all the others. In a few moments, tears began to run down the face of the old chief, who was upon his knees, his body erect, and his eyes closed. His prayer was going up to heaven, "O, Great Spirit, have mercy on poor Indian! O, Son of Great Spirit, have mercy on me! Jesus, come and cast the bad spirit out of my heart, and make poor, wicked Indian glad and happy!" By this time, all the Indians were so engaged, that they were praying with a loud voice, and their prayers ascended up to heaven, like a mighty cloud of incense. They felt the importance of the work, and with strong cries, and with tears, they petitioned the God of Sabaoth to save their wandering brethren. Soon all those pagans were weeping and crying aloud: "O, Jesus, save! O, I shall go to the bad place! O, Jesus, come and save me!" Our ministers were so overwhelmed with the solemnity of the scene, that they scarcely knew where they were. The old chief was still crying to God, but in less than ten minutes after tears began to fall from his face; he began to tremble and shake, like an aspen leaf in the wind, and in a moment more, he fell to the ground like a corpse. It seemed as though some mighty power had passed over them, for one after another of those pagans, with their leader, fell prostrate to the ground. But the Lord passed over them, and breathed upon them, and with joyous exclamations in their own tongue, they sprang to their feet, giving praise to God. When the old chief arose, with a shout, and a heavenly smile upon his countenance, he clasped his hand to his breast, saying: "O, happy here! O, Jesus, blessed Jesus, how I love thee! O, glory, glory!" Thus, one after another arose, uttering language similar to this, until twenty of the thirty were praising God for redeeming grace and dying love.

While preachers and people were giving praise to God, in songs and shouts of praise that could be heard afar off, I directed my footsteps to a house some two hundred yards distant, where were Bishop George and Dr. Bangs. They were sitting in the shade of the house, and as I approached them, I said: "Bishop, the Lord has just been converting twenty pagan Indians." The Bishop arose from his seat, and clasping his hands together, gave glory to God. The Dr. immediately started with me for the place where the Lord was giving life and light to the dead. As he entered the prayer circle, his eye fell upon the old chief, who had just been converted. Making his way to him, he commenced a conversation, through an interpreter, asking his views and feelings on the subject of religion, and the change he had experienced To all his inquiries he gave satisfactory replies, which showed, conclusively, that he was as soundly converted to God, as was St. Paul, when Ananias said to him : "Brother Paul, receive thy sight." The Dr. afterwards said, in a communication he gave us in the Magazine, that that chief made him think of the old Roman Generals.

O, who can tell the joy there was in heaven, among the angels and saints departed, when, as they stood leaning over the battlements of heaven, anxiously watching the first glimpse of a swift-winged messenger who, on wings of uncreated light, was speeding through realms of space, with the joyful news of sinners saved ! Who can paint the joy that beamed in their celestial faces, as they saw, far away, in the mighty deep, the messenger they were so anxiously waiting, his countenance, brighter than the sun, with the joy that thrilled his heart, and heard his voice, as he waved his hand high in air, and shouted forth in trumpet tones, that another score of precious souls had been rescued from the power and dominion of the devil, and saved from eternal ruin ! Let it be remembered that this was the first religious meeting they had ever attended, and that the first offer of salvation made to them, was accepted.

At this Conference, a new impetus was given to the missionary cause. Both preachers and people, from what they had seen of the work of God among these Indians, declared that pentecostal days had again returned, and that the prophecy of God was being fulfilled.

When our Conference closed, I received my appointment back to Grand River Mission. My field of labor had now become so extensive, that no time was allowed me for rest, and no time for study, except while on · horse back, or before light in the morning.

From the first year of my itinerancy, I had endeavored to follow Mr. Wesley's rule for preachers : "Rise at four in the morning." This gave me time for reading, meditation and prayer, before most of families would be out of their beds. There were now so many calls for preaching throughout the length and breadth of the Reservation, that I seemed to want to run a dozen ways at once.

In passing through the country of the whites, to reach the more distant tribes of Indians, I was often solicited to stop and preach, and relate what was going on among the Indians. I could now say : "In journeyings often, in perils of waters, in perils of robbers, in perils by mine own countrymen, in perils by the heathen, in perils in the city, in perils in the wilderness, in perils in the deep, in perils among false brethren ; in weariness and painfulness, in watchings often, in hunger and thirst, in fastings often, in cold and nakedness. Beside those things that are without, that which cometh upon me daily, the care of all the Churches."

In the care of all these new born babes in Christ, who needed instruction daily, and watching over continually, my cry was : O Lord, who is sufficient for this great work ! Yet, in the midst of all these labors and sufferings, my soul was happy, for the Lord was my sun and shield, as the shadow of a great rock in a weary land : a covert from the storm ; and as a river of water in a dry place. Often, when obliged to camp out in the wilderness, with the cold, damp ground for my bed, and the stars above me for my covering, with prowling beasts of prey around me as guardians of the night, often did I think of our Savior who spent many nights alone, in prayer, upon the cold ground, and I always found him near to bless and comfort me.

Within about four miles of our mission house, lived a tall Indian of the Oneida tribe. He was very wicked and very intemperate. He had a wife and two daughters, who were as smart and fair looking women as any I ever saw among the Indians. But they were all pagans. The father, as soon as he became intoxicated —and that was as often as he could get any of the fire-waters to drink—was like a mad man. He wanted to fight with every one he met, and would fight any-how, and he often became as bloody as a butcher. The Indians were all afraid of him when he had been drinking. To procure whisky, he would part with anything he possessed. On one occasion, he offered to sell the only bullock he had, that he might obtain whisky. But his neighbors would not buy it. He then attempted in his rage to destroy it.

At another time, when he had sold every thing he could get, even to the clothes upon his back, that were worth any thing, he stole from his wife, the few " traces of seed corn" which she had carefully laid away for another year. This he offered for whisky. Destitute as they were before, the poor woman now thought herself undone, for seed corn that year was very scarce, and this was their only hope of future harvest. The corn was purchased by a brother F——, a white man who was doing business with the Indians, and at whose house I often stopped. Br. F—— returned the corn privately to the afflicted woman, who was thereby much relieved. In his drunken fights this Indian would sometimes get bruised and scarred in a shocking manner, and in this plight return to his hapless family, destitute of clothing, and bearing the description in Mark v. 2, of one possessed of devils, and coming from the tombs. This Indian afterwards became converted. And what a change there was in him. He was like the man among the tombs, after the devils were cast out—"sitting at the feet of Jesus, clothed and in his right mind." He now left off his drinking, went to work, treated his family kindly, was well clothed, attended to his religious duties, and every Sunday morning could be seen with his wife and daughters—all of whom had experienced religion with him—threading his way to the chapel, Indian file, where he staid until after class-meeting in the afternoon. It was no uncommon thing to see this tall, gigantic Indian who, but a few months before, was the terror of his countrymen, while sitting in his seat, or on his knees supplicating God, fall to the floor as though an arrow had pierced his heart, and lay, apparently dead, for some time ; and when he would recover consciousness, he gave us evidence, by his spirit and language, that Christ had full possession of his heart.

One Sabbath, in the spring, he came to me after preaching, with a smile upon his countenance, and putting his hand into his blanket pocket, took out a very nice, white cake of maple sugar, which he presented me as a proof of his own and family's love for me. I received it with many thanks, which seemed to more than repay him for his trouble in preparing it. At another time I received a token of chief Davis' love for me. He had a garden in which he raised many melons. This year he planted, as usual, for a large crop, but all the vines, save one, failed to bear. This one vine had one melon upon it. "This," the chief said to his family, " this we must keep for our minister." So no one was allowed to meddle with it, and it was watched and tended with much care, until it was fit to pick. It was then taken in and kept until I came around. When I called to see him, he took a clean earthern plate, put the melon upon it, set it on the table, and then drawing his knife, which he always carried in his belt, he wiped it upon his blanket, and laid it beside the melon. He then very politely said to me : " Come, you go and eat," himself and family refusing to take any, for it was the minister's melon. I took his knife, cut the melon open, and ate a slice. It was very delicious. I then took another, and said : " Br., I have eaten. Come, you and your family, and see how good it is." They then took a piece and we feasted together upon it, and spent an hour in social converse, and in blessing God who gives us all the good things of this life which we enjoy.

CHAPTER IX.

As soon as the Mississaguas became comfortably
settled at the Credit, we established a school among
them, in which John Jones taught the branches of a
common English education.   This Br. Jones was a
Mohawk, and a half brother of Peter.   He had received a good education among the whites, and had
experienced religion at the commencement of the
revival on Grand River.   Being employed by the Missionary Committee, he accompanied his Mississagua
brethren to the Credit, and commenced his school with
about twenty scholars.   They had not been here many
weeks, when information was received from Col. Giv-
ins, their agent, that he would be at the mouth of the
river in a few weeks, with their annual presents.   Information of this event was conveyed to all the tribes
living west of us, and it was now certain that we
should have thousands of the pagan Indians, from the

AT THE DOOR.

"BEHOLD, I stand at the door and knock." At what door? The barred door of your heart, fellow-sinner; your heart, defiled, darkened, perverted, hardened, alienated from God and holiness, greatly needing the entrance of One who can change all this, restore it to God, and make Who stands there? Your best Friend; He who has done for you already what no other being could or would do—who has made possible the change you need, and now urges upon your acceptance the provided mercy. It is the Saviour who stands there.

How does he knock? By his word, pressed upon you from early childhood. By his providence, preserving life and health, or sending sickness. By his Spirit, awakening, convicting, reproving, melting, leading sinners to repentance, pardon, and peace; convincing you that you have only to accept the proffered mercy to be blessed.

Why does he knock? Because of his love for your soul: he would save it. You have shut and barred him out, and you persevere in excluding him. Yet he will hardly be denied. He has done and suffered so much to make salvation possible for you, that he beseeches you to be saved. Yes, he knocks again and again.

Hear that knock. Open and admit Him who knocks. Then he will come unto you, and make his abode with you. He will shed his love abroad in your heart. He will be your peace, through his precious blood, applied by grace to your soul, cleansing you from all sin. He will be your strength, enabling you to overcome the world, sin, and Satan. He will be your never-failing source of comfort under the many trials of your earthly condition. He will be your spring of joy, refreshing and gladdening your heart with the sweet sense of his presence and the assurance of his favor. He will reveal the prospect of heaven to your view, and enable you to feel that its glory and happiness shall be yours.

Will you refuse to admit such a guest? He seeks admittance to your heart *now;* but he may withdraw, and knock no more. Admit him, ere it be too late.

"How shall we escape, if we neglect so great salvation?" Heb. 2:3.

AMERICAN TRACT SOCIETY, 150 NASSAU-STREET, NEW YORK.

No. 179.

the chiefs and counsellors rushed down to the water's edge, to give their agent a salute and welcome. The sloop came up in a pleasant gale peculiar to the waters of Ontario—the anchor was thrown out, and the agent, with the governor and suite, embarked in the small boat, and rowed for the shore. During this time, the christian Indians remained in their tent, singing and praying, undisturbed by all the noise and bustle. The governor and his lady had heard much of the converted Indians, but could not believe that such poor, drunken, degraded creatures as these Indians had always been represented as being, could ever be made respectable citizens, and sober men and women. They had, accordingly, with several other ladies and gentlemen, come up on purpose to see these Indians, and on landing, they proceeded directly to the open tent, where the Indians were singing, and as they drew near, the governor and his friends removed their hats. After singing, they all knelt down, and one of the chiefs led in prayer, the governor and his company also kneeling. After prayer, they all arose, and advancing, shook hands with the governor and his suite.

The Col. now gave orders for all the chiefs and counsellors to arrange themselves, in order to receive their goods, that they might distribute them to the numerous families of the several tribes, according to their custom. He then ordered the sailors to bring on shore the presents, and also several kegs of rum, with which to "treat" the Indians. The presents consisted of guns, ammunition, brocade cloths, blankets, calico, and jewelry. When the Christians saw the rum, they went to the Col. and said: "Col., we don't want you to offer any of *our* people that rum, for we no drink any more rum, or whisky, and we not want any of it." "Well," said the Col., "then the rest shall not have any of it," and immediately ordered it back to the ship. This prevented intoxication on the beach, while receiving their presents; and this thoughtful act of their agent, together with the respect shown to them by the governor and company, produced a more favorable impression on the minds of the pagans toward the Mississaguas, and they began to say among themselves: "Guess the Mississaguas not so bad as white man say;" and so they ventured nearer them, and listened to their songs, and prayers, and exhortations, and many of them were made sensible there was something good which they knew not of. Some were saved, and many more would have been, had it not been for the powerful exertions made by the wicked whisky sellers, to keep them from listening to the gospel of light and life. They well knew that when the Indians once began to drink, they would continue drinking for several days, when they would part with anything and everything they had, in order to procure the "fire-water." In this way they would strip them of everything valuable, and then leave them. Sometimes one in each family would keep sober, in order to take care of the valuables. In such cases the traders found poor fishing among them.

One circumstance which occurred during the distribution of the annuities, is worthy of special attention. When the Col. was about handing over that part of the jewelry which belonged to the Mississaguas, our christian women approached their agent very modestly, and said : " Colonel, we would like it if you would give us the value of those jewels in money. We want it to help buy cows and oxen with, that we may work our lands. We don't wear jewels in our ears and noses any more ; you can sell them to the white women, for they love to wear them."

This request of these noble, christian women, with their christian deportment everywhere, had a wonderful effect upon the governor and his company, and on his return to York, he sent on carpenters and masons to build twenty neat, good houses, in village form, on the south side of the Credit river, and on the lake shore where we had previously marked off the grounds and divided it among each family. The houses were built as the governor had directed, and the expenses were all met by him ; not, however, from his private property, but from the public funds. He also sent on men with teams, who plowed up their fertile flats, and now they found themselves as comfortable and happy as any of their white neighbors.

The reformation still continued to spread among the Chippawas, as well as among the Six Nations. About one hundred miles north of the river Credit, there was a whole tribe converted, baptized, and brought into the fold of Christ. They, with those converted at the Hallowell Conference, moved on westwardly with their religious influence, until the wilderness resounded with the shouts of the redeemed tribes that inhabited the shores of Rice, Mud, Skawgan, Simcoe and Huron Lakes. Br. Wm. Case took the oversight of most of these tribes, as they bordered on his district, and with a view to supplying some farther particulars, I give a letter, written by him about this time, to the editors of the Methodist Magazine, at New York.

KINGSTON, U. C., June 30, 1826.

Dear Brethren:—In my last, a few days since, was announced the conversion of another body of Mississagua Indians, and that twenty-two had received christian baptism, and were received into society. This letter will detail to you a farther account of these people, as connected with the camp-meeting at Adolphustown, which commenced the 15th, and closed the 19th instant.

After the baptism of the native converts at Bellville, the 31st May, and having been strengthened in their faith by the pious exhortations of Br. Jones, who came down from the river Credit to assist on the occasion, the good work appears to have gained additional strength, and now and then an awakened soul was brought out of the sorrows of mourning into the joys of the Savior. As these brethren had signified a wish to be present at the camp-meeting, they were encouraged to attend, expecting that at a woods' meeting these children of the forest might not feel themselves less at home than they had done in the chapel at Bellville; it was hoped, too, that their faith might receive additional strength from a communion of so numerous a body of Christians of their white brethren. A portion of ground* was accordingly

* This encampment was situated in a most delightful and healthy part of the country, upon the north bank of Carnahan's bay, which deeply indents Adolphustown on the west. Opening in a broad view of the Bay of Quinte, and connecting with its deep waters, it afforded a convenient landing for the steamboat and other vessels. The ground for the encampment was enclosed by a gun fence, made high and strong, with two openings only, and these were secured by gates, which were opened and shut at pleasure. By this precaution the watch were able to keep out any drunken persons, should any such be disposed to disturb such meetings. About one hundred yards from the camp was an overflowing spring of cool waters, which, running from a sandy soil, were very sweet and healthful. During the night, lights were kept up, by inflammable wood placed about six feet from the ground, and in situations to illuminate the whole encampment. The fires appear also to have rendered harmless the night damps, for we have known no instance of ill health occasioned by these meetings in this place. On the contrary, numbers, we understand, have gone out of our villages with a feeble habit, whose health has been improving ever since. Probably an airy ride has been to their advantage, but the drinking freely at so pure a fountain, for several days, together with the respiration of unconfined air, and the gentle, reviving breezes of a summer month, could hardly fail to induce a better state of health.

assigned them, in the rear of the tents of the whites, but within the enclosure, that they might be as much as possible secure from the gaze of curiosity. By Thursday afternoon of the 15th, a line of tents had nearly filled the first circle within the fence, and the exercises of singing and prayer had commenced with spirit in different parts of the ground. We were now informed that the Mississagua fleet was in sight, when a few of us repaired to the shore to welcome our new friends, and conduct them into the encampment. We found between 50 and 60 landing from their bark canoes.* Their furniture of cooking utensils, guns, spears, &c., were taken out, with barks for covering their wigwams, their blankets rolled up, and all prepared to be borne on the heads of the squaws. When all were in readiness, the Indians took each a canoe, reversed, upon his head—the squaws in the rear—and the whole body advanced in Indian file to the encampment.

We had previously caused all the exercises to cease, not knowing what effect so many voices in different parts

---

* These canoes are the work of the natives, and display considerahle ingenuity. Being made wholly of white cedar, and hark taken from the birch, they are very light, and easily conveyed, on the heads of the natives, from one river to another. The ribs are of cedar, three inches wide, and half an inch in thickness, variously bent to form the hull of the vessel. These serve the purpose of knees for supporting other strips of cedar put on lengthwise, in the usual mode of planking. Over all is a sheathing of birch hark, similar to the copper sheathing which secures the hottom of shipping. With thongs of the cedar root, the whole, catching the ribs and hark, is sewed to the raves, which forms the finish of the vessel. The canoes employed in the Northwest trade are large, carrying from three to six tons; but those used by the natives in these parts are about twelve feet long and three feet wide; they are very convenient for the convcyance of a single family, and if necessary will carry from 6 to 8 men.

of the camp might have on the minds of the natives, who were unacquainted with such a scene; and we wished, too, that the entrance of the natives into a christian encampment for the first time, might be witnessed by the whole congregation. Two of the preachers having been placed at the head of the file, the party entered the camp, some of the men bearing the canoes on their heads, others the guns and spears, and the women their burdens of blankets and barks. As but few of the congregation knew that the Indians had arrived, their sudden appearance in this equipage created considerable emotion. The first was that of astonishment. They gazed with amazement; then reflecting on the former wild and wretched state of this people, contrasted with their present hopeful condition, and remembering their many prayers for the heathen, and seeing, too, their petitions fulfilled before them, surprise gave place to feelings of gratitude and delight; they broke forth into praises, and gave glory to God for the salvation of the heathen.

When they had arrived at that part of the ground which had been assigned to the use of the natives, laying down their burdens, they all kneeled and prayed for some time, the pious of the whites joining in the petitions for God's blessing on these strangers, and that *this gracious work might spread through all the wilds of America.*

In building their camp, the natives formed it an *oblong,* with their canoes, placing them at the same time on the sides reclining inward, to form a part of their shelter. Poles with one end in the ground, and leaning over the canoes, supported a roof of barks above. This completed their covert, to shelter them from the rains. The smoke from the fires in the centre escaped through the uncovered space above.   Their mats of bark unrolled, were then spread beneath the shelter, and served the double purpose of carpeting and couches.   The number of adults which occupied this camp was 41; their children about 17; in all 58.   Of the adults, about 28 had given evidence of a change of heart, two of whom officiated as exhorters.   The remaining 13 appeared somewhat serious; you will hear more of them at the conclusion of the meeting.

The natives being encamped by themselves, their meetings were generally held apart from the whites, except in the public preaching, when a portion of the seats on the right of the stand was reserved for their use.   At the conclusion of each service, the leading points of the sermon were delivered to the red brethren, being interpreted by William Beaver, one of the Indian exhorters. On several occasions the exhorters were called on to address their brethren in their own language.   The first exhortation was given on Friday, by Wm. Beaver, and from the peculiar earnestness of his manner, and the solemnity of his voice, together with the effect it appeared to produce on the minds of the natives, we judged the discourse to be powerful and awakening, for many wept, and some appeared to have been awakened from this time to seek a change of heart.   On Saturday and Sunday the congregation was large, we judged between three and four thousand.   Much order was observed, and great attention paid throughout the public services, but more especially when the native exhorters spoke.   They were heard with profound attention, and spoke with fluency, for some time.   When Beaver had concluded, we desired him to inform us what he had been saying.   After an apology for his bad English, he said, "I tell 'em they must all turn away from sin; that the Great Spirit will give 'em new eyes to see, new ears to hear good things; new heart to understand, and sing, and pray; all new! I tell 'em squaws they must wash 'em blanket clean—must cook 'em victuals clean like white woman; they must all live in peace, worship God, and love one another. Then," with a natural motion of the hand and arm, as if to level an uneven surface, he added, "the Good Spirit make the ground all smooth before you." During the meeting the pious Indians took an active part in the prayer-meetings, in behalf of the mourners, sometimes among the whites, but mostly among themselves; and it was principally by their means that the thirteen who came to the ground unconverted, were brought to the knowledge of the truth. At the close of the camp-meeting, every Indian on the ground appeared to be happy in the Savior's love. By constant labors, and frequent exercises of faith in prayer, several of the Indian brethren became very *skillful* in this mode of labor, and it was very striking to see the answers to their prayers in behalf of mourning penitents. On some occasions their faith was such, and their prayers so powerful, that the hearts of bystanders were melted, though they could not understand a word.

On Monday, the eucharist was administered, when several hundreds partook in the holy ordinance. The solemnity was great, and many were comforted in this joyful hour; yet our native brethren appeared to enjoy the greatest share of the Divine blessing. The late converts having signified their desire to receive christian baptism, twenty-one adults were presented at the altar as candidates for the ordinance. One of the ministers present having explained to them, by an interpreter, the nature and design of the ordinance, we proceeded to propose the apostles' creed and covenant, by the same interpreter, to all of which, with great solemnity, they severally assented, in the Chippewa, "Yoach." Baptism was then administered, and afterwards the communion. During these exercises their minds were considerably affected, and some of them so much as to be unable to stand, and were borne from the altar in the arms of their friends. After the meeting was concluded we repaired to the Indian camp, and administered baptism to ten children of the believing Indians. The whole number of converts now belonging to this tribe, and who have received christian baptism, is forty-three, and twenty-one children.

This camp-meeting we consider to have been, in some respects, one of the greatest we have witnessed in this country. We could not estimate the number present on the Sabbath, at less than three thousand; many good judges think there were at least four. Notwithstanding this multitude, good order prevailed throughout the assembly, and great attention was given to the word preached. The effects resulting from the exercises, have been apparently greater than usual. It is ascertained that about ninety persons professed to experience a change during the meeting; and besides, an impulse was given to religious feeling, in neighborhoods which have heretofore shown great indifference to the subject. Many left the ground under strong feelings of conviction, who, we hope, will be brought to a saving change. The marked attention and serious deportment of the multitude, we attribute to several causes. The improved state of religious society, which is apparent in this part of the country, together with the general awakenings which have prevailed during the past year, have had their influence to check disorder. The precautions in preparing the ground, together with the vigilance of the watch by night and day, must be considered essential to good order. But most of all, an unusual degree of spiritual influence attended the exercises. The inspiration of the Holy Ghost appeared to engage the pious in prayer, strengthening their faith and filling their hearts with joy and peace, and over-awed the multitude. The decent and orderly deportment of the Indians, too, was a standing reproof to ill manners.

The solemn attention which these natives paid to every point of religious order, could but be admired by all; and their devotions, in a barbarous language, hitherto unknown in these parts in the worship of God, all contributed to engage attention and promote the solemnity of the services. As yet, these Indian brethren have but one hymn they can sing, and they know but one tune. This they sing and sing, over and over, as if to them it was always good and always new. Some of their voices are remarkably melodious, and being softened and refined by the meltings of Divine grace, their singing is quite delightful. To give you a specimen of their language, I insert the first and fourth verses of the first and only hymn this tribe of the Mississaguas ever sung. It consists of four verses, and is a translation of the first four verses of the first hymn in our hymn book.

1.   "O à pa kish ke che go twàk
    Nege à ne she nà paig
    Che nà nà kà mootà waà wàt
    Ing ke sha mon ne toom.'

4. "Wune sà o kee mà mà she àn
   Mà che mà ne too wish
   Kee pe se qua pe na moo nunk
   Koo se non o me squeem."*

I will conclude my remarks on the natives by the relation of an anecdote: Jacob Peter, a sprightly youth of about eighteen years of age, belonging to this tribe, became pious about a year ago, at a camp-meeting held on the same ground. He has since been very zealous in behalf of his nation, and frequently exhorts with fluency and acceptance among his people. A few weeks since, Jacob, with a number of his brethren, attended an anniversary of the Missionary Society at Demorrestsville. In the evening, several of the white inhabitants gathered in to witness the devotion of the Indians, who had assembled by themselves for prayer-meeting. Esq. D. being present, requested Jacob to speak a few words to the English, by way of exhortation. Jacob arose, and in broken, but plain English, addressed them thus: "You white people have the gospel great many years. You have the Bible, too; suppose you sometimes read it, but you very wicked. You get drunk, you tell lies, you break the Sabbath." Then pointing to his brethren, he added: "But these Indians they hear the word only a little while—they can't read the Bible, but they become good right away. They no more get drunk, no more tell lies, they keep the Sabbath day. To us Indians, it seems very strange, that you have missionary so many years, and you so many *rogues yet*. The Indians hear missionary only little while, and we all turn Christians."

Jacob, with two more boys of his age, has lately gone

---

*The letter *a* marked thus à, has the Italian sound as in *father*, and has nearly the sound of *ar*.

to school on Grand River, to join the three sent there the last winter. A great field is opening for usefulness among this people. It is, indeed, *already white for the harvest.* In my next, which I hope to forward you soon, will be given some interesting facts relative to the origin and progress of this glorious work.

I remain, very affectionately, your fellow laborer in the gospel of Christ.　　　WILLIAM CASE.

So great and extensive had the work of God now become among the Chippawas, that we found we lacked many men and much means to give them the care and attention they needed, but wherever we could locate them, teach them agriculture and place their children in schools where the English language was taught them, we were successful beyond all our calculations, in christianizing and civilizing them, and making them happy, soul and body. In one of these western tribes, lived a man and woman, each over one hundred years of age. They were converted to Christianity, and baptised on joining the Church. As it was impossible to give an intelligible translation of their names as given in their native tongue, we called them, on account of their great age, Adam and Eve.

CHAPTER X.

The time of our Annual Conference now drew near, and as it was necessary I should visit my mother before or after Conference, I took this time, and made my preparations to be back in time to be at the opening of the session. On reaching home, I found the family all well, and working bravely to maintain themselves, and gain an honest livelihood. After a visit of a few days, I again mounted my horse, having divided my pittance with my mother, and turned my face toward the scene of my labors, leaving the family comfortable and happy.

I arrived, without accident, at the seat of Conference in time to be at the opening of the session, having made a journey some hundreds of miles entirely on horseback and on foot; for in those days a poor Methodist preacher had no other way of travelling. Bishop Hedding presided at this Conference. After listening to the first report of the Canada Conference

Missionary Society, which was formed the year before, Br. Loring Grant, being present at the first session of the Canada Conference, said he had never read of so great and powerful a work of God among the heathen since the days of the apostles. Here is the report, as read at the Conference:

"The managers, in presenting their first annual report to the society and the public, beg leave to call their attention to the fields of labor for their missionaries, and the prospects which lie before them, of probable usefulness, as well as to exhibit to them the state of their financial concerns. The fields of labor in this country, which are presented to the attention of the society, and which are now open to the labor of our missionaries, are the newly settled townships, and the Indian tribes.

"The new townships which have been surveyed, and opened for location since the late war, form a line of settlements in the rear of the old settlements, the whole length of the province—a length of about 600 miles. To these new townships are thronging thousands from Europe, and the older parts of America, who, in most places, would be without the means of grace, were it not for the labors of the itinerant ministry; nor can it be expected that any adequate supply can be afforded by any other means—such is the scattered state of the population, and so insulated are they by vacant lands. It is to these new townships and destitute settlements, that our missionaries are to continue to direct their attention, that the voice of grace with the sound of the ax may be heard, and that log cabins and chapels of devotion may continue to rise up together.

"The missionary ground which has heretofore been occupied by our missionaries, was the new settlements on the river *Rideau*, and the newly settled townships at the head of Lake Ontario. These are now embraced in the Perth and Toronto circuits, and supplied by the labors of the circuit preachers, the inhabitants being at length both able and willing to support the expenses of regular circuits.

"By the labors of the late missionaries these circuits have been organized—order in society much promoted—the altar of devotion erected in many families, and many sinners converted from the error of their ways, and thus added to the church of Christ. The duty of the missionaries, and the services which they were expected to perform, are to labor daily for the welfare of their flocks, by preaching the word in every destitute settlement; to distribute the Holy Scriptures to the destitute; to exhort to peace, and the support of the cival authorities; to encourage the establishment of Sabbath Schools; to recommend economy, decency, and industry; to press the worship of God in every family; to visit the sick, and assist the poor; to administer the ordinances; to labor for, and suffer with their flocks; and to do all in their power to bring sinners to repentance, and thereby endeavor to extend the interests of the Redeemer's kingdom.

IMPROVEMENT OF THE CONDITION OF THE INDIAN TRIBES.

"Of the natives, there are two bodies which present themselves more especially to the benevolent consideration of the christian public, viz: the Six Nations, and the tribes of the great Chippewa nation. The Mohawks are the leading tribe of the Six Nations, having been rendered more intelligent by some advantages of education. By British liberality, schools have been kept up in the Mohawk for many years, by which means, principally, several have been matured to a state of intelligence and genius sufficient to prove that the native mind is capable of virtues and excellencies the most refined. These remain monuments of real greatness amid the depravity of the nation, who, by the destructive use of ardent spirits, are hurried on to the dreadful precipice which threatens their utter extinction.   Nothing, in our opinion, can rescue this people but the power of the Gospel.

"That the truths and power of grace are capable of producing great alterations, we have evident examples at the Grand River, some of the most dissipated of that nation having been changed from confirmed habits of drunkenness and irreligion to habits of sobriety, and to a virtuous and pious deportment, worthy, indeed, of Christians of more enlightened communities.   At the mission house on the Grand River, there are about thirty Mohawks, who adorn the gospel of their profession; among these is a chief* of considerable distinction, who is much devoted, and takes a deep interest in the welfare of the society and of the schools.

"The Chippewa nation, in its various tribes, is by far the most numerous.   They spread out the whole length of the province, extending also far to the north.   Their tongue is said to be the prevailing one, and is held in such esteem that the chiefs in every tribe must speak it in general councils; and thus, with a knowledge of this tongue, the traveller may pass through to the western ocean, conversing with every nation.   The Mississaguas,

*Chief Davis.

once a powerful tribe of the Chippewas, have been much reduced by former wars, and in later times by the use of ardent spirits. Such a thirst have they for the taste of spirits, that they have been known to barter the most valuable of their presents for a small quantity; and not unfrequently have they continued their drunken revels till the whole of their property was expended. In this state they are frequently exposed to sufferings and death, by the waters and frosts; and to this cause principally may be attributed their present degraded and wasted condition.

"Their religion, too, is another proof of the benighted state of their minds. Among their sacrifices are dogs; their offerings are made to the sun and moon, and when influenced by apprehensions of danger, they have been known to pay their worship to the evil spirit, in order to induce him to do them no harm. Their views of a future state are altogether sensual, for they appear to have no higher idea of happiness than plenty of game and pleasant huntings. Thus do these unhappy people appear to be entirely without God, and without hope in the world. Their wandering state and manner of life have been supposed to be insurmountable obstacles in the way of their conversion; for they are everywhere at home, seldom long in one place, never erecting any permanent habitations, but residing in temporary huts, covered with matted flags, or with barks from the trunks of trees. For such a people, then, where is there any foundation for hope? 'Can these dry bones ever live?' Yes, verily, for he that made them, can he not redeem? Is there any tribe of all the nations for whom the Savior did not die? And did not our Savior command that the gospel

of his grace and mercy should be preached to every creature? By how much farther these pagans have wandered from the true God, by so much the more is the
power of the gospel manifested, and the riches of his
grace exalted in their conversion.

"Of the degraded Mississaguas, more than sixty during
the past year have embraced the gospel; and such have
been the changes wrought in their feelings and manners,
as to be matter of astonishment to all who knew them,
and of especial encouragement for the society to persevere in their labors. Native schools, for the improvement of the mind, must be considered of importance,
whether for the purposes of civilization, or to fix more
permanently in the mind, the principles of Christianity.
Where this has been already received, and even where
strong religious feelings are experienced, 'line upon line,
and precept upon precept,' are necessary. A knowledge
of reading, then, will greatly aid in such a course of
instruction. By opening the Bible, and whole libraries,
to the astonished minds of the native disciples—thereby
unfolding the works of the Creator, the plan of redemption through the Savior, and the wonders of his love—
it will prepare them for teaching these great things to
their friends and neighbors. To the schools, then, and
the revivals of grace, we must look for native ministers,
who may hereafter preach to the surrounding nations of
their red brethren, 'the unsearchable riches of Christ.'

The natives themselves perceive the importance of
education, especially wherever religious awakenings have
commenced; immediately they solicit schools for the instruction of their children. It is now about two years
since a school was commenced at the Upper Mohawk,

where from 25 to 30 children have been taught to read in English. During the same time, a Sabbath School has been kept up, and well attended. Through the summer, both schools have been prosperous—the Sabbath School on some occasions consisting of about sixty youths and children. The improvement of the school has been considerable, and some of the scholars give indications of superior capacity. To brothers Crawford and Johnson is due the gratitude of the society for their assiduity and perseverance as teachers in the school. The house at this station was erected for the double purpose of schools and meetings; and is of hewed oak, neatly plastered, and made comfortable by a stove for winter. It was built partly by the labor of the natives, but mostly by liberal donations of benevolent persons in the adjacent settlements. Before the house was erected, no room could be obtained for the school, till an aged chief, lately converted, offered his own house for the purpose, and retired to a cabin in the woods. At this station, (*Mohawk*) about 100 adults of the Mississaguas have their tents erected, with a view to afford their children the advantages of education,—the principal chief* of the tribe, setting a suitable example, by encouraging his young wife to attend the school.

"A strong and increasing desire is waked up in the youth for learning to read; the following is an example: A few months since, a lad of about seventeen, having heard of the school at the Grand River, and prompted by a desire for education, set off on a journey of one hundred miles to visit the place where Indians are taught to read. Being hospitably received by the Indian breth-

—————————————
*Capt. John.

ren, he entered the school, and is now making proficiency in his studies; and what is farther encouraging, he appears to have experienced a change, and begins to improve his gifts by prayer in his native tongue.

"Among the Muncey Indians, a tribe of the Delawares, on the river Thames, a school was opened in the month of May last. Its commencement was discouraging, and was attended with circumstances of unpromising nature, among which was the reluctance of some of the chiefs to consent to the school. Had the pious youth who commenced the undertaking, possessed less enterprise and perseverance, the attempt would probably have failed, and thereby much good been prevented. After several visits, and much labor, he at length succeeded in getting a school of seven children. The school has since become more popular, for on the first of the present month it consisted of fifteen scholars. Through the exertion of the preachers, and the liberality of the friends in the Westminster and Thames circuits, materials have been procured for erecting here a convenient building for schools and meetings. In two other places teachers have been solicited by the natives; and such are the prospects that we are encouraged to hope that their solicitations will be complied with, and two more schools be in operation before the opening of the spring. Besides, it is expected that provision may be made for the board and education of several Indian boys from a distance, who have signified their wishes to attend the school.

TRANSLATIONS.

"For two years past, Doctor A. Hill, an intelligent Mohawk chief, has been engaged in the translation of the evangelists, St. Matthew and St. Luke; and having corrected a former translation of St. Mark and St. John, the whole are now nearly completed, and will be ready for the press in a short time. A princess of the same nation, and well qualified for the work, it is understood, is engaged in the translation of the Acts of the Apostles : so that the Six Nations may hope, at no very distant period, to possess the invaluable treasure of the whole New Testament in the Mohawk language—a tongue which most of the Six Nations understand. A number of excellent hymns have also been translated by the doctor, and are now ready for printing. In this compilation, care has been taken to select the most spiritual of our hymns, as well as to furnish variety ; such as for evening, morning, Sabbath, sacramental, &c. When this book shall be in the possession of our pious native brethren, we expect the melody of their devotions, (already excellent,) will be greatly improved, to the advantage of public worship, and for the advancement of personal piety.

NATIVE TEACHERS.

"Considerable hopes are entertained, that teachers and preachers from among the natives will be raised up, and prepared to carry instruction and the *Word of Life* to many nations of our vast wilderness. In this hope we are encouraged, from the fact that several promising and useful gifts have already appeared, both among the Mohawks and Chippewas. Among the former, native teachers of schools have been employed for many years by the Church Missionary Society, by which means a very considerable portion of that people can read intelligibly in their native tongue.

"In our school at the Grand River, a Mohawk convert has been engaged for some time as a teacher. Others, both Mohawks and Chippewas, are well qualified for use-fulness in this department of the mission. Teachers of righteousness, also, in whom is seen the excellencies of grace as Christians, and the power of the gospel as ex-horters, are rising up from among their brethren, and promise much for the interests of religion among the natives. We have already stated to what an extent the Chippewa language is understood among the tribes of the west and north. When, therefore, this favorable circumstance is taken into view, together with the effect of religious instruction on the minds and manners of this people during the past year, we cannot think it too much to hope that the Gospel of the Savior may be made known to these nations by means of native teach-ers; that churches may be formed among the wild men of the woods, and that the high praises of Jehovah may yet be sung throughout the vast forests of America; 'then shall the wilderness and the solitary places be glad for them, and the desert shall rejoice, and blossom as the rose.'—Isaiah xxxv. 1.

EFFECTS OF THE GOSPEL ON THE MINDS AND MANNERS
OF THE NATIVES.

"We are aware that objections have been raised against any attempt for the improvement of the natives—be-cause 'they have grown worse by their intercourse with the whites'—thence it has been inferred that 'all instruc-tion to the natives has a demoralizing, rather than a vir-tuous tendency.' To this we reply, that if the acquaint-ance of the natives generally had been with the most virtuous part of the community, who had afforded them instruction, enforcing the same by examples of piety and virtue; and if, in consequence of *such* intercourse, the natives had become more immoral and worthless, there would then be some force in the objection ; but when it is considered that the instruction of the natives has been generally neglected, and that, in the meantime, their manners have been debased by the vices of the immoral whites, who have thought it their interest to introduce the means of intoxication among them ; the objection at once appears without weight, inasmuch as the vicious taint which the natives have received is from another source than that which is contemplated by this society, and altogether foreign from the precepts of the gospel. The natives of America, we have no doubt, are as capable of improvement as any other people of similar advantages, and that religious instruction may be as salutary on the savage mind, we are prepared to exhibit proofs, which will not be questioned.

"We refer to the changes which have taken place at the several missionary stations, and particularly at the Grand River, where by the plain preaching of *repentance toward God, and faith in our Lord Jesus Christ*, about one hundred natives have been reclaimed from confirmed habits of vice and irreligion, to be sober, virtuous, and industrious people. Of this number, sixty-eight are Mississaguas, who, with few exceptions, were entirely pagan ; and who, from their love of spirits, were among the most filthy and wretched of the savage tribes ; but since their conversion, all is changed. The drunkard's whoop and savage yell, have given place to the voice of supplication, and the orisons of pagan worship are exchanged for the melodious songs of grateful praise to Jehovah. The Christians are aware of their weakness, and they deny themselves altogether the use of ardent spirits. In this respect, they exhibit an example worthy of imitation to their white brethren of the like infirmity; for when these Indians have been urged to 'take a little,' they have been known to reply, 'No, me drink no more. Once me drink too much, and me fear if me *drink a little*, me drink too much again.'

"The Indians, by becoming a sober people, find their condition more comfortable in many respects. Their presents of clothing from the Government, being saved from the waste of intoxication, they are enabled to appear more decently, and to live in a more comfortable manner. By the same means, the comfort of the Indian families is also promoted. In the former state, the females were made unhappy by excessive toil, and more so by abuse from their drunken husbands; they are now treated in a manner more suited to the delicacy of their sex. By the industry of their husbands they are better provided for; and the cleanliness of their persons, and the neatness of their apparel, are a handsome comment on the change which has taken place in their husbands and fathers.

"The peace and amity which prevail among the converted Indians, is another proof of the happy effects of the gospel. Between the five Iroquois nations, (among whom the Mohawks have stood conspicuous,) and the great Chippewa nation, a deeply rooted animosity has existed for ages. This hostility was founded in the bloody wars which long prevailed, in a severe contest for the sovereignty of the great lakes. From that time, the two great bodies were entered into confederacies, never mingled in general councils, never pitched their tents, nor held their festivals together; but since their christian profession, their animosity has ceased. The Mohawks, who possess the fertile flats of the Grand River, have invited their Mississagua brethren to occupy their lands, and reside among them. They now both plant in the same fields, send their children to the same school, and worship in the same assembly. The Mississaguas, since their conversion, have shown a desire to commence a civilized way of living; and from the experiment of planting, the present season, we are encouraged to hope they may do well in this new mode of life. Their fields of corn have been pretty well cultivated, and promise a good harvest.

"Having signified to the government their wishes to settle on their lands, for civilization, they have received assurances of encouragement and aid beyond their highest expectations, and they hope to be able to commence an establishment on the Credit, in the course of another season."

It is hardly possible for the reader to conceive what effect the conversion of these Indian tribes produced upon the minds of our Canadian brethren. That God was in this work, is shown in the outward events and circumstances that continually transpired to further on the great work just begun. At the Conference when I received my first appointment to the Indians, a Conference Missionary was appointed to pass through the bounds of the Conference, organizing missionary societies, and waking up an interest in the cause.

Rev. Loring Grant, one of the most talented and

efficient ministers then in the Conference, a delegate to the late General Conference, and noted for his extensive business capacity, and great tact in financial matters, was appointed to fill this arduous post, which he did with the greatest success.

After travelling through the various parts of the Conference embraced in the States, he crossed into Canada just at the time we needed his help most. Passing from one end of the Province to the other, and visiting all the principal places, by his admirable manner of presenting his work, he enlisted many prominent men in every place, who made no profession of religion, but their sympathies being enlisted, they joined the societies, and gave both money and influence to help the Indians become civilized. The following letter which I have lately received from him, relating to the subject, will be of interest to the reader:

My Dear old Friend and Br. Torry: . . . You ask me about the formation of Missionary Societies. I answer: In January, 1819, the friends of missions, in the city of Philadelphia, took the initiatory steps towards the formation of a missionary society. Preparing a rough draft, they sent it to the General Conference, which was to hold its third session as a delegated body, the first of May, 1820, in the city of Baltimore. As a delegate of the General Conference, I had the satisfaction of listening to the proposition, and of assisting in perfecting the organization of the Missionary Society of the M. E.

Church. At the Annual Conference in Vienna, July 24, 1822, the Genesee Conference formed itself into an Auxiliary Missionary Society, and recommended the appointment of a Conference Missionary, who should be President of the Society, in the absence of the officiating Bishop. When the appointments were announced, I felt, as you may well suppose, surprised to hear my name announced as the missionary referred to.

Judging from the remarks of the various friends of the enterprise, showing the importance of such an appointment and the many things to be done by him, I felt the task an arduous one; however, I determined to do the best I could, although in much weakness. I expected to receive at least *oral* instructions, from our worthy Superintendent, but he left without giving the much desired information. I was thus left to my own resources, but calling to mind what was said in Conference by the President and various others, I found meeting houses were to built, which I attended to, without leaving any debt upon the Church. Our work was then divided into large circuits, generally embracing as much territory as is now contained in a Presiding Elder's district, and in some cases even as much as an entire Conference. In cases of revival upon our large circuits, it was considered necessary to have some one to call upon for help in such places, which was made my duty. These calls I obeyed whenever made. Another and important part of the work of the missionary was to organize societies for the purpose of creating a feeling of interest in the heaven-appointed enterprise of converting the world, and to raise the requisite means of carrying this good work forward.

After ranging through the bounds of the Genesee, Oneida, Wyoming, and portions of Black River Conferences, as now organized, I determined to visit the Canadas. Accordingly, in the spring of the following year I visited all the principal places in the region bordering on the Niagara River, from Lake Erie and Lake Ontario, and around to its head over on Dundas-St., &c. I enlisted the principal citizens of different denominations, and also those making no profession of religion, and although they were the first Missionary Societies formed in the provinces yet the people have sustained them with a zeal and energy showing their cause to be a good one.

Societies then formed have not only kept their organization, but have manifested an interest truly commendable, so far as we have been informed. The hope of doing the red man good, seemed to inspire all. Christians thought and talked of bringing them to Christ and heaven, believing, as you know they were taught by the examples before them, that a growth in education and every good, would follow a genuine work of grace in the hearts of these savage men. The red man's seeking God and a genuine Christianity, resulted from the use of a sanctified education brought to bear upon them. Consequently, when you went among them with your heart burning with love to God and the souls of the degraded sons of the forest, and pointed them to Calvary, telling them that God so loved the world as to give his Son to die for them, that they might be saved, with what interest they listened you know; and, thank God, the Church and the world are ready to bear testimony that your labors were so far from being vain, that scores and hundreds were brought to God as the fruits of your untiring labors and abundant zeal in a work that angels might have delighted to engage in.

Hearing of your great success, while on the Buffalo District, in 1825–6, I determined to visit you. Accordingly, on Monday, after my winter quarterly meeting for Niagara circuit, I crossed the river and proceeded up the Lake, calling on the friends at the different places, where, a few years before, I had formed societies, and found them delighted with the result of your labors, and glad they had entered into the work of raising funds for the support of the mission cause, especially the Indian mission. They spoke of the great change among the Indians; that it had made them new creatures; that they were sober, pious persons, giving up their old habits of vice, and instead of the lazy, filthy, drunken savage, they were now cleanly, somewhat industrious, deeply pious, and orderly.

Feeling much interested, I determined to press forward, although suffering from a severe attack of influenza. Some friends taking me in their sleigh, we found you, the second day after crossing the Niagara river, some four miles from the mission house. It was just beginning to grow dark, and now we had an opportunity of seeing and feeling what religion had done for these Indians, for, as you met them on the way, as we proceeded towards the mission house, and told them a missionary from the States had come to visit them, and preach to them that evening, their eyes brightened, joy played over their countenances, and they hastened on to inform their friends.

On arriving at the mission, we found Br. Crawford and wife, with a large number of girls, who were learning to knit and sew. You informed Br. Crawford of my design to preach, although quite sick. The long tin trumpet was immediately sounded, and after a brief space we saw the Indians coming rapidly from every direction. So thoroughly had they been trained, that, with one look at the missionary from the States, they fell on their knees, and spent a few minutes in the most devotional manner. This, with other evidences of a genuine work of grace, so inspired me as to make me forget my pain.

I was told I might have my choice, preach plain, or have an interpreter. I chose the former, and was still further helped by the attention and responses of, to me, this new class of hearers. I felt myself greatly favored with such an audience, that gave the best of evidence of sound conversion. After I had finished, Capt. Davis, one of the most eloquent men I ever heard address any audience, arose by request of the Missionary, and, as I was afterwards told, repeated the sermon *verbatim*, not substituting, or omitting one word, although he spoke in Mohawk, and I in English. I felt God was in it. I should have listened with rapture a vastly greater length of time, for I never was more delighted. The class-meeting that followed, would have compared favorably with any in any place, and under the most favorable circumstances. For strict decorum, great spirituality, and a knowledge of, and a strict adherence to, the usages of our Church, they were excelled by none; thus showing the indefatigable industry of their spiritual guide. As I had a quarterly meeting at Buffalo, the Saturday following, and as this was the only opportunity I could have of worshiping with them, we continued the meeting till near 12 o'clock at night. As I passed from Grand River to the ferry at

Black Rock, I was pleased to learn from friends, all along the route, that the mission had the deepest hold upon their feelings and confidence.

Very respectfully and affectionately yours,

LORING GRANT.

Auxiliary societies being now formed in almost every part of the Province, our worthy brethren began to hand over of their abundance, some five, some ten, and some twenty and twenty-five dollars, until our annual missionary collection amounted to over one thousand dollars, whereas, two or three years previous to this time, not a dollar of missionary money was raised.

The reason for this absence of missionary funds was, that no call had been made, as I always found our people of British North America to be the most liberal of any part of our wide spread Zion. They have always taken better care of their ministers than many of the brethren of the States ; always paying them their full salaries, and giving the superannuated their full disciplinary allowance, never even dreaming that a man ought to work his whole life for them at half pay, and then be turned upon the cold charities of the world to *beg*, or suffer and *starve*, because he can no longer work. Their religion partakes more of the "live and let live" policy, and less of the sordid, miserly meanness of some Christians, who will pinch a sixpence into the size of a half dollar, whenever any

call for the support of the gospel is made, but who
can spend their money by fifties to gratify their pride
or love of aggrandizement. Such Christians are always trying to get into heaven with all their bonds,
their stocks and mortgages, their farms, and all they
can hoard together during their brief stay upon this
earth ; but it only serves as so much weight to drag
them down to eternal woe and perdition. Such a
thing as a *stingy Christian* never was heard of in
heaven, and never will be, and no chart is laid down
in the Bible, by which such a person can get there.
But it does say, "He that giveth to the poor, lendeth
to the Lord," and "Give to him that asketh of thee,
and from him that would borrow, turn not thou away."
But we do not call it giving when a church-member
pays his preacher, or his missionary bill, or gives for
the Bible cause, or tract cause, or any of the many
calls which go to support the gospel, whether it be to
feed those who are now laboring, or those who are
beyond the age of labor, and who, that they might be
instrumental in spreading the gospel, have been content
with a mere support while laboring, trusting to God,
and the honor and honesty of their brethren, for help
in their declining years, but through culpable neglect,
are suffering, and starving, and dying for want of
the necessaries of life. You will find them scattered

through the land, some of them living in houses that many of our farmers would refuse to stable their cattle in, wandering over the hill-sides, gathering a few scanty sticks here and there, to keep themselves warm during the cold of winter, or forsooth, if they are able, sawing wood for their rich neighbors who, in return, dole them out the smallest possible wages, never once asking why they are thus employed. They, who should have their places among the first in the land, who have labored their lives long in the noblest of all business, not only are left to suffer, but too often, insult is added to injury—the well to do passing them by with the contemptuous remark that such must be poor economists, or poor financiers, or they would have been as well off as other people.

God has placed men upon this earth as stewards of his property ; he has given them full and explicit directions as to the use of it ; he has told them he shall require his own again with usury, and then he leaves them for a season. But think ye the cry of the hungry, perishing for bread, the cry of the beggar who is turned from your door to perish in the street, the cry of the widow and the fatherless, whose faces ye grind in the dust, think ye the cry of all these, as they lift up their despairing voices to heaven, enters into an ear that heareth not ? I tell you nay ! God is long-suffering, but he is just.   When he shall come at the latter day to make up his account with his stewards, ye will hear his voice thundering in your ears, saying, "Thou wicked and slothful servant, thou knewest that I reap where I sowed not, and gather where I have not strewed ; thou oughtest, therefore, to have put my money to the exchangers, and then at my coming I should have received mine own with usury."   Then shall he say unto his angels, as the king said unto his servants ·in the parable, "Take therefore the talent from him, and cast ye the unprofitable servant into outer darkness ; there shall be weeping and gnashing of teeth."

CHAPTER XI.

After the work of God became general among the natives, the standard of piety in our Church throughout the provinces was raised fifty per cent. It was not unfrequent that our white brethren from different parts of the provinces, who would visit the natives and worship with them, would say to me: "We are ashamed of ourselves, when we see how far beyond us the Indians go in their devotedness to God, and in their enjoyment of his grace." The secret, if any, was, the natives made a full surrender of soul and body to the Lord; they fasted once a week, and prayed to God always; and thus they made true the declaration of the Savior: "He that honoreth me, him will my Father honor." And the Father did honor them with a cloud of his divine glory, and made them to drink from the rivers of his pleasure, and he fed them with the bread of heaven continually.

There lived, on the Grand River, about ten miles

from our first establishment, a pagan Indian, by the name of Jacob Hill. He was a sober and industrious native, and could speak good English. The Lord converted this man, and shortly after, his whole family were walking with him in the way to heaven. We soon established an appointment for preaching in his neighborhood, collected the native children, and commenced a school, and it was not long before we had a good society of converted Indians, giving glory to God for redeeming grace and dying love.

A good work of the Lord also broke out among the Delawares near the mouth of Grand River, and also among the Senecas, and we now could sing:

"O, Jesus! ride on till all are subdued;
Thy mercy make known, and sprinkle thy blood!
Display thy salvation, and teach the new song,
To every nation, and people, and tongue."

I append some extracts from the "State of the Mission under the direction of the Missionary Society of the Methodist Episcopal Church," as found in the Methodist Magazine for 1827:

MOHAWK AND MISSISSAGUA INDIAN MISSIONS.

The Rev. Wm. Case writes under date of Dec. 25th, 1826:

"The work is progressing and extending to other bodies of Indians in the back wilderness. We hope to give you further accounts soon. Thus much we now say, that it exceeds our highest anticipations. I cannot forbear saying that Br. Ryerson, at the River Credit, is making progress in the knowledge of the Chippewa. He has advanced far enough to ascertain that the structure of the language bears a resemblance to the Hebrew."

In another dated Jan. 4th, 1827, he observes :

"If we now had four or five native missionaries, they might be employed to great advantage. The work is mightily prevailing throughout their border, on the Rice Lake, Mud Lake, and Skoogog Lake. On this account, I think the speakers we have, cannot be spared at present."

In another dated Bellville, Jan. 10th, 1827 :

"The society at the mission house, on the Graud River, continues to advance in its christian course. Its numbers, however, have been lessened by the removal of the Chippewas, and the society has met with a heavy loss, in the death of one of its most faithful members. The faithful warnings and triumphant death of the pious Jacob Hill, will be long remembered by the Mohawks on the Grand River.

"The conversion of another Mohawk chief in the same neighborhood, has again renewed their strength. And the addition of several families of the Chippewas, lately from the forest, has increased the society to the number of forty. The Chippewas, who were converted at the Grand River, now reside at the River Credit, where twenty comfortable houses have been provided for them, by the kindness of the governor. With the exception of a few families, the whole tribe have embraced Christianity, including the two chiefs. The whole number of souls is about one hundred and eighty ; the society, one hundred and ten ; the school, between thirty and forty ; the Sabbath School between forty and fifty children. In November, I heard eleven of the children read intelligibly in the New Testament. At this establishment are to be seen the effects of Christianity on the manners of a rude and barbarous people. Here are industry, civilization, growing intelligence, peace, and grace. And those who have witnessed the change, have expressed their persuasions that this new nation of Christians enjoy a sum of religious and earthly felicity, which is not always found in the civilized societies of longer standing, and greater advantages. How great the change ! A nation of wandering, idle drunkards, destitute of almost every comfort of life, have, in the course of twenty months, through the influence of Christianity, become a virtuous, industrious, and happy people ! All praise to HIM who changes the heart by the power of his grace, and who gives to his people by the same Spirit to delight in the work of enlightening the heathen ! The conversion of the tribe in the vicinity of Bellville, is as remarkable as those at the River Credit. Ten months ago, these were the same unhappy, sottish drunkards. They are now, without an exception in the whole tribe, a reformed and religious community. They number about one hundred and thirty souls, and the society embraces every adult, about ninety persons. We have now been engaged four days in a course of instruction to about one hundred, in the chapel in this place, during which time they have made considerable improvement in singing, and a farther knowledge of Christianity.

"By the aid of the interpreters, Wm. Beaver and

Jacob Peter, the congregation is taught to memorize the commandments, the Lord's prayer, and other portions of the Scriptures, which have been translated into the Chippewa. The interpreter pronounces a sentence in the Indian, when the whole assembly together repeat it after him. This method of instruction was commenced last fall, on Grape Island, with about one half of the tribe, (the others being gone to their huntings in the north,) and it succeeded so well, that now, on the return of the hunters, we proceeded to teach the remainder of the tribe in the same way. During the exercises yesterday, they were much affected while we proceeded to explain the ten commandments. At the conclusion of each, we applied the subject thus: 'Now, brothers, you see you have broken this law, and being guilty, how will you stand before your offended Judge?' By the time we had concluded the exposition, sobs and groans were heard through the assembly, and we proceeded: 'Now, brothers and sisters, you have sinned, and you have no goodness to plead. But you are sorry for your sins; yet where will you go for relief? I will tell you, brothers, there is but one path for your feet, but one wigwam that can defend you from the storm: *Jesus Christ* is a strong rock to defend you—run to him; he loves you, for he died for you; and your Great Father receives you, and forgives all your sins, because his beloved Son died for you, and now pleads for you ; yes, he gives you his Holy Spirit to comfort your hearts, and to assure you that your sins are forgiven.' "

CONVERSION OF ANOTHER BODY OF THE CHIPPEWAS.

"On Monday afternoon," (says the same writer, under date Jan. 16th,) "we proceeded to an examination of the assembly in regard to their christian experience; and the result was, that the whole body, of about sixty adults, had become reformed in their manners, so as to give up the use of spirits, and all but about ten professed to have received the hopes and joys of the gospel. The converted natives we invited forward for baptism, while those who had more recently been awakened, were told that, when they should be able to declare the mercy of God to their souls, they also would hereafter be admitted to the ordinance, and they were requested to retire in the rear of the congregation. When they arose to retire, they began to weep, and then to pray, that the Great Good Spirit would now have mercy upon them. When we perceived how deeply they were affected, we sent some of the most experienced Indian brethren to engage in prayer in their behalf. During the exercise of prayer, the spirit of grace appeared to be powerful on the minds of the penitents, and in the course of about an hour, nine persons professed to have found peace to their souls. The most of those present, had been reformed from their drunken habits for several months, and having now become so deeply impressed with a sense of their sins, and of the blessings of their Savior, we concluded to admit all the converts, with their families, to the ordinance of baptism. The nature and design of the ordinance were now explained, and we proceeded to propose the formula, 'Dost thou renounce the devil, with all his works?' Again we paused to give them further instruction in regard to the extent of Satan's power and influence, for the natives of the Chippewa have been terribly afraid of the evil spirit, (Muchemuneto) and to avert his displeasure, have made their offerings and paid their devotions generally to him.

"We informed them from the Scriptures, that Satan had no power but to tempt to evil, and to punish the wicked; that those who believed in the Lord Jesus Christ, had nothing to fear from him, and in the Lord Jehovah there was everlasting strength ·to tread Satan beneath their feet. While on this subject they appeared unusually moved, and when we again proposed, 'Dost thou renounce the devil, with all his works?' they responded, with great earnestness and a strong voice, 'Ah!' and some of them put down their feet as if treading the power of Satan beneath them. Seventy-five now received baptism, about sixty of whom were over the age of ten years. On the same evening, the Lord's Supper was also administered to the adults who had been baptized."

MISSION AT MUNCEY TOWN.

Extract of a letter from the Rev. Thomas Madden, dated March 8, 1827:

"I have lately visited Muncey town, and I think there is a prospect of good being done there; and although the school is small at times, and has not been attended with that punctuality we could have wished, in consequence of the unsettled state of many of the Indian families, yet those whom we have clothed, and whose parents have food and raiment for them, have made good progress in reading and writing.

"There is no opposition at present to the school, or ministration of the Word. Some have become reformed, and are preparing for christian baptism. A local preacher who is well acquainted with their manners, has settled among them, and his labors are acceptable and useful. I hope there may be something done for him.   Br. Carey is doing what he can.   We expect to get things in a more settled state in the course of the season.   We have a second school in operation on the Grand River, which commenced about the first of January.   There are about twenty-five native children who attend, and make fine progress in learning.   A Sabbath-school was commenced at the same time, which is well attended by the parents and children, so that the prospect in that place is more favorable than it has ever been before.   The school and society are still going on at the mission house.   A number of the Mississaguas were brought in at the mission house last autumn, and baptized, but have since removed to the Credit, so that the society remains about the same."

Br. Crawford, who became our first Indian teacher, was faithful and successful in his work of teaching, as also in his office of class-leader and exhorter.   The converted natives improved rapidly in piety, and in them were all the christian graces seen.   Their progress in agriculture and the arts was rapid, for the Lord blessed them spiritually and temporally;   and while I staid with them, they were the happiest people I have ever known, and with them I would have lived during my earthly pilgrimage, had not my health failed.

The natives of North America have always been noted for surpassingly sweet voices for singing, wherever they have any chance for cultivation, and we found the Indians of Canada easy to learn anything relating to vocal music. At first they had but one hymn in their own language, yet they never grew tired of it, but sang it over and over at all their meetings.

As the work spread, and the number of Christians increased, the demand for a larger supply of music became more apparent, and accordingly I selected about thirty of our most spiritual hymns, some for evening, morning, Sabbath, sacramental occasions, &c., and taking them to Dr. Aaron Hill, engaged him to translate them into Mohawk. The Dr. was a Mohawk by birth, a very intelligent man, and quite a skillful physician. He had a good English education, and was one of the best translators of the Indian into Mohawk we had in the Six Nations. We also employed him to translate the New Testament into Mohawk, and as he had no particular place of residence among his people, we engaged his board with a white family residing on the Reservation, near what is now called Brantfordville, and within a few miles of our missionary establishment, where I called upon him in my regular rounds.

He entered upon his work with much spirit and ambition, for we had promised him a compensation if he succeeded in his work. He first translated the Gospel according to St. Matthew and St. Luke, and having corrected a former translation of St. Mark and St. John, he soon finished the collection of hymns, and they were immediately sent on to New York, where our Missionary Society printed them, and sent us back a neat hymn-book, containing the English and Indian on opposite pages. The art of singing by patent notes being at that time much in vogue, we obtained some note-books, and by singing a tune with them a few times, they so mastered it as to sing correctly and harmoniously each part of the tune. So great was their improvement, and so marked their progress, that hundreds of whites who visited them at their devotions, acknowledged that they excelled, by far, the whites in that branch of divine worship.

At the last session of our Conference, Br. Egerton Ryerson, a scholar learned in English, Hebrew and Greek, was appointed to labor among those Indians who were now settled at the Credit. He, with Peter Jones, now translated a number of hymns into the Chippewa tongue, which is entirely different from the Mohawk, and thus were the Chippewas favored equally with their Mohawk brethren. Br. Case, in a letter to New York, thus notices the pleasure with which the natives received their hymn-book:

"The work of religion among the natives here continues to prosper. Of another body of Chippewas, in the vicinity of Kingston, about ten have been converted, and the whole body, of about forty, have renounced spirits, and have come up to Grape Island for instruction

Peter Jones is now with us. The condition of our Indian friends is every day improving. You would delight to hear our whole assembly, about 130, singing the Indian of

> "How happy are they, who their Savior obey,
>   And have laid up their treasure above;
> Tongue cannot express the sweet comfort and peace,
>   Of a soul in its earliest love."

> Nah kooh shà a she
> Pah pe na tah mooh wàdt
> Kee sha moon ne toon kane wah mah chik
> Ah pe che sah kooh
> Cepe pah he na tah moogk
> Pe je nuk shah wane one kooh se wadt. *

"The Indians are much delighted with the new hymnbook, and their desire to read is, by this circumstance, much increased. We are exceedingly happy in seeing the progress of this good work, and we are much encouraged by the deep interest which is taken in their welfare, both in this country and by strangers. To-day we renew our labors on the Island. I arrived here about two weeks since. Several of the preachers from the Hallowell and Bellville circuits accompany us in the labors of this week — of building a scow, making a harrow, planting, shingling houses, and teaching these new Christians the way to heaven."

Br. Ryerson, being mostly stationary at the Credit, was able to give his time closely to the affairs of our

---

* It may be proper to add, that the Indian words are divided into syllables, to enable the young learner to read with more case. It is therefore, not to be understood that in every division is contained a word. It frequently occurs that a single word extends throughout the line, and that the same word contains a whole sentence of the English.

Mississagua brethren.   The board shanty erected by them for a church at their first settlement, was unfit for use in cold weather, as it afforded them little or no protection from the winds and sifting snows. Br. Ryerson, therefore, formed the project of building a new and comfortable church, and he succeeded so admirably in his noble enterprise as to complete, in a few months, a fine church, which was the pride of the Indians, and the ornament of the village.   Br. R. acquitted himself like a man, and a noble minister of the Gospel, in the work assigned him as missionary. We give a letter written by him at this period to the Missionary Society at New York:

"INDIAN MISSION AT THE CREDIT, U. C.,
April 18th, 1827.

" *Rev. and Dear Sir:*—I now sit down to discharge a duty, which, for various reasons, I have long neglected. I arrived at my station the 16th of Sept., 1826, when I commenced my labors among this new made people. I was at that time a perfect stranger to Indians, and but little acquainted with their customs; but the affectionate manner in which they received me, and the joy they appeared to feel on the occasion, removed all the strangeness of national feeling, and enabled me to embrace them as brethren, and love them as mine own people. I found them happy in their spiritual circumstances—of one heart and one soul, rejoicing daily in the Lord, and their children attentive at school.

"How changed the scene, thought I, while visiting their

several camps; this flat,* which had heretofore resounded
with the yells of drunkenness, and teemed with intoxicated Indians and white men, is now covered with wigwams of *Christians*, and vocal with the praises of
Jehovah! This injured people, whose thousands have
dwindled to a little more than five-score, are now regard-
ed by the Sun of righteousness, and are admitted to
behold a light which is shrouded from the view of many
of their more wise and refined neighbors. The grace of
God was manifest among them, but they needed to be
instructed more perfectly how to cleave unto the Lord
with full purpose of heart. Order and discipline were
wanting, and a house that would answer the double purpose of literary and religious instruction.

"As the cold weather now began to pinch, so that we
could no longer have morning prayers in the old board
chapel, it was necessary to erect a house immediately.
We thought it advisable to make the first attempt towards procuring the means for building among ourselves.
Accordingly, the Indians, men, women and children, were
collected together by the sound of the horn, and the
matter was explained to them by Peter Jones, and a subscription presented. In half an hour, one hundred dollars, lacking four-pence, were subscribed, and (it being
the season for catching salmon) forty dollars were paid
at the time. Many of the Indian women, when they
saw others go forward and present the widow's mite,
(for they gave all they had, which was from one shilling
to three dollars,) expressed their sorrow that they had
nothing to give, but added, they would have some soon.

---

*The Indians were encamped on a level piece of ground near the
river, where fishermen of every description had formerly been accustomed to resort.

"They immediately plied themselves to the making of baskets and brooms, and soon presented their dollars and half dollars, and had their names set down among the others. Little boys from eight to twelve years, brought their shillings and two shillings, the product of their little fingers, to help in building a house where they could learn to be wise like the white boys, and pray to *Re-sha-mun-ire-to*, (the Great Spirit.) How astonishing the contrast! A short time ago these Indians would sell the last thing they had for one tenth its value, to get a little whisky; but now they will labor and exercise economy to get something to build a house, wherein they can worship the Lord of Hosts. Perhaps some of the intellectual and refined may be tempted to impute the zeal and benevolence of these poor Indians to their ignorance and imbecility. But, sir, is it ignorance and imbecility to be zealous for the King of kings—to love Jesus with our whole hearts and honor him with all our substance? How would he, who possesses all the treasures of wisdom and knowledge, decide in this case? He has decided it in Luke xxi. 3, 4. Ah! sir, were all our white Christians as much attached to our blessed Savior and his house, as these babes and sucklings in Christ are, how would the temples of Jehovah rise to our view in almost every part of this extensive and populous continent.

"In the evening, when I retired into our temporary *wiki-wam*, and reviewed the scenes of the day, and called to mind what several Indian women had said while presenting their offerings, 'now we will have a house where we can hear about, and pray to Jesus, without getting cold,' I felt to exclaim with the old patriarch, when he heard of his long lost Joseph, 'It is enough—it is the Lord's doings, and it is marvelous in our eyes.'

"About the middle of November, the house (which is thirty-six feet long by twenty-eight feet wide,) was suficiently finished to teach school in. The white inhabitants in this part of the province, have shown a very commendable zeal and liberality, by aiding in the erection of the building. It is also worthy of particular notice and grateful acknowledgment, that some benevolent individuals of the London district, (nearly one hundred miles west of this,) hearing that we wanted a stove, purchased a very handsome one, and sent it to us at this place. The house is now finished, except the seats, which would have been made before this time, could lumber have been procured and paid for.

"Order and discipline were now to be established. For this purpose we (myself and Peter Jones) divided them into classes, and selected two of the most intelligent and experienced men to take charge of each of these classes. Each class meets once a week. We meet the class-leaders every Sabbath, when we enquire into their own, and the state of their classes, and give them severally, the most suitable advice of which we are capable. We also endeavor to explain to them how they should watch over, and talk to their brethren, and what particular duties they ought particularly to enforce. These class-leaders are thereby preparing for more extended usefulness; and in part, become interpreters of good things to their respective classes. They feel themselves as shepherds (which is a comparison I often use in explaining to them their duty,) over their little flocks, and often communicate the state of their classes in the most interesting manner. As some of them speak English, I have often heard them say, ' We are weak children." "But I think my class is getting stronger and stronger, and I do believe that Jesus will, by and by, take all up in his arms into heaven.'

" There have been three instances of intoxication since I came here. Two of the offenders were restored by deep repentance ; and the other, in the anguish of his soul for what he had done, terminated his existence by suicide. Each of these improprieties was the effect of white men's impiety and baseness. In one instance, the Indian was pursued more than a quarter of a mile, and then was, as it were, compelled to take the poisonous draught ; in the other instance, the poor victim was persuaded to ride in a wagon, when similar means were used to destroy him ; and what is horrid to relate, whisky was secretly mingled with cider. Alas! sir, how does the blood, not of an individual only, but of tens of thousands, cry from the ground of America, for vengeance upon her inhabitants ! What woe shall be too severe for him who causes one of these little ones to offend, and puts the bottle to his brother's mouth ?

"The school consists of about forty scholars, and is taught by Mr. Peter Jones, whose exemplary life, and inde-fatigable labor, will doubtless give the most perfect satis-faction to the Missionary Committee, and be a lasting blessing to his pupils. About twenty. Indian children have learned those catechisms which teach the first prin-ciples of the christian religion, and a number of Watts' hymns for children. About the same number can read the Holy Scriptures—twelve of these can repeat the greatest part of our Savior's sermon on the Mount, and are beginning to write intelligibly. The children are generally exemplary in their conduct—several of them have professed to experience a change of heart from nature to grace; and some of them show signs of superior capacity and genius, and will, I doubt not, be seen at no distant day, standing as daysmen between the Great Spirit and their heathen brethren, crying to the one, 'Spare us, good Lord;' and entreating the others in the language of the ancient Gentile missionary, 'We pray you in Christ's stead, be ye reconciled to God.'

"The Indians have commenced their spring's labor, and appear to improve in habits of industry. However, their former habits of hunting and fishing, on which their whole dependence for support has *always* been placed, prevent them from feeling that deep interest in their agricultural success, which we could wish. But in this respect, judging from the past, we anticipate great improvement. By means of their funds invested in the hands of the government, they have purchased two yoke of oxen, one wagon, three ploughs, chains, harrow teeth, hoes, and other implements of husbandry, in order to commence the important and interesting business of agriculture. They have likewise received from their affectionate York and Yonge-street brethren, the present of a very elegant Scotch plow, which will be of great utility in breaking up the soil. Our village consists of twenty houses, (besides the chapel,) built on half acre lots, which are now fenced in, and will soon be prepared for planting. A number of heathen Indians, having heard that their brethren at the Credit had learned to live in a new and better way, have come here from different parts of the province—have embraced Christianity, and now appear to be established in the faith as it is in Jesus. The society contains one hundred and twenty members, who are steadfast and immovable, and seem to be growing in grace and in knowledge. I never experienced more affecting marks of sincere friendship, christian affection and tenderness, than among this people. I must defer the details of any further particulars till a future period.

"Yours affectionately,

"E. RYERSON."

Br. Carey succeeded admirably in his work at Muncey town, and showed himself to be a hero indeed. He continued teaching, under many dangers and difficulties, and under many discouragements, until the whole tribe were brought under the influence of the Gospel of Christ. During the earlier period of his teaching, and before many of the natives had renounced their old customs and habits, one of the Indians, having gone to the white settlement for whisky, was told that unless he should drive Carey away from his nation, he should have no more whisky. Accordingly, he determined to shoot him. So, loading his rifle, and drinking whisky enough to make him brave, he started back for the place where Carey was teaching. He crawled stealthily up to the door of the wigwam, which was open, and raising his rifle to his shoulder, he aimed at Carey, who stood with his back to the door. A little girl sitting near the door, saw the Indian when he came to the house, and watching his motions, saw him raise his rifle. Quick as thought, she sprang from the seat, and seizing the end of the gun, pushed it to the floor. Br. Carey, hearing the noise, turned around, when the Indian, seeing himself discovered, fled to the woods.

When our friends abroad heard of Br. Carey's danger, they advised him to leave so dangerous a place; but he, like a good soldier and faithful sentinel, said: "No! I will not leave my work, for I do not believe the Lord will allow a drunken Indian to take my life while engaged in his work." And so it was, though the same savage tried the second time to murder Carey; the Lord was round about him like a wall of fire to guard his servant, and to show those wicked whisky dealers that they were dealing with some power greater than man's.

CHAPTER XII.

It was a very general opinion of skeptics, and, indeed, of our christian friends and brethren at large,
that our Indians, who had been converted so suddenly
from heathenism to Christianity, would relapse soon
into their former habits of drinking and degradation,
that they would soon return to their former mode of
worship, and cling with greater tenacity to their
pagan rites and ceremonies.   But in this, happily, all
were disappointed, for when they became soundly converted to God, they also became the most devotional
people I ever saw.   When we explained to them the
requirements of the Gospel, and the great good the
Lord had in store for the humble, persevering Christian, who sits at the feet of the blessed Jesus, to learn
from him of his law, they seemed to lose all thought
of worldly cares, of personal distinction or aggrandizement, but gave their whole souls as an offering to

their blessed Redeemer, to do with them as he saw fit ; and this they did day after day, spending much of their time in prayer and devout meditation, morning and evening ; for as they considered it their chief business to save their souls, they could find time every day in the week, as well as on Sunday, for their devotions ; and when the pale horse and his rider appeared for them, summoning them away to the land of spirits, to dwell with him whom they had served so diligently, and loved so fervently here on earth, they hailed the messenger as the harbinger of eternal rest, and with song, and shout, and glad hosannah, they entered the dark river of death, and the sound of their voices could be heard even as they reached the other shore.

Among those who died in the triumphs of faith, was a young girl of the Mississagua tribe, at the River Credit. She was about twelve years of age, and among the first converts of this tribe. She entered the school at Grand River, and while staying there, showed herself a diligent scholar, as well as devout Christian, remarkably consistent in all her intercourse with her friends and fellow-scholars. She soon became able to read and write. A nice Bible was presented to her by a friend, as soon as she became able to read in it. This she read day and night, as she carried it with her wherever she went, and it may truly be said, "In it she meditated day and night." This course of conduct continued until the day of her death, which occurred some two years after her conversion to God. She seemed to ripen for heaven as days and months wore away, and when at last the message came for her, it found her ready to enter the cold stream of death without a sigh, or a word of sorrow, at parting with all those she held dear to her on earth, but, with hands clasping her precious Bible to her bosom, her faith strong in its precious promises, she calmly awaited the final dissolution of the bands which held her from a closer communion with her God, and leaning on his strong arm she sweetly fell asleep. On the day of her burial, one of her class-mates bore in her hand, as she followed her to the tomb, the Bible the departed had held so dear, and which had been a lamp of life, guiding her in the paths of righteousness.

Another instance of the power of religion over the last foe, was shown in the death of a woman of the Tuscarora tribe, who had become a subject of converting grace, but in consequence of ill health, had never received the rite of baptism. As her health continued to decline, it was thought best, by her friends, for her to leave her family and journey a short distance down the river, for the purpose of procuring medical aid. Accordingly, she was placed in an Indian canoe, and they started down the Grand River. After traveling some fifteen or twenty miles, she suddenly became worse, and it was found necessary to land immediately. She was taken to a small Indian house close to the river, and belonging to a native of the Delaware tribe. As Providence would have it, I was passing just at that time on the opposite side of the river, on my way down to the mouth, then some ten or twelve miles distant. When I came opposite the house where the sick woman lay, I was espied by one of the attendants, who informed her that the missionary was passing. She immediately requested them to send for me. Accordingly, an Indian sprang into a boat and made on down the river after me. He soon came within hailing distance, and beckoned me to stop. As he came up, he informed me there was a sick woman on the other side of the river, who wished to see me. I immediately hitched my horse to a tree, and crossing the river with the Indian, was soon standing in the presence of the dark-winged angel of death.

As I approached the bed of straw whereon lay the sick woman, I enquired how she was. She said she must soon die, and requested me to baptize her before her death. I administered the ordinance, and it was a solemn time. She seemed happy in God, and now took leave of her husband and friends. Last of all, and hardest to give up, was her infant. This, with all a mother's yearning, she pressed to her bosom, as though she could not give it up; but the grace of God was sufficient for her, and, with one last fond look, she gave it into the hands of those around her, and folding her hands, she awaited the coming of those bright ones commissioned to bear her spirit to its eternal rest. While we were thus standing, expecting every breath would be her last, the door opened, and her mother, a pagan, quickly and anxiously approached the bedside of her dying daughter. She had heard at a distance of her daughter's illness, and hastening on, she reached her bedside in time to see her die.

The daughter eagerly grasped the hand of her mother, and for a few moments all was silence, save the quick, deep sobs of the sorrow-stricken mother. At length the dying daughter, in a feeble voice said : "Mother, I am going to heaven, to live with Jesus, my adorable Savior; and I want you, before I die, should promise me you will get religion and meet me above." The mother, strong in the religion of her forefathers, hesitated to give an answer to her dying daughter. Seeing her reluctance to part with her old customs, the dying daughter, still clasping the hand of her mother, said, while the tears were streaming down her icy cheeks: "O, mother! I cannot die until you promise me you will get religion and meet me in heaven." The mother, trembling, while the tears showed the deep feeling of her heart, at length said: "I will try to be a Christian, and live so as to meet you in heaven." Then this dying saint let go her mother's hand, and, as she heard the rumbling of the chariot wheels that were to bear her away, and saw the bright and shining angels fluttering above her, as they waited to escort her to the mansions of bliss, she closed her eyes, and with a smile of ineffable joy upon her features, she joined the waiting band of heavenly ones, and passed on to her home beyond the skies.

One other instance of death among these Christians I extract from Rev. Peter Jones' Journal:

"SUNDAY, June 4th, 1826.—Rode this morning to our settlement at the Credit. Found the Indians engaged in the Sabbath School, and all pretty well, except Br. Geo. Youngs, who was very ill.

"MONDAY, 5th.—Towards evening, at the request of the sick man, (Geo. Youngs,) we had prayers with him, that he might be resigned to the will of God, as there was little hope of his recovery. He said there was only one thing on his mind, 'He should have liked to live a little longer, to have known more of this good religion, but for that, he was willing, if it pleased the Good Spirit, to die then.' O Lord, spare thy servant a little longer, if thy holy will; nevertheless, not our will, but thine be done.

"TUESDAY, 6th.—In the morning prayed with Br. Geo. Youngs, who was evidently sick unto death. He appeared very prayerful, and resigned to the will of God. Dr. A. called; he informed us there was no hope of his recovery. About ten o'clock, word came to me that he was dying, so I hastened down and got there just as he was breathing his last. He fell asleep in the arms of Jesus, to join with the glorified spirits above, where, in the paradise of God, he will rest from all his labors. Blessed be God, that he died a Christian! At our prayer-meeting in the afternoon, we had a solemn time. O Lord, continue to carry on thy work till all the natives of the forest become Christians!

"WEDNESDAY, 7th.—At 11 A. M., I preached a funeral sermon to the Indians, on the patience of Job. While addressing them on the duty of resignation to the will of God, under all the dispensations of his providence, there was a solemn joy on every countenance, and frequent bursts of praise. After this service, I committed to the grave the remains of our good brother, in sure and certain hope of a glorious resurrection. This is the first Christian Indian buried at the Credit."

In contrast I give another incident, most melancholy in its details, of one who, through the satanic intrigues and influences of wicked white men, fell from his high estate, and in his remorse committed suicide. The fisheries of the Credit were very profitable, and the whites, availing themselves of the indifference of the natives, were in the habit of resorting there yearly, and carrying off barrels of fish. As the natives depended much upon these fisheries for food during their season, they were always there in large numbers, and always willing to barter what they did not want for immediate use, for anything the whites had to offer, and which most generally was whisky. When the Indians once began to drink, they would part with anything and everything they possessed, even to the clothes upon their bodies,.to get more fire-water; and those avaricious traders would take the last blanket they had, leaving them without covering from the weather. It was no uncommon sight to see these natives, both male and female, lying drunk upon the beach around the traders' shanties, with scarcely any clothing, having been robbed, as it were, by the traders, who intended, when they became sober, to sell back the clothing at exorbitant prices, to be paid in fish.

After our converted Mississaguas settled there, the traders came as usual, with their barrels of whisky, but not one Indian could they get to touch one drop of their poisonous stuff. At this they began to think .their craft was in danger, for if they could not make Indians drunk, there would be no profit in buying their fish.   They therefore laid their heads together, and with the help of their father, the devil, who was chief counsellor, they laid their plans to entrap the natives unawares.   They tried many schemes, in vain. They arranged their decanters and glasses in their most attractive form, and put on their blandest smiles, but all to no purpose.   At one time, one of the traders, seeing a christian Indian and his family passing his door, invited them to enter, and offered them whisky as a token of his pleasure at seeing them again.

The Indian said, "Have you Bibles?"   "O, yes!" said the trader, and handed one down.   The Indian, taking the Bible in his hand, and looking at the trader said, "Much gospel; little whisky!"   The trader, surprised and foiled in his attempt to intoxicate them, said nothing, and they passed on.   They next tried force, and in one instance they pursued a native more than a quarter of a mile, when they forced him to drink of their liquor.   Again, they changed their tactics, and offered the natives *sweet cider*, telling them that though they could not drink whisky, there surely was no harm in drinking a glass of sweet cider, as that was not forbidden them.   After much specious reasoning of this sort, they prevailed upon one Indian to drink a glass of cider.   But these demons incarnate, had mixed whisky with the cider, and as they plied him with glass after glass, he soon began to feel the maddening fire coursing through his veins. Feeling he was undone, he started for home. As he entered, his wife seeing his state, cried out in her anguish, "We are ruined ; you have let the white man make you drunk !" The Indian paused a moment, as she thus bewailed their misfortune, then taking down his rifle, he left the house, unnoticed by his wife, who was deeply lamenting this unhappy event, and making his way to the grove near by, shot himself through the body. The Indians, hearing the report of a gun near by, went out, and there they found him, lying on the ground, rolling in his blood, and writhing in his anguish and agony of spirit, mortally wounded. They carried him to the house, and laid him upon his bed. The christian natives had gathered in, and now with his family fell upon their knees, and offered up prayer to God that he might be saved. When asked, how he felt in his mind, he said, "All dark ; no feel happy— no feel like praying ! Though every exertion was made to save him, he gradually sunk into the embrace of death, wailing out in his last breath, "All dark, dark !"

As they arose from their knees, and stood mournfully around the bed-side of their unfortunate brother, and heard his dying exclamation, as he entered upon the dread unknown, and learned the story of his fall, how, with many professions of friendship and fond regard, those servants of darkness had enticed him to do what in itself he thought no wrong, they determined to drive those traders from their midst, and henceforth to allow no white man on their land, with anything in the shape of drink, and never to take anything from the hand of a white man that could contain anything intoxicating.

I have often thought what an account those men, who trafficked with the aborigines of our country, must give ! The blood of thousands cries from the ground for vengeance against their destroyers.   Surely, if there is any work too mean for the devil to do, it must be this rum-selling, whisky-making business.   That there is work so mean and so dirty that the devil disdains to touch his hand to it, although gloved, we do not doubt ; and when those men who have been his most faithful servants here on earth, who have cheerfully performed his vilest drudgery, come into the presence of their Master, as he sits on his throne, in those lurid, sulphurous regions below, and claim an exalted station near him, because of their zeal in his service, he will spurn them from him in contempt, and tell them that the darkest, farthest, hottest corner of his dungeon is only too good for them.

CHAPTER XIII.

From the commencement of my labors with the Indians, my path seemed to lead me to those who had not as yet received any knowledge of the Bible or a plan of salvation. My business was to break up the fallow ground, and having sown the seed, leave others to water and gather in the harvest. Thus, as soon as a station was formed at the River Credit by those natives converted at Grand River, and who, because they had no particular abiding place, settled there, I left them in the care of a missionary stationed among them by the Conference, and only occasionally visited them afterwards, as I was pressing on to carry the gospel to others yet in their pagan state. Among such I labored while they were wandering about, but as soon as they settled down in one place, they required some one to watch over them, and guide and instruct them daily, until they should become men and women in Christ.   And as there were, as yet, but few who would take their lives in their hands and wander through the wilderness, hunting up the wild man of the forest to tell him of a crucified Savior, it became necessary for me to take this post of exposure and peril, and be continually pushing on the outposts of the work.

Peter Jones had begun, at this time, to preach, and travelled much among his brethren, telling them what God had done for him, and inviting them to come and possess themselves of the same joy ; but his heart was with his brethren at the Credit, and he was loth to leave them until they could better guide themselves. The result consequent upon the privations I was called upon to endure, of breasting storms of wind and rain, of snow and ice, of sleeping upon the cold, wet ground, wherever night overtook me, oftentimes without fire or food, toiling through trackless swamps, or swimming deep and swollen rivers ; such things, after three years of hard labor, began to undermine my constitution, and as I entered upon my fourth year, I found I was overtaxing my strength.   My constitution had not fully recovered from the effects of my sickness while travelling among the new settlements of the whites, and my constant exposure to wet and cold, was not in the least beneficial to me.

As I looked into the future I could not hope it would be any better for me, for we were constantly making aggressive warfare upon the powers of darkness, and this necessarily kept me among the wild, untaught savages much, or most of my time, save when, that I might recruit my strength, I would spend a few days' time enjoying the hospitalities of my white brethren. At times I felt mightily strengthened, and nerved to the conflict, while storming some of the strongholds of the Prince of Darkness, and especially when we succeeded, through the name and strength of the Captain of our salvation, in unlocking the prison doors of death, and in leading forth into the light and liberty of the Son of God, those who had been long bound down in the chains of hellish darkness. To listen to the songs and shouts of victory, and to witness the glory and peace which filled their happy, liberated souls, seemed enough, at times, to fully compensate us for all the toil and suffering we endured.

Often I felt like saying, "Let me live and die on the battle-field ;" but at other times the voice of duty warned me to leave the field, before I should be compelled to do so for want of health. Under these impressions, I wrote to Br. Case, stating my circumstances, and my convictions that I ought to leave my post.

He soon answered my letter, in his affectionate and fatherly way, calling my attention to the manner the first successful missionary effort commenced under Brainard, who labored among the natives of South America with glorious success, but after three years' toil and privation, was brought to the gates of death. When on his dying bed, he called a brother of his, studying for the ministry, to him, and in a solemn charge, gave the care of his flock into his hands. But this brother, though a good man, lacked that missionary fire which burned so brightly in the heart of young Brainard, and the mission, so well begun, soon dwindled away. "Now," said Br. Case, "here we are, with this mission just begun. You have been among the Indians until they have confidence in all you say. We have other good ministers who would be employed in the work, but they are unacquainted with the Indians ; and the natives distrust all white men whom they have not proved. Now, brother, you must not think of leaving this work. There is a hereafter, and who knows the stars that will be added to your crown, if you continue on in this blessed work."

About this time, chief Davis, hearing me say I soon must leave them, in consequence of my ill health, came to me, and taking his seat beside me, said : "Be you going to leave us ?" I replied, "I think I shall be obliged to, on account of my health, which is failing ; and I find I cannot do the work expected of me." "Brother," said the chief, "let me tell you. You must not leave us now. We not strong yet. You leave us now, we all go down." I replied, "If I leave you, our good Bishop will send you another good minister to preach to you and live with you." He quickly replied : "He not know Indian ; Indian not know him ; Indian not mind him. You know Indian ; Indian know you ; Indian mind you." This was said with so much feeling and concern for his people, that with what Br. Case had said in his letter to me, it nearly discouraged me from entertaining any more thoughts of leaving the mission field at the coming Conference.

On my way to our Annual Conference, while traveling through a roadless wilderness, I became so unwell as to faint and fall from my horse. I lay some time senseless, how long I know not. My horse had gone a few paces ahead, when he stopped and waited for me. On recovering, I arose to my feet, moved slowly on after my horse, and taking the bridle in my hand, sat down by the roots of a tree, and lifted up my heart in prayer to God, that he would direct me and assist me. I now looked ahead of me, in the direction I expected to find a settlement, and saw a white man and woman coming towards me. As they came near, and saw me sitting on the ground, they asked me if I was sick. I told them I was; that I had fainted and fallen from my horse, and asked them how far it was to a settlement of white people. They informed me I was near what was then called the Dundas road, and that I would find a public house but a short distance ahead. Upon this, I arose, and walking slowly along, soon came in sight of the house spoken of. Here I had my horse taken care of, and then went to bed. After a few hours I felt better, and again mounting my horse, proceeded on my way to Conference.

Much of the time, while on this journey, I was hardly able to ride; but I persevered, and finally reached my destination. Bishop George presided at this Conference. He and all the preachers saw the state of my health, yet would they not consent to release me from my work. The Bishop said I might visit my friends in the States, and in spending a few weeks with them, I would probably recover, so as to continue my work. Accordingly, I made the best of my situation, and started for my home in the States. Here I spent several days, in that quiet and rest I so much needed, and on returning to Canada, my health was much improved, so that I entered upon my work with strong hopes of pushing forward the victories of the cross, with all my former strength of physical endurance.

About this time, we were called upon to mourn the loss of one of our most efficient and pious Indians, Br. Jacob Hill, of whom I have spoken as being converted some two years previous. The society we established at his house, and which consisted, at first, of himself and family, had continued to increase, until nearly all his neighbors became members, and a flourishing school was now in operation. Br. Jacob evinced great interest in the success of the school, and also in the work generally. While in his pagan state, he was much respected by his white neighbors, for his honesty and temperate habits ; and after his conversion, he was one of the most happy, devoted and consistent Christians in the nation. During his last sickness, he exhorted all who came to see him to prepare to meet him in heaven. He was very happy, and spent most of his last hours conversing with his family and christian brethren, warning them to be faithful, humble Christians. He told them they might expect the Lord would yet convert and save a great many of their brethren. Though his stay with us as a Christian was short, he died in the full triumphs of faith, and has taken his place among the blood-washed, around the throne in heaven.

About ten miles below our first establishment on Grand River, were a number of wigwams belonging to the Oneida tribe. They had established themselves at this place because of some salt springs, where, in years gone by, Indians had manufactured salt. The place was known as "Salt Springs." I succeeded in drawing the attention of these Indians to the importance of establishing a school among them, and I also left an appointment for preaching at this place.

Winter had now set in upon us, and my head, hands and heart, were overcharged with the great interests of these natives who were just emerging from the cloud of heathenish darkness that enveloped them, into the clear and dazzling sunlight of gospel day. I found it necessary, during the winter, in consequence of the increase of scholars and hearers at Salt Springs, to build a house which should answer the purpose of church and school-house. The Missionary Society as yet did not afford us any help in building among the Indians. I had only drawn on our fund for one hundred dollars a year, with a few dollars more as expenses, that being my salary while among the Indians. Some of our teachers were receiving small salaries yearly, but when we commenced building, I was obliged to go out amongst our white brethren, and presenting my cause before them, rely upon their benevolent contributions for assistance.

I now devoted all my spare time, when not upon other parts of my large circuit or mission, to the gathering together of materials and collecting funds, that we might commence building as soon as spring opened. As winter wore away, I found my health, which had not fully returned since my sickness of the previous summer, was continually failing, under the care and exposure necessary to meet my appointments, and to oversee all the different portions of the work. Preaching every day at stations miles apart, made it necessary for me to be out in all weathers, when possible for a man to travel. The spring had just opened ; materials for building were all collected and on hand, and everything was prospering when I was taken sick and confined to a small unfinished room, in a house about one mile from Grand River.

Here, for four weeks I lay, the physicians expecting I never would leave my bed alive. The Indians from all parts called to see the Missionary. They sympathized very much with me, and wanted to do something for me. They would come to my room and weep while listening to me, as I talked to them of the good things of the kingdom of heaven, and morning and evening their prayers arose to the Great Spirit, that my life might yet be spared. At the end of four weeks I was able to sit up, and soon began to walk about. This was about the first of May, in the fifth year of my labor among the Indians.

At Salt Springs there lived a pagan woman, very industrious, temperate and economical in all her habits. She had settled on those fertile flats bordering the river, and by carefully tilling the soil, which yielded profusely when properly worked, and hoarding all she raised, amassed quite a property, and was known among the Indians as the "rich woman." When I commenced preaching to her tribe, we invited her to come to the meetings, which we informed her were to benefit the Indians, and cause them to leave off the use of fire-waters, &c. She said she would wait and see if our religion reformed the drunkard, or made them any more industrious. She soon had evidence that the Gospel could reform the most dissolute among them. She then became friendly, attended our meetings, and seemed inclined to be pious.

My brethren in the ministry, with myself, now thought it best for me to leave the mission field ; accordingly, as soon as I became able to ride my horse, I started for my mother's house, in Chenango Co., N. Y. On mounting my horse, I found I should be able to ride but very few miles in a day ; but when I was fully under way for home, and had been several days among white people, where I could have comfortable beds and wholesome food, my health improved rapidly, and at the end of a week's journeying on horseback, I reached the village of Penn Yan, in this State.

Here I met with Abner Chase, of the Genesee Conference, and Presiding Elder of the district. He thought it best for me to take an appointment on his district at the approaching Conference, which held its annual session in Wilkesbarre, Pennsylvania. In order to this, I must take a transfer from the Canada Conference. As my health had improved very fast after crossing the Niagara waters, up to that time, and as I was growing stronger every day, I consented to let Br. Chase present my case before the presiding Bishop and Conference, and if it was thought best for me to take an appointment within the bounds of his district, to do so. I now continued on for my mother's house, which I reached in the course of a few days. Here I spent the few weeks intervening before Conference commenced its session, at which I was transferred by the Bishop to the Genesee Conference, and received my appointment, according to my request, as junior preacher. I was appointed to labor upon the Ulysses circuit, with R. M. Evarts as senior preacher.

I immediately took leave of my mother, and started for my circuit, which was some sixty miles distant. My colleague was taken lame, and did not join me in the work. Thus, again, the whole care of a circuit fell upon me. This circuit embraced all the country lying between Cayuga and Seneca Lakes, from the town of Enfield to Ovid. Within the bounds of that circuit, there are, at the time of my writing this, nine different stations, with as many ministers.

As it was necessary for me to be at the Canada Conference, which met in September, in order to report the state of the mission at Grand River, after going once around my circuit I started for the Canadas, and reached Grand River the week before the Conference commenced its session. Having one Sabbath to spend before the opening of Conference, I concluded to preach at the Salt Springs, where I had commenced building, and where the Indians were just beginning to listen to the truths of religion.

Everything remained about as when I left. It was announced that I would again preach at that place, and when Sunday came, we had a general rally of the Indians and whites from all parts of the country round about. While I was preaching, the Spirit of the Lord sent home the truth of the Gospel to the hearts of nearly all present, and a general weeping and crying out for mercy was heard in all parts of the house. We all fell upon our knees and commenced praying. Soon the Lord began to lift up the bowed down, and shouts of victory were heard among those who were weeping and wailing because of their lost and ruined condition.

The Lord was present to save and bless. Among those who rejoiced in the love of a new found Savior, was the noble Chief, Doxtader, one of the most influential chiefs of the Six Nations, and a part of his family. His son William, a young man of great promise, noted for his sagacity and shrewdness, together with the reputation of being one of the best Mohawk scholars in all the reservation, was arrested by the Spirit of God, soundly converted, and, like St. Paul, began to preach to his people almost as soon as he was brought into the light of the Gospel. He seemed like a burning seraph, such power accompanied his prayers and exhortations.

We had witnessed but few instances among the Indians of a more powerful meeting than this. Over a score were converted that day, and were rejoicing in the Savior's love. I stayed with this people several days, and the Lord wrought gloriously for us here. I was obliged to tear myself away, that I might attend Conference. The news of this glorious work had preceded me, and Christians everywhere were rejoicing at the wondrous displays of Divine love.

While stopping at Salt Springs, and during my illness in the spring, I had made it my home at a Mr. Tuthill's, who died during my absence in the States. As his death was quite sudden, and the events relating to it somewhat remarkable, I will relate it as given to me by his widow. A short time before his death, while lying in bed, he heard three raps at the head of his bed. He immediately informed his family some of them would soon die. The day on which he was killed, he had business away from home, which required him to start early in the morning. He arose about four o'clock, and was on his knees, praying, much longer than was usual, for him. On leaving, he bid his family farewell, which was an unusual thing for him to do. He drove his own team. The distance he had to go was ten miles. He had travelled that distance, left his load, finished his business, and started for home. He seated himself in his empty wagon, with a man by his side. The man said he seemed not inclined to talk, save, every few minutes he would say, "We are alive yet," and thus they moved along for his home. Their road was smooth and sandy, passing, now and then, under dry oaks, which had been girdled. As they were passing under one of these trees, a large limb fell from the tree, striking him on the head, and killing him instantly. He was a member of our Church, and a respectable, friendly, good man. He and his family had shown me much kindness during my sickness, and I had often been blessed while praying with and for them, and at my last meeting with the Indians, I had the pleasure of seeing two of his children made happy in the love of God.

I reached Hamilton, the seat of Conference, the second day of its session. Bishop Hedding in the chair. At this Conference we had trouble with Henry Ryan, an aged minister, who had been one of our most efficient and successful ministers, for thirty years. He was Irish by birth, of a tall, gigantic frame, inclined to corpulency, and weighing near three hundred. He was by far the largest man I ever saw. He had a voice like a lion, and when speaking in the open air, to a large assembly, he might be heard distinctly for miles. Br. Case once said of his preaching at camp-meetings, that "when fully roused to his subject, and raising his voice, it was like throwing handirons and crowbars among the people." His greatest success was in his early ministry, which was mostly in the Canadas. When a young man, he was a colleague of Bishop Hedding. Probably no minister braved more difficulties, or encountered greater hardships than

Henry Ryan. He was presiding elder in the Canadas for many years. I remember hearing him relate some of his adventures, of which he had many. During the war of 1812, he had charge of all the societies and circuits both in the Upper and Lower Provinces, as the British Government would allow no American preacher in the Canadas. Father Ryan, as he was called, when I entered the Canadas, was a British subject by birth, and the people had such unbounded confidence in his integrity and loyalty that he was allowed to travel in any part of the Provinces of British North America. During this war, an Indian came to his dwelling to sell him a quarter of venison. He bought it, and gave him in return a silver half dollar, with the American eagle stamped upon it. The Indian looked at it and said, "You Yankee ; I kill you;" and drawing his knife, made towards him. Father Ryan, being unarmed, caught up a sled stake, and raising it above his head, said, "If you come one step nearer, I'll kill you!" The Indian, having no other weapon than his knife, durst not venture further. "Now," said Father Ryan, "you lay down that piece of money." The Indian laid it down. "Now," said he, " take your venison, and be gone." The Indian picked up the venison from where Ryan had thrown it, and was soon out of sight. "And would you have killed him ?" said I to him, when he related to me this incident. "Kill him !" said he, "I would have killed him as quick as I would a bear !"

At another time, while travelliug to one of his appointments, he stopped at a public house, to feed his horse and refresh himself. Two ruffians, who were angry at him, placed themselves at the outside of the door, intending, when he came out, to clinch him and give him a pounding. The landlord, knowing their design, told Father Ryan the facts, and advised him not to go out until they had left. But Father Ryan was no such man. Taking hold of the little end of his riding-whip, he walked deliberately to the door. Opening it, he said to the fellows that stood there, "Stand back !" They looked at his gigantic frame, then up into his flashing eyes, and immediately fell back, as they were told, while Father Ryan went on his way unharmed.

At another time, a number of the baser sort of men determined they would whip Father Ryan, at a place where he was expected to preach. The old hero had received timely notice of their intentions, and at an early hour entered the pulpit, which was one of the olden sort, six feet from the floor, breast high, and doors on each side. The people were all assembled to hear Father Ryan preach. Soon the wicked fellows made their appearance, and began crowding up towards the pulpit.   Ryan rose suddenly to his feet, pulled off his coat, rolled up his sleeves above his elbows, doubled up his huge fist, and stretching out his mighty arm exclaimed, as he shook it at them, "Look here, you ruffians, God Almighty has not given me this arm and fist for nothing ; come here if you dare !"   At this, these desperate fellows made a pause, when Father Ryan immediately began preaching one of his thunder and lightning sermons, and in a few minutes his enemies were glad to get outside the door, and the preacher with his congregation had a great and glorious time in worshiping the Lord God of hosts.

This mighty man, while in the spirit of his work, seemed not to be daunted or discouraged by the most trying circumstances.   As long as Father Ryan counselled with such men as Br. Case, he gave general satisfaction to both preachers and people upon his district ; but when he rejected them, and chose for his counsellors such men as James Jackson, who were full of all mischief, he began to err from the path of right, and it was soon discovered that he was laying plans which, if carried into effect, would destroy the harmony of the whole Methodist Church in Canada. The Bishop was requested to remove him from his district, which highly offended him, and he, with Jack-

son and several others, resolved on a revolution in the
M. E. Church in Canada. He believed his influence
with the people to be so great, that he could readily
persuade them to his faith, and thus draw off nearly
the whole laity in the Provinces. Br. Case becoming
thoroughly acquainted with his plans and movements,
and believing it necessary for the peace of the Church,
that they should be arrested and exposed, preferred a
bill of charges against him. During the examination
of the character of ministers, when the usual question
was asked, "Is there anything against Henry Ryan?"
Br. Case arose and said, there was; and proceeded to
read his bill of charges. Upon this, Ryan took his
hat, bid the Conference good bye, and walked deliberately out of the house, James Jackson following.
He soon notified the Conference that he would not
stand a trial, and they might do as they pleased with
him. He returned no more to his seat in the Conference, but commenced the dreadful work of stirring up
strife, and making divisions among brethren.

Hundreds of our good people, with many ministers,
both local and travelling, for a time believed Ryan
had been wronged, and that he was yet seeking the
best good of the Church, as he formerly had done.
He was at length taken ill, and was unable to speak
a word for six months before he died. We may hope

he repented of his wrong, found mercy at the hand of the Lord, and is saved.

The Indians, finding my health was much improved, plead with me to stay longer with them. I would have done so, notwithstanding I had already received my appointment within the Genesee Conference, and had commenced my labors there; but I·knew that though my health was much improved, yet I was far from being able to enter upon the mission field and endure even one-half what I had been obliged to, during the nine years of my stay in Canada, among the whites and Indians.

Bishop Hedding and Br. Case, after learning the true state of my health, said they would not press me back into the mission field, but thought it would be necessary for me to accompany the missionary now stationed among them, and introduce him to the Indians of Grand River and surrounding places.

During the exercises of our Missionary Anniversary, a large handful of silver jewelry was placed on the table. A message accompanied it from one of the western ·tribes of the Chippewa nation, praying us to come to them with some of the great good Book, which the Great Spirit had given us white people. They had heard that Indians could have it; that it made them good and happy, and they wanted to know more about it. Had my health permitted, I would gladly have gone, bearing the tidings of great joy to those poor, wandering men, and preaching Jesus and his resurrection to their waiting minds.

When the Conference closed, Br. Mesmore was sent to Grand River, James Richardson to the Credit Mission, Solomon Waldron to the Grape Island Mission, and Peter Jones to the native tribes of Chippewas. Thus, from a beginning which some of our preachers and people ridiculed as useless, saying, it was folly for me to stay among such a besotted people, as they could never be converted—from such a beginning and under such circumstances, had in five years grown up a work which required four men to manage, and a continual call for more.

The fire, which at first was lighted with a single match among those swamps and forests, had, by careful watching and feeding, spread itself into one vast conflagration, lighting up the whole province with its glorious blaze, and, sweeping on to the westward, was devouring every sin and all uncleanness. The white pagans, hearing the roar of its oncoming strength, became frightened, and swinging their whisky barrels on their shoulders, hastened from its track. The poor Indians, roused by the unusual sound, raised themselves in their darkness, and seeing the treetop lighted up in the blaze of gospel fire, eagerly watched its approach and hailed its coming with joy, as the harbinger of that glorious day which should drive all sorrow, darkness and night away from them, and leave them in the full blaze of light, life, and liberty. And still that fire is sweeping onward. To the north and west it spread, crossing those vast upland plains of inland North America, gathering strength in its onward march, until upon the peaks of the Rocky Mountains it blazed forth, lighting up the eternal snows with its brilliancy, and shedding its welcome, beacon-like rays far and wide into the surrounding darkness. And now it has descended the western slope of those mountains, and among the gigantic forests of Oregon and western British North America, can be heard the roar of its ever devouring elements ; and the crash of falling superstition ever and anon echoes in the distance, while the crisp and withered leaves of Indian rites and ceremonies only serve to feed the flame. May the fire continue to burn until the whole continent shall be wrapped in one broad sheet of gospel flame, and all men, like the poor Indian, shall rejoice at its coming.

Br. Mesmore and myself immediately left Hamilton for Grand River Mission. We steered our course for Salt Springs, as at that part of the Mission we had so lately received a pentecostal shower, that we were still favored with a sight of the blessed drops as they fell here and there among the people. We called the Indians together, and once more I worshiped with those people whom my soul loved.

At the close of our exercises, I arose and thus addressed them : "Brothers and sisters, the time has now come, when I must leave you. Our good Bishop has sent you this good minister," pointing to Br. Mesmore, "who will live with, and preach to you. Brothers, listen to what he says to you ; love him and he will love you, and do you good." I then sat down when chief Doxtader arose and said : "Brother, we thank you for coming to us. We thank you for showing us how we might be saved and become happy. We thank our God for what he has done for us."

As he finished the last sentence, he began weeping aloud. Sobs were heard from all parts of the house, and I could not refrain from joining with them. I looked at Br. Mesmore, and he too was weeping. For a while we gave vent to our full souls, and then taking the parting hand, Br. Mesmore and I started for our horses, which were hitched to some of the trees around the house. As we mounted and made off, I turned my head to take one more look of the people who had become so dear to me. They had left the house, and were leaning on the fence and against the trees, still weeping aloud.

Before reaching Salt Springs, Br. Mesmore had said to me, "I do not believe I ever can love Indians as I love my own people." After our parting at the church he said, "Well, Br. Torry, I never saw anything like this in my life. You ought never to leave these Indians. I believe, after all, I shall come to love them as much as any people I ever labored with."

Having now taken a final leave of the Canadas, I hastened back to my appointment in the States, and after a long and tedious journey, through the mercy of the Lord, I arrived at Townsendville church about nine o'clock one Sunday morning, and found our people gathering from all parts for a love-feast.

CHAPTER XIV.

On reaching my circuit, I found that my colleague,
R. M. Evarts, was unwell, and had not as yet commenced laboring on the circuit. I was again alone
on a large circuit, with plenty of preaching and travelling to do. As I travelled from one part to another,
visiting and praying with the people, I found the Lord
present to bless the people, and we had many a happy
season together, and many sinners were converted to
God. At the close of the year, the Official Board
petitioned Conference for my return, and I was sent
back as preacher in charge. My colleagues for this
year were Brs. Gideon Laning and Schuyler Hoes.

Br. Laning still survives, an honored member of
Genesee Conference, and though sustaining a superannuated relation to the Church, he still labors as he

can, and through the columns of the Northern Christian Advocate occasionally gives us glimpses of olden times, as he portrays the itinerant, travelling over the hills and through the valleys of his extensive circuit, waking with his clarion voice, thousands of careless, slumbering sinners to the claims of the gospel, as it is in Christ Jesus. May he long live to enjoy a green old age, and may his last days be unclouded by a single sorrow, and may his death be triumphant.

This was the first year of Br. Hoes' experience as a travelling preacher. Br. Hoes was a pious, zealous, and successful preacher. Possessing a powerful mind, with more than ordinary ministerial talents, united with a fervent zeal to do his fellow men good, he preached and prayed as though life and death were the result of his labors, and he would surely be held responsible for the influence he exerted. Preaching he considered serious business, therefore he never tried to ring the ear with pleasant sounds, or dazzle the eye with shining things. He viewed his fellow men as mortals hastening on to the final day of judgment, there to receive their sentence for eternal happiness or woe, and as such he raised his voice in trumpet tones, warning the sinner of the terrible retribution that awaited him, if he died in his sins. He took for his motto that passage, "Whatsoever thy hand findeth to do, do it with thy might," and his preaching or praying was like a storm of thunder bolts falling upon the heads of sinners.

The last time I saw him he told me some of his brethren had advised him to be more moderate in his manner of delivery, and he had tried it, but, said he, "I cannot get happy in so doing, and the words I speak do not take hold upon the hearts of my hearers ; and now I have made up my mind to preach so as I can please God, get blessed, and bless the people."

Br. Hoes was a strong opposer of American slavery, and he boldly denounced it as a great sin, striving with his brethren, to show them the enormous guilt of slave-holders ; but some of his quondam conservative brethren, looking upon him as a dangerous innovator and disturber of the peace of Zion, and being in authority over him, dealt so severely with him as to cause him to leave the Church and join the Wesleyans. Subsequently, some of these men have, by their actions, acknowledged him their superior in judging the signs of the times, and now tacitly, as an atonement for their want of penetration, they follow in the path marked out by him, and, in their zeal, carry their measures to such extremes as were never advocated by him. After joining the Wesleyans, he became a distinguished minister, and for several years labored with great success. For a few years before his death he travelled extensively in the South, for his health, which was fast declining. His last trip was to California, where, finding his health did not improve, he finally came back to his family in Fulton, New York, and after a few months' illness, died. When he approached the river of death, it was with a firm step, and an unshaken confidence in Jesus Christ, the mighty conqueror of death and hell. When, as it was supposed, the last struggle was over, he revived, as one waking out of sleep, and exclaimed, " Have I come back again ? I have taken two steps into the river ; I shall go over next time." And so it was ; for in a few moments he passed quite over, and found his resting place with the redeemed ones in heaven.

This year was abundant in work and revivals. We all had plenty of work to do, and in the course of the two years, we built, repaired, and finished five churches. During this year, my mother had taken her leave of earth, and gone to dwell in the mansions of the blest in heaven. I visited her some six weeks before her death, and found her waiting the coming of her Lord, with her lamp trimmed and burning. I staid several days, doing all I could for her comfort ; and then took my leave of her for the last time ; no more to hear her voice, or see her face, until the resurrection morning shall wake the slumbering dust to life, and the dead shall come forth clothed in immortality. The Lord had given her twelve children, and for these she never ceased to pray, till her pulse ceased to beat, and her eyes closed in death. Five of the twelve had passed on before, and, doubtless, were among the first to hail her ransomed spirit, as it entered the abodes of the blessed.

This year the Genesee Conference was divided into two; the eastern portion taking the name of Oneida, and the western retaining its original name. My field of labor being in the eastern portion, I was transferred, with several others, to the Oneida Conference, which held its first session at Cazenovia, where I received an appointment to Pompey circuit, Isaac Puffer being preacher in charge. As Cazenovia was near the centre of the circuit, I made my home there. We had some good revivals, and I was continued the next year upon the same circuit, with G. Stoddard and Benjamin Phillips as colleagues. During this year we also had several powerful revivals. At Delphi we had a small chapel, well finished, a small society, and a small congregation.

One evening, while preaching to these people, the Lord so directed the truth declared to them, that they were pricked in their hearts, and a cry like that heard in the days of the Apostles, when Peter was preaching, rose from the congregation. As soon as I finished my sermon, I hastened to the altar, and invited all who wanted religion to come forward, and we would pray for them. More than twenty immediately crowded around the altar, and began to plead for the pardon of their sins. In the course of an hour, nearly every one found peace in believing. I appointed next day morning, which was Monday, at 9 A. M., for a love-feast. During the night, many of the converts went from house to house, telling their neighbors what great things God had done for them, and inviting and urging their friends to accept of the same for themselves.

In the morning, before the appointed time, the people were seen gathering from all quarters, to see and hear for themselves what all this stir and noise should mean. It seemed as though all Delphi valley was aroused and alarmed for its safety, and now came flocking to our little chapel, as doves hasten to their windows before a mighty tempest. Our altar was crowded with penitents of all ages, from the youth of twelve, to the white-headed father of three score and ten. We continued our meetings from nine in the morning till ten and eleven at night, only giving the people time for food and rest. This meeting lasted eight days, during which time over one hundred were converted to God.

The Divine power manifested among the people at this meeting, was similar to that we had been accustomed to witness among the red men of the wilderness of North America.

I soon discovered that many of our converts were favored with visits from the Baptist minister of Delphi, as he felt it his duty to inform them of the importance of being baptized without delay; that they must be immersed, if they expected to be saved, as the doctrine of sprinkling, held by the Methodists, was no doctrine at all, and as the Methodists disbelieved in immersion, they must, as a consequence, be baptized by him ; that we believe in being saved by works and not by faith, which was a very pernicious doctrine, and ought not to be inculcated.

In order that the people might not be misled, or form erroneous opinions respecting our belief and practice, I read to all the congregation, our Articles of Faith, as laid down in our Discipline, which, of course, would show satisfactorily and conclusively, that his statements were incorrect.   I also told them if any of them wished baptism by immersion, I could accommodate them in that way at any time.   After explaining our rules and creed. to them, they nearly all seemed satisfied, and our Baptist friends did not have the pleasure of seating many of our converts around their close communion table.

Among the inhabitants of the valley were several "heads of families," belonging to the Presbyterian Churches at Cazenovia and Pompey Hill. Many of their children were converts, and they thought it best to organize a Church at Delphi, that their children might join the Church of their fathers. Accordingly, a day was appointed for the meeting, and as they had no church of their own, we offered them the use of ours. They had taken pains to circulate what they call "Pamphlet Articles," among those converts whom they expected would join them at their organization. One of these pamphlets was handed to me a few days before the meeting, and as I had a copy of the "Saybrook Platform" in my possession, I compared the two, and found they were unlike. As this "Platform" contained their whole "Confession of Faith," I thought it best to show it to these Presbyterian brethren, and ask why the Pamphlet Articles differed from their "Platform." They immediately disowned . the Saybrook Platform, as not containing their true Articles of Faith, and more than hinted that I had procured them to pervert the minds of the young converts. One lady said to me, "I have been a member of the Presbyterian Church for more than thirty years, and I never before heard such doctrine preached as you have in that book." Very well, said I, "when your minis-

ter comes, you will abide by his decision, I suppose ?"
"Certainly, he ought to know ; but he never will say
that is part of our creed."

The· part referred to, is that part treating upon
election and foreordination. That all may see the inconsistency of such a creed, and know why the good
woman referred to, disowned them, I will insert them
as I find them in the book I then had with me :

"CHAPTER III.   OF GOD'S ETERNAL DECREE.—God
from all eternity did, by the most wise and holy counsel
of his own will, freely and unchangeably ordain whatsoever comes to pass, yet so as thereby neither is God
the author of sin : nor is violence offered to the will of
the creature, nor is the liberty or contingency of second
causes taken away, but rather established.

"II.   Although God knows whatsoever may or can
come to pass, upon all supposed conditions, yet hath he
not decreed anything, because he foresaw it as future, or
as that which would come to pass, upon such conditions.

"III.   By the decree of God, for the manifestation of
his glory, some men and angels are predestinated unto
everlasting life, and others foreordained to everlasting
death.

"IV.   These angels and men, thus predestinated and
foreordained, are particularly and unchangeably designed ;
and their number is so certain and definite that it cannot
be either increased or diminished.

"V.   Those of mankind that are predestinated unto
life, God, before the foundation of the world was laid,
according to his eternal and immutable purpose, and the

secret counsel and good pleasure of his will, hath chosen in Christ, unto everlasting glory, out of his mere free grace and love, without any foresight of faith or good works, or perseverance in either of them, or any other thing in the creature, or conditions, or causes moving him thereunto; and all to the praise of his glorious grace.

"VI. As God hath appointed the elect unto glory, so hath he, by the eternal and most free purpose of his will, foreordained all the means thereunto. Wherefore, they who are elected, being fallen in Adam, are redeemed by Christ, are effectually called unto faith in Christ by his Spirit working in due season; are justified, adopted, sanctified and kept by his power through faith unto salvation. Neither are any other redeemed by Christ, effectually called, justified, adopted, sanctified, and saved, but the elect only.

"VII. The rest of mankind, God was pleased, according to the unsearchable counsel of his own will, whereby he extendeth or withholdeth mercy as he pleaseth, for the glory of his sovereign power over his creatures, to pass by, and to ordain them to dishonor and wrath for their sin, to the praise of his glorious justice.

"VIII. The doctrine of this high mystery of predestination is to be handled with special prudence and care, that men attending to the will of God revealed in his word, and yielding obedience thereunto, may, from the certainty of their effectual vocation, be assured of their eternal election. So shall this doctrine afford matter of praise, reverence, and admiration of God; and of humility, diligence, and abundant consolation, to all that sincerely obey the gospel."

Upon the day appointed, the people gathered themselves together.   The minister from Pompey Hill came and preached what the people called a good Methodist sermon ; not a bit of election or foreordination was in it.   After closing his discourse, he organized a Church of those who were already members of the Presbyterian Churches at Pompey and Cazenovia, and gave notice of an intermission of an hour, after which an opportunity would be given for any who wished to join the newly organized membership.   During all this time I had remained a silent, though attentive spectator, of all that transpired.   As soon as the benediction was pronounced, and before the people left their seats, I stepped into the alley and approaching the altar where Mr. S., the minister, stood, spoke in a voice loud enough for all in the house to hear : "Mr. S., I hold in my hand a book which I wish you to examine, and determine whether it contains the Articles of your Faith, as recognized by your Church."   He took it, and turning to the title-page, said, "Why, yes, I presume so ; I see the name of our printer and others here."   "One more question, sir," said I.   "Do your Pamphlet Articles contain the same doctrine as set forth in this book ?"   "Why, yes ; the same in substance, but we don't circulate this book among our people much."   "Why not ?" said I.   "Well, because our people can't understand them very well.'   I replied, "I should think your

Articles of Faith ought to be plain enough for any one to understand." Upon this, our conversation closed, for having proved them to be what I had said they were, I had cleared myself from the imputation of any underhanded means in the matter, and I now left the young converts to do as they wished. When I stepped forward, the people paused and remained silent in their places while we were talking. As soon as we had finished, there was great commotion among the people, and many opinions were expressed, so that when the afternoon services commenced, and the opportunity was given for any others to join their Church, not one of all the converts arose, they having determined they never could believe in such a doctrine, and never would join a Church that professed them.

I now told the people I wished them to examine carefully and prayerfully the creeds and doctrines of all Churches, that they might decide in an enlightened manner which seemed most christian-like in its sentiments ; that we had but one Discipline, and that contained all our Articles of Faith ; that, if after carefully perusing them, they could not conscientiously fellowship them, we had no objections to their going elsewhere. Soon after this, I gave an opportunity for those who wished, to join our Church. Nearly all of the converts took upon them the vows of a Christian as laid down in our Discipline.

During this powerful revival, there was converted an aged man by the name of Hill. He had spent his whole life without an interest in Christ, and now at the eleventh hour he called for mercy and found pardon through Jesus Christ. His wife had long been a member of our Church, and he was ever friendly to the cause, making his house the home for ministers of the gospel, and sustaining the principles of Christianity as far as a moral life, and honorable dealings with his neighbors, were concerned. He had long been skeptical in his belief of an experimental religion, but at one of the series of meetings he became convicted of his sins, and after groaning under the weight of guilt which seemed like mountains pressing him down to hell, light broke in upon his mind; the chains of death were broken asunder, and his redeemed soul was set at full liberty. He died soon after his conversion, and we have reason to believe, but for that revival he would have been lost in an eternity of misery.

It may seem somewhat strange to the reader, that I have said nothing of my colleagues helping me in this meeting. At the time it commenced, Br. Benjamin Phillips was in the eastern part of our circuit, laboring in a revival which was in progress there. It being some thirty miles distant, he did not receive the news in time to reach the place, until just before the

meeting appointed for the organization of a Presbyterian Church. * Br. Stoddard was journeying in the far
west, and did not return until sometime after. Br. S.
Seager, now Dr. Seager, with Br. Cole, students at
Cazenovia Seminary, rendered us timely assistance.

At Conference, I received my appointment to Fabius
circuit. This was a very extensive field of labor, and
I was directed to employ one or more men, as the work
seemed to require. Within the bounds of old Fabius
circuit are now stationed ten Conference ministers, to
such an extent has the work since spread.

Until this year, (1831,) I had remained a single man,
with a salary of only one hundred dollars a year, and at
no time since have I ever received, while an effective
preacher, over two hundred dollars yearly, except while
at the Oneida Mission, and all who know the manner
in which a Methodist preacher's salary is made up to
him, will remember that a fifty-cent piece is more
often stretched into a dollar bill, than contracted to
the size of quarter of a dollar.

By the permission of my presiding elder, John Demp-
ster, I invited Br. North, a local preacher, living near
the circuit, to assist in meeting the wants of the people
on our extensive circuit. He accepted my invitation,
and thus commenced his itinerant career, which he has
followed until within a few years ; when, by reason of

the infirmities of age, he retired from active duties, and now sustains a superannuated relation to the Oneida Conference.   The Lord grant he may have grace to sustain him in his declining years, and that his last days may be days of peace.

After our first quarterly meeting, our presiding elder gave us Calvin Danforth, a young man of fine talents.   He was sent, the year following, to labor at Utica, where he was attacked by the cholera, and brought to death's door.   He however recovered, but with a broken constitution, and but indifferent health. He afterward went South, where he lived several years, but was never able to preach much.   He was a young man of great promise, but God took him to himself, and he now stands with the angels around the throne in heaven.

We had several powerful revivals this year.   God was with us, and nearly two hundred souls were gathered to the fold of Christ.   At Preble, where we had a small society, with a good-sized church, we commenced a "meeting of days," and in about a week sixty professed to be converted to God.   One young man converted at this meeting, became an itinerant minister of our Church.   This was the beginning of good times for the Methodist Church in Preble.

At a northerly point of our circuit, South Onondaga,

we had a small society worshiping in a Union Church, built by the Presbyterians, Methodists, Universalists, and surrounding community, who belonged to no persuasion. The Methodists had an appointment æt 2 P. M., Sunday, once in two weeks. The Universalists had appointed theirs the same day, at 11 o'clock A. M. As I had to preach at Cardiff, at 10 1-2, attend a class meeting and ride four miles, I never arrived at my afternoon appointment until the congregation were assembled and seated. It often happened that the Universalist speaker would continue his services until time for me to commence the exercises of the afternoon, and often many of his congregation would stay during both services.

On one occasion, as I entered the house, I found him still speaking, and the house crowded full with both congregations. I took my seat among the congregation, and waited patiently for him to close; but he continued, until he had trespassed upon my time to such a degree, that I found it would be impossible for me to preach and get through in any season. As usual, his theme had been universal salvation—heaven for all, and hell but a myth. After he had closed, and left the pulpit, I ascended it, and told the congregation that, in consequence of the lateness of the hour, I should not preach that day. "But," said I, "let us pray."   I immediately kneeled down, and if the Lord ever helped me to pray, he did at that time.   I had perfect liberty to say what I pleased, and the believers in Universalism quaked and trembled as they saw the subtle fabric they had woven for themselves, melting away before the gospel light and the power of divine truth.   Such was the divine influence that pervaded the whole assembly, that it seemed as though the heavens and earth had joined themselves together, so evident was it that the Lord was with us, to help us on to the rescue.   After prayer, I dismissed the people, telling them that we would commence a protracted effort to save the lost and wandering ones.

Our plan of proceedings at a "meeting of days," was to have a love-feast in the morning, followed by a prayer-meeting for penitents—as we were always sure to have some who were concerned for their soul's welfare—preaching in the P. M. at 1 or 1 1-2 o'clock, and prayer-meeting, or preaching and prayer-meeting in the evening.   Thus, while making an especial effort for souls, we devoted our whole time to the work ; and to the fact of continually pressing the claims of the Gospel upon the hearts of sinners, together with a burning zeal among the members for the salvation of souls, and a full sense of the responsibility resting upon them, as professors of the religion they invited their friends and neighbors to receive, we owe much of that wonderful success which always crowned our protracted meetings in those days.

We commenced the meeting. I had a few valiant soldiers to help me, who knew how to wield the weapons of faith and prayer, and we commenced an attack upon one of the strongest holds of darkness then within the bounds of the circuit. In about twenty-four hours we had broken the enemy's ranks, and the Lord gave us victory over the powers of sin and death. Thus we made it literally true in that mighty conflict with earth and hell, that we took the kingdom by storm. Such was the terror thrown into the enemy's ranks, that even the leading champion of Universalism (a military man,) was arrested by the power of God as he sat in the congregation. When he felt the invisible power of Almighty God fastening upon him, he sprang from his seat, rushed towards the door, swinging his arm as though brandishing his sword, and swearing fearfully as he retreated from the field of battle.

When fairly out of the house, he made for his dwelling, not far distant, but the groans of the wounded and the shouts of the victors, as they beheld the powers of hell fall before their onset, reached his ears even as he sat by his own fireside, and as shout after shout fell upon his ear, they seemed like terrific claps of thunder in the mighty tempest that surged through his soul. He tried to shut from him those fearful sounds, but the walls of his dwelling were as paper ; and still he listened, till it seemed he heard voices from the spirit world, ringing forth his fearful doom. In sheer despair, he, with some eight or ten of his strongest men, returned to the battle field, threw down their arms and cried aloud for mercy.

In that hour, was the old castle of Universalism shaken to its foundations ; its walls crumbled and fell to the dust, as did the walls of Jericho, amid the shouts and hallelujahs of the redeemed of the Lord, and now from the mouth of him who but an hour or two before had uttered horrid imprecations and blasphemy, was heard "salvation to our God, who sitteth upon the throne, and to the Lamb for ever and ever." Then in quick succession, from the sacramental host of God's elect, rose the victorious shouts of "amen ! hallelujah!" and in less than a week that gallant little band of South Onondaga were rejoicing in the acquisition of over sixty converts, who had now enlisted in their ranks, and from that time till this, Universalism has never dared set foot upon the ground where it was so signally beaten. May the Lord ever save his people from this delusion of the devil !

One of our laborers, Br. Wilson Newman, who distinguished himself in those glorious achievements made for our Immanuel, has since taken his leave of the Church militant, and joined the Church triumphant. He died in holy triumph. Shouts of victory fell from his tongue till he found himself with the redeemed and blood-washed throng around the throne of God in heaven. Others, also, Br. Cole, and sister Seeley, have gone up from South Onondaga, to join their leader and swell the song of redemption. Peace to their memory! The leader of Universalism afterwards became a circuit steward, and an humble follower of Jesus Christ. Several young men, also, fruits of this revival, are now active and successful ministers of Oneida Conference. To God be all the glory. Amen, and amen.

During my second year upon this circuit, I was brought, for the first time, in contact with Mormonism. Two Mormon preachers had entered the town of Spafford, and were preaching what they called the "Apostolic doctrines," professing to have the gift of tongues, and of working of miracles. They claimed a special commission from God to pronounce a woe upon all christian Churches in the world, for having forsaken the commandments of the Lord, unless they returned to the doctrines of primitive Christianity, which they professed the Lord had in a very marvelous manner discovered unto them.   They also claimed to possess the last portion of divine revelation to fallen man, engraved on tables of gold, which they affirmed were found in the earth, where they had been hid from the earliest ages of Christianity, but which the Lord, a short time since, had revealed unto a certain individual, the founder of their sect, who had transcribed it, and formed it into a book, which they denominated their bible, that the world might, as they said, know what great honor the Lord God of heaven and earth had conferred upon them.   One of our leading brethren, of Spafford Hollow Society, Br. S., a man of good sense, and great respectability, and also a licensed exhorter in our Church, hearing that these men had entered the town, resolved to visit them, and hear for himself those wonderful accounts, as the Mormons were but a few miles from him.   Accordingly, without forming any opinion, either good or bad, as to their merit, he went and listened to their doctrine.

For some time previous to this, he had felt a conviction in his mind that he ought to know more of the power and love of God in his soul, and it was with much prayer, and an ardent desire to have more of religion in his heart, that he entered the place where the Mormon preachers were holding forth their doctrine. They commenced by telling the people that they were commissioned of God to preach primitive Christianity ; that he had given them the power to cast out devils, to speak in any language necessary, to heal diseases, and to raise the dead ; that these were gifts from heaven bestowed upon their Church ; that whosoever believed them to be divinely appointed of God, embraced their doctrine, believed their Bible to be inspiration, would have all these gifts conferred upon them, after being baptized by immersion. In order more fully to deceive the people, they commenced muttering over something, which they called "speaking in unknown tongues."

Br. S. sat all this time listening with great attention to everything that was said, when suddenly his mind became impressed with the belief that these men must be sent of God in order to revive primitive religion ; and as he began to cherish the impression, which he thought divine, his belief in Mormonism became stronger and stronger, until he had faith to go forward and receive baptism from one of these men. They then told him he must expect to meet with great persecutions ; that his friends, and even his family, would turn against him ; but that it must make him only the more zealous for the faith which he had now received.

That he might be well fortified in argument against

his opponents, they furnished him with one of their bibles, and he returned to his home wrapt up in his wild enthusiasm, and thanking God that he had at last shown him the good old apostolic way. When he showed to his wife and children his bible, told them he believed it divine, and that he had been baptized and joined the Mormons, they were, as it were, struck dumb with astonishment and mortification. His friends, on hearing of it, treated him with impatient contempt, which only served to make him stronger in his faith, as the ministers had told him he must suffer for truth's sake.

Soon after this event, I called upon him. He received me rather coldly. I told him I had come to put up with him during our meeting of days, which I had appointed at a neighbor's barn, near by, and which was to commence next day.

"Very well," said he, "I will put out your horse." So we walked out together. On leaving the house, he said:

"I suppose you have heard that I have joined the Mormons?"

"Yes," said I, "I have heard so," and then continued my conversation with him about other matters, in the same friendly manner that I had formerly been accustomed to. Very soon he began to appear like himself, friendly, open and free in conversation, until we again entered his dwelling, and were seated. I then, in a pleasant way, said :

"Br. S., have you the Mormon bible ?"

"Yes."

"I would like to see it, as I never, as yet, have come across one." He readily handed it to me. I took it, and commenced reading. I soon found the author had stated many things which were as absurd and false as the Mohammedan Koran. Said I, "Br. S., I find many things in your bible that I do not understand ; will you explain them to me ?" He drew near, and listened to me, as I read and exposed the sophistry of the author's reasoning. When I had finished, he exclaimed, "Well, I had not noticed that before !"

I continued reading, pointing out its errors, and showing the utter impossibility of its being a revelation from God, until his faith in it began to be shaken. I then said to him, "Do you really believe this book to be a revelation from God, and that the Mormons have come in possession of it in the way they inform us ?"

"Yes, I do."

"Then," said I, "you really have become a Mormon ?"

"Yes."

"What did the Mormon preachers tell you, when you were baptized ?"

"They told me I would receive the gift of tongues, and have the power of working miracles, as the Apostles did."

"Well, did you receive any special gift when you were baptized ?"

"No."

"What do you think was the reason ?"

"The preachers told me I had not faith enough, but if I held on the good way, I would soon receive all they had promised me."

"Well, you are going to attend our meeting of days ?"

"O, no, the Methodist brethren don't want me with them."

"Well, I want you to attend, and I am calculating to put up with you during that time ; and now, Brother, you perceive there is something about this new bible, we cannot understand ; and then, again, you have not received the gift of the Holy Ghost nor the power of working miracles, &c., as your preachers said you would, and my advice to you is, that you attend our meeting and make it a matter of special prayer to God that he will show you whether Mormonism is true or false."

He finally agreed to my proposals. On the following Sabbath morning we had a love-feast in Br. O'Farrall's barn. Br. S. attended ; took his seat in one corner, as much out of the sight of the assembled multitude as possible, and commenced praying to the Lord to show him the right way in this matter. During the love-feast, the Lord revealed himself in a very special manner ; a flood of light and glory broke in upon us, and the whole barn seemed lighted up with the glory of God. In that hour, the scales fell from the eyes of our brother, and the snare of the devil was broken.

The love-feast closed. I informed the people there would be an intermission of fifteen minutes, and then public preaching would commence. I then left the barn, but had gone only a few rods when Br. S. came up by my side and said, "Br. Torry, I am now convinced Mormonism is of the devil, and I want you to allow me to tell the people how I have been duped by him, and to warn all against this dreadful heresy which is gaining ground in our land."

I promised him the opportunity, and we soon returned to the barn, where we found a large body of people collected from every part of the town. I said to Br. S., "Now you take the stand and say what you want to." He did so. He told them how, by yielding to a sudden impression of mind, he had been led away by the evil one ; and then and there renounced his belief in Mormonism, and warned all to take the holy Bible as their guide, and to measure all isms by it, that they might know whether they were of God or the devil. The whole assembly were melted into tears ; and from the assembled multitude one universal shout of thanksgiving to God arose, that Br. S. was at last free from his delusion.

Had not this brother been reclaimed, he would, in all probability, have sold his farm, and with all his property emigrated to Nauvoo, where the Mormons were then engaged in building a city. His family, one of the finest in the country, would have been broken up, and that good brother would have lost all he was worth in this world, if not his soul forever.

Dear reader, in the relation of the facts of this case, you see how very possible it is to be led astray from the path of duty, and to embrace great errors, even while trying to do right. If we do not bring our feelings and notions of christian theology up to the Word of God, and ask of God in faith, to show us plainly the way he has cast up for us to walk in, we are liable to be duped by wicked men and the devil. May the Lord save you and me from his wild delusions, and may we who have professed faith in Christ, be kept by the power of God unto full salvation. "Then shall we know, if we follow on to know the Lord, his going forth is prepared as the morning, and he shall come unto us as the rain, as the latter and former rain ;" so shall we be ripe for heaven. When the Lord sends forth his angels with a great sounding trumpet, to gather in the harvest, may we hear from our Judge, "Well done, good and faithful servants, enter ye into the joy of your Lord !" Amen !

During my second year, we had a daughter born, who only lived six months. She faded from earth like the morning flower, for the angels loved her, and bore her away to Him who said, "Suffer little children to come unto me—for of such is the kingdom of heaven."

The next year I was stationed upon Norwich circuit, and had for my colleague Br. Stowell. During the year our circuit was divided. Br. Stowell took the north, and I the south part, which embraced Norwich village, where was no church. We started a subscription, and commmenced building the first Methodist church in that place.

In the east part of the town, the *Christ*-ians had circulated their pernicious doctrines, until many of our membership embraced those views of the doctrine of the Trinity, and of the Divinity of Jesus Christ. As Mr. Millard, the leader of that sect, had published his views and doctrines in two letters to the public, I advertised that I would preach two sermons for the purpose of meeting and refuting his arguments. I did so, and the Lord helped me in such a manner that I was enabled to successfully refute all his dogmas, and to convince the people that his doctrine was but a species of refined *deism*. So thoroughly convinced were the people of their error, that they renounced all fellowship with the doctrine, and in the public congregation confessed their wanderings, and ever since then, that doctrine has been unable to obtain scarce any foothold among those people.

CHAPTER XV.

I was next stationed upon Chenango circuit. Within the bounds of this circuit I had spent the most of
my time from four years of age, until I commenced
my itinerant life. When my father moved from Connecticut, he settled in the town of Butternuts, and
his house was the first in the town where Methodist
preaching was heard, and from this place spread the
gospel, until all the hills and valleys of that and ad-
joining towns, were vocal with the praises of a people
redeemed through the blood of the Lamb. But after
the lapse of a score of years, Methodism was scattered
from that part of the town of Butternuts where she
had achieved her greatest victories, and for a number
of years it was among the things of the past. But
the Lord returned again the captivity of his people,
and once more the heralds of the cross planted their

ever victorious standard upon the hill-tops, and again, in all its loveliness, appeared the waving banner of Methodism.

During the year I labored on Chenango circuit we preached at what was called "Gregory Hill," a place where, in an early day, Methodism had builded a church, but which for many years had been given up to the moles and bats. I could well remember the time when that house was thronged with devout worshipers, as it was only two or three miles from the place where I was raised, but now it was entirely deserted, and as there were but two or three families who were the true worshipers of God, preaching was had in a private house near by the old church.

One night, while preaching, the Lord blessed his word to the awakening of souls. The work continuing, I soon gave out for a two days meeting at the old church. Our meeting commenced on Saturday, and on Sabbath evening the Lord revealed himself to us in great mercy and power. We continued the meeting for a number of days, and sixty professed the love of God in their hearts, as the fruits of that meeting. During the meeting, a young man who was skeptical in his religious views, but who considered himself a man of some importance, attended the meetings with a troop of followers, for the purpose of making sport of the work of God. He finally told his companions he could and would go forward with other mourners, take his seat with them, kneel when they kneeled, and pretend, finally, to experience a change of heart, and shout, and sing and speak, and thus deceive both preacher and people.

On the evening fixed upon for the trial, he, with all his fellows, was on hand. When the invitation was given for those who felt the need of religion, to come forward and present themselves for the prayers of the people of God, this fool-hardy young man took his seat with the crowd of others. As he sat down he placed his elbow upon his knee, his face upon his hand, and thus waited until they all kneeled. At the request of the minister, the others kneeled to pray, but he remained in the position he had at first taken. The meeting progressed, the Lord was with us in great power, and many souls were saved that evening ; but still no one said anything to that young man who sat with his head upon his hand, apparently unmoved by the scene around him.

The meeting closed. The people had nearly all left the house, but still he retained the same position as before, neither moving nor looking up at anything that passed. Finally, as the house was about being closed, some one went and spoke to him, but not a muscle moved.   They took hold of him, and shook him, but he could neither stir nor speak.   Finally, as he afterward said, he resolved to change his course of life, confess his motive in coming there, and ask the forgiveness of the people and of his God.   Then his physical strength returned to him, and he could walk and talk as well as ever.

This proof of God's power in punishing such high-handed wickedness, so wrought upon the fears of those who came to disturb the meetings, that no more trouble was experienced from them during the meeting, or at any subsequent period of my stay upon the circuit.   The Lord did great things for us this year.

During this year our second child was attacked with the scarlet fever.   When the disease left him, he became convulsed with a fit which lasted seven hours. Though he grew up to manhood, and was a bright, active child, he was never free from fits.

I love to go back in memory to those days, and call up these triumphs and trials which occurred upon the old battle-ground of the Butternuts and Unadilla river, and to talk of the wonder-working power of God to save sinners from their guilt; and I love to speak the names of those veterans who bore with me the burden and heat of the day ; who used to gather themselves together in barns and groves, and speak often one to another, of the glorious love they felt in their souls, and strengthen each the other to go forth to labor more effectually for their master, and to contend more earnestly for the faith once delivered to the saints. There were Daniel and John Eastwood, the Brs. Chamberlain, Brs. Wood, Hyer, Corkins, and a host of others, both male and female, who fought the battles of the Lord valiantly, and achieved victories for Christ that will tell upon posterity through all coming time.

At Sidney Plains, which lies near the south end of this circuit, lived Arvine Clark, one of the best men I have ever met with. Though engaged in public business, and much of the time abroad, he always seemed devotional, a man of much prayer and great faith. "Through his influence and untiring efforts, the M. E. Chapel was erected at Sidney Plains ; for the accomplishment of that enterprise, his contribution was large and liberal." He was always looking to the wants of those who were sent by the Church to minister the word of life, and was ready to divide his last dollar with them, if necessity required. He loved the Church as he loved his own household, yet he was ever ready to extend the right hand of fellowship to his brethren of other denominations, and his influence was widely felt, for his life was a fitting commentary on his profession of love to the Savior. ' He was blessed with an amiable family, who all became members of the Church of his choice, and one of his sons has since become an able and successful minister in one of our eastern Conferences. He left the shores of mortality some three years since, and has joined the ransomed host above. May his mantle fall upon his sons, that they, with their honored father, may meet above, to share the rewards of the faithful, amid the glories of the throne.

My next field of labor was Otego circuit. I had for my colleague, Br. J. Soule, a good and zealous young man, then in his first year of itinerant life. He became a successful minister, and after twenty years' labor within the bounds of Oneida Conference, was transferred to one of the western Conferences, where he soon finished his labors and entered into his rest above. This circuit extended on the east to the Susquehanna River, the eastern boundary of our Conference. We had some especial manifestations of Divine power, to bless and save lost men from sin and ruin.

My next circuit was Canajoharie. My colleague was Isaac Grant, who has finished his work and gone to his reward in heaven. The Lord gave us souls as seals to our ministry.

The next year (1837) I was appointed to the Oneida

and Onondaga Indians. Some six years previous to this, these Indians had been visited by William Doxtater, one of their countrymen from Canada, son of the noble chief, Doxtater, who was converted at my last visit with them at Salt Springs. Soon after his conversion, he gave evidence that the Lord had destined him to carry the gospel to his countrymen, and with his soul filled with burning zeal for his Master's cause, he went from place to place, declaring the will of God towards his countrymen. He felt as did the Apostle of old, "Wo is me, if I preach not the gospel!" Under such impressions he visited his brethren at Oneida Castle, N. Y., and with his soul filled with love for his Lord and Master, he told them of his mission to them, and entreated them, as they valued their happiness in this world and the world to come, to turn from their ancient customs and follow his Lord and Savior. So eloquently did he plead, and with such a masterly hand did he portray the sufferings and death of Him who came into the world to save fallen man; and such was the power from on high that accompanied his preaching, that a gracious revival broke out among them, and a goodly number forsook their old customs and mode of worship, and became meek and humble followers of the Lamb of God.

Some of the Onondagas invited William to visit

them, which he did several times, going by stage, the mode of conveyance at that time. William dressed and appeared like other gentlemen travelling, and as he saw many well dressed, gentlemanly appearing men step into the bar-room, whenever the stage stopped at any station, and call for "something to drink," and as he was often invited to join them, he at last yielded, drank once, twice, and soon became intoxicated. He was called to an account by the authorities of our Church, and immediately silenced. He returned to Canada, where, among his friends, he was finally reclaimed from his backslidings, and died, we hope, in the Lord. William was a young man of superior talents. He was considered the best Mohawk scholar in the Six Nations, and had he been watched over and taken care of, as all young men should be, when first converted, and on entering the ministry, or had a different course been pursued towards him when he first fell, he might have been the honored instrument of the conversion of thousands of the pagan tribes who now sit in the shadow of death. I can never think of him without being deeply affected.

On entering upon my work at the Oneida Castle, I found the training of the Indians had been such that they were in the habit of mingling with the dissipated whites, who sold much spirituous liquor to them, and made them discontented and uneasy. We found much trouble in keeping them in the right way, as they were so prone to follow their own desires. They seemed entirely different from their Canadian brethren, not having as much stability and strength of purpose about them. During my stay with them, they received the principal of their annuity, and afterwards sold out, some going to Canada, some to Green Bay, and a few families remaining at their old homes. Those who have stayed have been doing well, spiritually and temporally. Two of their number are local preachers, Thomas Cornelius and Br. Johnson, both smart men and good preachers. May they, with their little band, continue steadfast in the faith, as once delivered to the saints, that they may be able to comprehend the breadth and length, the depth and height, and know the love of Christ which passeth knowledge, that they may be filled with all the fullness of God.

After staying with the Oneidas two years, my health became so much impaired that I was obliged to ask of the Conference a superannuated relation to the Church. It was granted me; and I, with my wife and three little sons, the youngest only one year old, moved to Andover, Allegany Co., N. Y., where I had a brother and two sisters living. At the time we moved to Andover there was no Methodist preaching in the place. I succeeded in establishing stated appointments and we soon had a revival of religion, in which many souls were converted to God. One of the leading men of the place, Jason Hunt, joined the Church, and has since become a local preacher of our Church. By his exertions, a new church was built, and since then Methodism has taken a strong hold of the hearts of the people in that place. Great good has resulted to the people of the surrounding country from the zeal and piety manifested by the leading members of Andover society. May the Lord continue to favor them with the redeeming and saving influences of his grace, until the whole village and surrounding country are saved in Christ.

During the time of my superannuated relation to the Church, I continued to preach, and do all I could to advance the kingdom of Christ. As soon as I thought myself able to do effective service as an itinerant minister, I returned to my Conference, and took an appointment to a field of labor. I entered upon my work with strong hopes that my health would allow me to push on the victories of the cross, and bring home trophies of redeeming grace to the fold of Christ. For the few months of warm weather I was able to work as in other years, but as soon as the cold of winter came, I found I could not labor in evening meetings, nor be out much in stormy weather, without serious injury to myself. For three successive winters I made the effort, and then was obliged again to leave the itinerant field, and seek a shelter for myself and family. The health of my companion had also become very much impaired with the labors of an itinerant life, and the care of four small children, one of them being sick much of the time. My horse and carriage, which had been moving us from circuit to circuit for sixteen years, was as nearly worn out as ourselves, and we were without any earthly home to go to, or means to get one.

As I have before observed, my salary had never been over two hundred, and often, very often, I received but part of the sum stipulated for my maintenance, which, with the continued sickness of our oldest son, who was constantly under the care of some physician, obliged us to use the utmost economy to make our means hold out, and pay all our debts, which we always have been able to do. As a superannuated minister, my yearly claim upon Conference, according to the Discipline, was a hundred dollars for myself, a hundred for my wife, and twenty-four for each child under fourteen years of age ; but all that I ever received of this sum was from eighty to one hundred dollars per year, and for several years back we can depend only on sixty or seventy per year.

This diminution in the pittance doled out to superannuated preachers, widows and orphans, must be
caused, I suppose, by the continual passing of resolutions by our venerable body of ministers, assembled in
Conference, who yearly declare their solemn intention
of raising, by a tax of less than twenty-five cents a
member, the whole amount necessary to pay off the
whole claim of their superannuated preachers, their
widows and orphans. We sincerely hope they may
yet be successful in fulfilling, even to the letter, their
resolutions. But continually resolving and never per-
forming, can only have the effect to defeat the object
at which it aims.

Our friends at South Onondaga, hearing that my
health had again failed, and that we were left without
the means to purchase a home for ourselves, kindly
wrote to us, and offered to meet us with teams at Syracuse, and convey us and baggage to their village.
Our furniture was not much, for we had moved from
Dan to Beersheba, until it was marred, and broken into many fragments, and two hundred a year did not
allow us to purchase much to replace the old. We
accepted the offer our friends had made us, and according to appointment, met them at Syracuse, and were
taken by them to the house prepared for us. We enjoyed their hospitality, and I in return, was able to

preach some, and pray with and for them, and some good, I trust, was done them during the fall and winter I staid among them, which will have a lasting effect upon some who attended our meetings.

In the spring I moved one mile from the village, into an old school-house, that I had preached in thirty-five years before. It had been fitted up as a dwelling house, and for a little garden spot with it, I paid fifteen dollars a year as rent. During our stay here, our oldest son experienced religion at our family altar, and united himself with the Church. Soon after his conversion he was brought very low with a very severe attack of fits, and from that time until his death, they increased in number and severity. We paid, this year, over fifty dollars for medicine, which we hoped might do him good, but it was without avail.

I was without horse or carriage to get around with, and therefore visited my friends at a distance, for the purpose of preaching or praying with them, only when they came for me. By the kindness of our neighbors we had been able to purchase a cow which became our main support. As winter approached, so large had been our expenses for sickness, that I found myself destitute of money to purchase any hay for our cow. Hay was high, and a cash article that year. In my extremity, I carried my case to the Lord and asked his assistance.

Just at this time I was requested to attend a meeting about twenty miles from home. I did so, and on my return, when within two miles of Syracuse I called upon Br. Horton, a member of the first M. E. Church, of Syracuse. As I drove up to his gate, he met me and took my horse to the barn.   While taking care of my horse he said to me, "I have a son who has come home sick with the consumption ; we have just had a counsel of physicians over his case, and they have decided he cannot live. He has no religion, and does not seem inclined to seek it."   We went into the house and seated ourselves around the fire, for it was now cold weather. The sick son lay in another apartment, and while visiting with Br. and sister Horton, I had no chance to see him, but he was continually on my mind. His mother, without my knowledge, had spoken to him when I rode up to the gate, telling him an old Methodist minister was coming in, and asking him if she should invite me in to see him. He told her it hurt him to talk, and he wished to see no one. After staying with Br. Horton a couple of hours, I told him I must be on my way home, "but," said I, "I should like to speak to your sick son before I go."

"Very well," said he, "while you are visiting him, I will get your horse."

I accordingly entered the sick room and found Albert

sitting in a rocking chair, his morning gown on, and with a pale, sickly looking countenance. I said to him: "Mr. Horton, you seem quite out of health."

"Yes," said he.

"Do you enjoy religion ?"

"No."

"You believe religion is necessary, I suppose, for as you have had a religious training, you cannot think otherwise."

He looked at me earnestly for a moment, and then said: "If the Bible is true, I suppose I am a great sinner, and need religion."

I replied: "There can be no·doubt of the truth of the divinity of the Holy Bible. It is a revelation of God to man, and it plainly shows us that all men, by nature, are sinners, and need regeneration by the Holy Ghost." I then endeavored to show him how man, in his fallen, sinful state, may come to Christ Jesus and be saved, at the same time urging upon him the all important necessity of an immediate application to the Great Physician of souls.

While thus talking, his father and mother entered the room and I said, " Let us pray." We knelt, and while supplicating a throne of grace, I felt in my heart that God would save their dear son Albert. On taking my leave, I took hold of his hand and said, "Now give your heart to the Lord and know the blessedness of the religion of the Bible."

The tears flowed from his eyes and I knew the Spirit of the Lord had found a lodgment in his heart. As I passed from the house to my carriage I said to Br. Horton, who accompanied me, "Br. Horton, the Lord will convert your son."   I returned home.

The second day after, while standing near my shanty, Br. H. drove up, and after shaking hands, and enquiring after each other's welfare, he said to me, "Br. Torry, I have come to take you home with me."

"For what," said I.

"Albert has been deeply concerned for his soul ever since you left my house, and is very anxious you should visit him again.   He says, he believes if you come and pray for him, he will get religion."

"I cannot go with you to-day, but to-morrow morning I will make an effort to be there."

Accordingly, he returned.   I went into the house, told my wife, and said, "You must go too, for you can help sing and pray, and we shall see that young man converted."

She consented, and accordingly the next morning we started, and reached Br. Horton's about half past twelve.   Br. H. met us at the gate, and as we passed in, I saw a man leaving the house, and going away.

Upon enquiry, I found it to be another son, who lived in the city. We took our seats by the stove to warm us, and sister Horton immediately commenced preparation for our dinner. She told us Albert was very anxious to see us ; that he had told his brother while visiting with him, "I am going to have religion to-day. Father Torry is coming to pray with me, and I shall get religion." Was not this faith like that of Cornelius of old, when Peter met him at the door of his house, "And Cornelius said unto Peter, 'We are all here present before God, to hear all things that are commanded thee of God ?'"

As soon as I became warm, I went into Albert's room. As I approached him, he grasped my hand, exclaiming, "I am glad you have come ! I am glad you have come ! I hope you have come full of religion ! full of religion !" I took my seat and commenced singing,

"Come, ye sinners, poor and needy."

Just at this moment, the door opened, and sister Horton said, "Your dinner is ready;" but I was too much engaged to think of eating dinner, and continued singing. My wife and sister Horton immediately entered the room, and as Br. H. had also now come in, I proposed prayer. We knelt. Albert fell upon his knees, and I commenced presenting the case of this humble suppliant before the throne of God. All were praying, and in less than five minutes, salvation from heaven came. Albert was converted. He sank to the floor ; we raised him up, placed him in his chair, when he exclaimed, "O, how happy I am ! Is this religion?" We assured him that he had found the pearl of great price. Then was there joy in that house. If there was not dancing, as when the prodigal son returned to his father's house, there certainly was music, for we all could but rejoice and praise God that another soul was saved from sin and death. In half an hour, Albert rejoiced and praised God, as the rock of his salvation ; then, all at once, he paused, looked at me as I sat near him, and uttering a deep sigh, said, "Do you think this is religion ? I feel distressed here," laying his hand upon his heart. "Ah," said I, "the old adversary has come ; the devil always makes an attack upon young converts."

Albert had indulged in skeptical notions regarding the emotional part of religion, as, in fact, many others, even those who call themselves Christians do, and now the devil had said to this redeemed soul, "You are laboring under excitement ; you are not converted to God." And as he paused to listen, the temptation took fast hold of him, till it seemed like an arrow piercing his heart. We again used our weapons of faith and prayer, and Satan was soon driven back and this redeemed soul was again filled unutterably full of the love of God ; and through the entire night he was unspeakably happy.

The next morning as we took our leave of him, he slipped a five dollar note into my hand, and at the next visit I made him shortly after, five more, thus making just the sum I had asked of the Lord a few days previous.

My last visit with Albert was a few days before his death.   As I was leaving him, I took his hand and said, "Br. Horton, we shall see each other's faces no more until we strike hands above, for I see you are ripening fast for that world of bliss,

> " 'Where God the Son forever reigns,
> And scatters night away.' "

He quickly replied, "Do you ?"   "Yes," I said. Then with an ecstasy of feeling he shouted, "Glory to God !   I have nothing in my heart but love ; love for everybody !"   "Thank God," said I, "that is perfect love."   Then came the farewell ; and in a few days his happy soul found its home beyond the storms of earth, in that sunny clime not measured by the flight of years.

His funeral took place at the first Methodist Church in Syracuse.   A numerous assembly attended, to pay their last respects to the deceased. He was universally respected as a good citizen, and an accomplished gentleman. As a scholar and a business man he was rarely surpassed. His conversion to God, and triumphant death, proved a blessing to his brothers and sister, and others who visited him during his last days. He exhorted all who visited him to seek the blessed religion of Jesus Christ, telling them it was the only thing that could make them happy here, and give them a glorious prospect of immortality hereafter.

During this winter, our neighbors made us a donation of thirty dollars, and we were thus able to get along quite comfortably. While visiting an old friend, Stephen Houghtaling, in the town of Lafayette, he said he would give ten dollars towards buying a small place then for sale some three miles from him. We mentioned the proposal to the Rev. Aaron Cross, who had several times called upon us, and who was very friendly towards us. He immediately wrote to Br. Hosmer, editor of the Northern Christian Advocate, who kindly consented to insert a notice in his paper, calling upon my friends to help me in this undertaking. They nobly responded to the call, and donations from fifty cents to ten dollars came in, until some four hundred dollars were pledged. A good brother in Pompey, Oliver Watkins, assisted me in collecting the money, and we purchased the place, and took possession in the spring of 1857.

I have retained on paper, and in my memory, the names of those who generously assisted us at that time, and I hope never to cease praying for them and theirs while life shall last. Br. Aaron Cross and Br. Watkins, who not only donated of their own substance, but also spent many days in collecting what my friends had subscribed, will have their reward, I trust, not only in this life, but also in that which is to come. My earnest prayers shall ever rise for their continued prosperity.

As soon as we had taken possession of our new home, I invited my neighbors and friends to my house on Sunday afternoons and evenings, for the purpose of holding meetings. There was no meeting of any sort within from three to five miles of our neighborhood, and many had grown up, who seldom ever heard the sound of the gospel. The congregations soon became so large that I was obliged to fit up my barn for their meetings, which increased in interest continually. Many of my brethren on surrounding charges, hearing that meetings were held weekly here, left their own societies, and came to help us.

Some one thought it best to report to the preachers on a circuit some three miles east of us, that I was holding opposition meetings for the purpose of disturbing them. They, without speaking to me, informed the Presiding Elder of the, as they supposed, correct statement of facts, and he came to me with the matter. I gave him the particulars, but finding that the course some were taking in order to break up our meetings, would cause much hard feeling in high places, I gave up the endeavor, and the people again relapsed into their former state. Though years have elapsed since that period, there has never been any real revival of religion among that people, and they still sit in darkness. While I stayed among them, I tried to do my duty as a minister, as far as the Church would allow me to. I finally sold out, and moved to Tully. While living here, I received news of my brother Daniel's death. He entered the itinerant field about twelve years later than myself, as his obituary will show, which I copy entire, as written for the Advocate.*

"Rev. Daniel Torry, of the Wyoming Annual Conference, died at Brooklyn, Susquehannah Co., Pa., Sept. 30th, 1857, in the 57th year of his age.

"Br. Torry was born in Stafford Co., Conn., in 1800. He removed with his parents to Western New York, and at the age of twenty was converted to God, under the labors of Israel Chamberlayne at a revival in Plymouth, Chenango Co. He soon united with the M. E. Church, and very early in his christian experience began to feel that God had called him to the work of the ministry. Being naturally diffident, he strove to banish the impression, but his convictions of duty deepened, until he felt, "Wo is me, if I preach not the gospel." In order

The next year, (1858) news reached us of the death of our aged and much honored father, Nathan Clark, my wife's father, who died Sept. 9th, 1858, in the 96th year of his age. Father Clark was born in 1763, and served for awhile as a soldier in the Revolutionary war. In 1810 he moved from Vermont, his native State, to Madison Co., N. Y., where he lived until his decease. In early life, he and his wife both belonged to the Baptist Church, but on moving into this country, they were deprived of their former privi-

---

to get rid of his impression, as he informed the writer, he removed to Norwich, in the same county, taking his certificate of membership. He held it in his own hands, and, being among strangers, he did not openly profess religion for a time, till a little circumstance occurred, which rendered it impossible for him longer to conceal his real character.

"A young lady, who had formerly been a classmate of his at Plymouth, being on a visit among her friends at Norwich, met young Torry at the house of Reuben Reynolds, of precious memory, and, as was quite natural, the good sister began to talk over the precious seasons of the past, which soon brought Br. Torry from his hiding place, and before parting that evening, Br. Reynolds proposed having a family prayer-meeting, and called upon young Torry to lead in prayer. He dare not refuse, and as he bowed with one of his classmates, it called up many of the touching reminiscences of the past, and awakened all the devotional feelings of the soul, and such was the fervency and faith of the suppliant, that an overwhelming Divine influence came down upon their heads and hearts, until many were attracted to the place by their shouts of victory. This family prayer-meeting not only brought young Torry from his religious seclusion, but greatly encouraged the pious few at Norwich, and led to efforts to secure regular preaching at that place, by the Methodist preachers.

"Soon after this, a small class was formed, and Br. Torry was appointed leader and steward. His first license to exhort is dated July 8th, 1825, and signed by Isaac Grant, in behalf of the Society at Norwich. He was licensed to preach, some time during that year, leges, and commenced meetings at their own house, where a revival soon broke out, and in the spring of 1811 a Methodist society was formed by James Kelsey, of those who had experienced religion during the winter, and also a few who were professors on coming into the country, among which were Solomon Root, Sen.,

---

which license has been lost or mislaid. The first license to preach that we find among his papers, is dated April 29th, 1826, and signed, by George Peck, Presiding Elder. This year (1826) he entered the regular work, on old Wyoming circuit, with Geo. Peck and Philo Barberry as colleagues. The balance of his labors was on the following charges: In 1827-28, on Bridgewater; 1829, on Binghamton; 1830-31, on Broome; 1832, on Spencer. This year he was married to Betsey Smith, daughter of Isaac Smith, Esq., of Brooklyn, Pa., who still survives him. In 1833-34, he travelled on Lanesborough; 1835, on Brooklyn; 1836, on Vestal; 1837, Skinner's Eddy. In 1838 we find him on the superannuated list for one year. In 1839-40 he travelled on Pike circuit; 1841, on Orwell. Here, again, his health failed, and from 1842 to 1847 he was on the superannuated list. In 1847-8 he travelled on what was then Montrose and Great Bend, where he ended his itinerant career, since which time he has resided at this place, only preaching occasionally, as his feeble health would admit.

"He possessed a naturally strong constitution, but his excessive labors and exposures early induced a complication of diseases that baffled all human skill, and hurried him from labor to repose. When I came to this charge last May, I found him rapidly sinking into the arms of death; yet his stay was protracted much beyond my expectation. He was a great sufferer, yet he bore his afflictions with christian fortitude, and met death with the heroism of a christian philosopher. As a preacher, he was above mediocrity, and had he been favored with early mental culture, might have shone among the stars of the first magnitude. He was an acute observer of men and things, a thorough scholar in human nature, a firm disciplinarian, a safe counsellor, a fast friend, and a faithful minister of the Lord Jesus. His end was peace. His hope was big with immortality. The last words I heard him utter were, 'I am only waiting!' and after a long pause, he added, 'Almost over, almost over!'

"A. H. SCHOONMAKER."

and his wife and mother, Justus Root and his wife, and also father Clark and his wife.

This was the first M. E. Society in the town of Madison. But few of those old soldiers now remain, after the lapse of half a century, to tell of the trials and triumphs, the losses and crosses which followed that little band of settlers who, away in the wilderness of a new country, gathered themselves together to strengthen each other in the way they had chosen, and to call upon God as the Captain of their salvation.

Mother Clark, a woman of strong faith and earnest piety, mighty in prayer and abounding in good works, departed this life many years ago, leaving her husband to wait " yet a little longer," even until his head was frosted with the snows of many winters, and the corn should be fully ripe for harvest. Though Father Clark lived to an advanced age, he retained his mental faculties unimpaired to the last. When asked, some time previous to his death, how his mind was in regard to a future state, "Strong in God," said the aged saint, and then he repeated,

> "On Jordan's stormy banks I stand,
> And cast a wishful eye."

"This is my situation," said he, "and I am only waiting the call of my Master, when I shall join forever in the song of the redeemed." As might be expected from such a life, his end was peace. "Mark the perfect man, and behold the upright, for the end of that man is peace."

CHAPTER XVI.

Having in view the writing of this work, and knowing that I needed some information in regard to the Canadas which I did not possess, I concluded to make a journey thither, visit once more the old scenes and battle-grounds of my youth, collect what information and material I needed for my work, and once more look into the faces of those old friends who once with me were young, and who stood shoulder to shoulder, as we drove on the battles of the cross. Accordingly, upon the fifth day of July, I started with my horse and carriage, from my residence in Homer, Cortland Co., N. Y.

A few weeks previous to this, I had visited my old field of labor, lying in that part of the country then embraced in the old Cayuga circuit. I found many old friends scattered all through the country, many of whom were members of the Church when I preached to them forty-four years ago, and many more who claimed me as their spiritual father. It was refreshing to me, and I spent many precious hours with them in calling up old times, and in bowing once more around their family altars, where for many years they had offered daily sacrifice.

My first visit was at Br. Brown's, who lives near where he did when I first knew him, forty-four years ago. He was then a member of our Church, and with his wife, is still making on for that heavenly country, to which they have so long been journeying. It is refreshing to meet with these old pilgrims who are already in sight of their future home, and who, as they stand upon the bank of the river, can feel the sweet breezes as they blow from those celestial fields just upon the other side of Jordan. At the Mack settlement I found some old friends, the brothers Lambert, with whom I used to worship thirty-two years ago. I had a good time in praying with them and their families. One of them has since fallen asleep in Jesus, to awake again in the first resurrection, over which the second death hath no power. May his two sisters, who administered to his every comfort in his last sickness, receive, like Martha and Mary of old, the blessing and sympathy of the blessed Jesus.

As a camp-meeting was to commence at Millport, I concluded to attend it. This was within the bounds of old Ulysses circuit, and I expected there to meet many friends whom I otherwise would not see. When within fourteen miles of the camp-ground, I stopped for the night at Br. Barker's. For more than thirty years, this good brother and his wife had braved the storms and trials of a christian life, and were still contending for the faith, with all that zeal and perseverance becoming valiant soldiers of the cross.

During the night a swelling began upon my face, just above one of my eyes, and by morning, it had increased much and become so painful that I was forced to give up all thoughts of attending camp-meeting, and immediately set my face for home.

Near evening, I stopped at Mack settlement, where a good sister kindly made a poultice for my face, which much relieved it, and as it became much better the next day, I finally concluded to return to the Millport camp-meeting. I reached the ground on Monday, and tented with Br. Mallett, a local preacher of the M. E. Church, whose wife claimed me to be the instrument, under God, of her conversion. In their morning love-feast, before closing the meeting, my friends made me a present of the sum of twelve dollars, for which may the Lord reward them.

I have made this little digression, in order to show the manner in which Providence opened my way, and supplied me with means for my journey. The route which I had chosen for my journey, led me to the head of Seneca Lake. Here the village of Watkins is situated, and here I found a son of Br. Dodson, an old superannuated preacher of the East Genesee Conference. With Br. Dodson and his now sainted wife, I had spent many precious hours around their family altar, and in the house of God, while travelling Ulysses circuit, and now, as I visited him again, we enjoyed another blessed season of prayer, which seemed like former days. He, like myself, is sinking under the weight of years, and the excessive labor of former times. He has a son and daughter living here, who both belong to the M. E. Church of this place.

The next day I called upon a Mr. Matthews, son of the widow Matthews, at whose house I used to preach thirty-two years ago, and where the Lord often blessed us. Sister Matthews is still walking in the straight and narrow way that leads to life eternal. I found this son of hers, with his wife, very friendly, kind and hospitable ; his wife a member of the M. E. Church, and deeply pious.

My next stopping place was at the Rev. Loring Grant's. Found himself and wife in tolerable health, surrounded with the good things of this life, and with blooming hopes of entering their rest above, when done with the things of this earth.   I spent a Sabbath with them, and talked over our toils, and sufferings, and triumphs of other days.   Monday morning I left their hospitable mansion, and pursued my way to Canada.   At Canandaigua I stopped for the night with Br. McKinstry, pastor of the M. E. Church of that village.   He with his lady treated me very kindly, and in the morning he showed me through their splendid church.

I continued on my journey until I reached Lewiston, on the Niagara, opposite Queenstown, in Canada. Forty-two years ago, I crossed this ferry in an old scow boat ; now I drove over upon the suspension bridge, which has been erected at this place within a few years past.   I passed on through the village of Queenstown, one mile north, and stopped with a brother who lives in the house where General Brock expired, after being shot from his horse at the battle of Queenstown height, in the year 1812.

Next day I passed on to St. Catherine's, a large commercial town upon the Wellington Canal.   In its harbor lay a number of splendid vessels bound to different ports upon the lakes, and other parts of the British Empire.   Thirty-two years had passed since I stood upon Canadian soil, and in that time how changed had everything become.

I continued my journeying until I reached Fifty Mile Creek. On Sabbath morning I entered one of the Wesleyan churches and took my seat among the congregation who were all strangers to me. I looked around upon the assembly, thinking, perhaps some familiar face might greet my view, but no man or woman had I ever seen before. Years before, I had travelled and labored and preached through this country, and many people lived around here who were well acquainted with me, and whom I loved to see. But they were gone, and a new generation had taken their places. The old church in which the Methodist Conference held its session thirty-five years before, when I was one of its members, was now filled by a new race of people. The preacher in the pulpit was a fine looking young Englishman, who commenced the services by reading a portion of the Holy Bible, after which, he gave out one of Wesley's hymns. After reading the hymn, the congregation rose, and all together, commenced singing the first two lines as the minister had read them. They then paused; he read the other two lines of the first verse and they sung again. In this manner they proceeded through the hymn. When the minister kneeled for prayer, the whole congregation, without exception, kneeled with him. Accustomed as I was to the mode of worship in the States, where even members do not kneel, I asked myself if all these persons were professors of religion, not at the time thinking that this was the mode in which they were formerly instructed, and that they had not departed from it.

After the sermon, came the class-meeting. Here my eye fell upon a man, who, by his resemblance, I called a son of old father Lewis, one of the old standbys in days past and gone.

After class-meeting was over, I introduced myself to the minister, and enquired who that person might be. He told me I was right in my conjecture, and immediately introduced him to me. I enquired after his father, and others of the old settlers. He told me they were all slumbering in the tomb; that he lived upon the old homestead, and invited me, with the preacher in charge, to dine with him.

The same Sabbath I attended service in one of the most splendid Wesleyan churches in Hamilton, where, as I was informed, was stationed the most talented minister in all the Canadas. As I entered the porch, the sexton, perceiving me to be a stranger, offered me a seat just in front of the pulpit. The house was large and spacious, well fitted up, with a large organ just back of the pulpit, and a vestry opening near the pulpit stairs. The house was soon completely filled with seemingly devout worshipers, for not a whisper did I hear, or a smile did I see, upon the face of any one. The minister, a large, portly looking man, read a portion of Scripture in a deep, full and sonorous tone of voice, then his hymn, which he lined, as did the minister I had listened to in the morning, and all the congregation joined with the organ in making melody in the house of God.

During the prayer, all kneeled except a few Presbyterians or Baptists, who stood upon their feet, as is the custom in their own churches. The minister gave us a good sermon, though not as great as I had expected, from the reputation he seemed to have among the people.

Hamilton is a city of more than 21,000 inhabitants, with many churches, flourishing schools, and enterprising and industrious business men, who, by their trade and influence, are continually advancing its interests, and beautifying its surroundings. When I left the Canadas, thirty-two years ago, the greater part of the ground where this city now stands was covered with heavy oak timber, with only a few houses to be seen, and those scattered here and there, according to the fancy of the settlers.

From Hamilton I journeyed on until I reached Brantfordville, a large village on the Grand River.

This village is beautifully situated, containing many large and spacious buildings, both public and private, and is rapidly increasing in wealth and population. Forty-two years ago, this village consisted only of a few shanties, and a tavern or "liquor-hole," on each side of the river. It was a great resort for drunken whites and Indians, and so notorious had the place become when I came into the country, that the two taverns bore the names of "Sodom and Gomorrah."

At that time there was a certain white man who was in the habit of drinking to excess occasionally. These drunken frolics were periodical, and at such times it was almost impossible for him to pass either Sodom or Gomorrah without getting pretty well "corned." Some of his friends speaking to him on the subject, he said he could form a resolution to pass both places and not touch a drop of liquor, and he could keep it. Accordingly he started out, and true to his word he passed both Sodom and Gomorrah without stopping to touch anything. But after he was quite past them, he became so elated with his success in resisting temptation, that he determined to go back and "treat resolution!" which he did, and soon was as much intoxicated as ever. It was only about one mile and a half from this that we built our first mission house for the Indians. Now the village contains several splendid churches, all of which are well filled every Sabbath.

One mile from Brantfordville is the elegant and spacious mansion of the late Rev. Peter Jones, built by him after he superannuated. Here he lived until his Lord called him to join the ransomed host above, and occupy the mansion prepared for him at the right hand of the Father. I found her who had been his companion in labor and suffering, living here with four fine sons, the eldest nineteen, and the youngest eight years of age. She is now the wife of our much esteemed brother, John Carey,* who was one of the first to help on the work of christianizing the Indians.

When I first called upon Br. Carey and his wife, they were both absent from home ; I therefore drove on, and on my return, a day or two after, as I drove up to the gate, I espied Br. John walking through the beautiful grounds that surround their mansion. As soon as he saw me, he started across the garden upon a run, and without waiting to pass around to the gate which opened upon the road, he placed his hands upon the high picket fence which surrounds the grounds, and with one bound was at my side. Grasping me in his arms he exclaimed, "Why, Alvin Torry !"

---

*This will not appear strange, neither will the elegant paper which follows, when it is remembered that Mr. Jones, on his visit to England in 1830, married an English lady.—ED.

I found this old friend in excellent health and spirits, with a fine property which he had amassed at Muncey town, living in ease and elegance, and spending the evening of his days in peace and prosperity. The time I spent here was busily employed in narrating to each other the eventful portions of our lives since our separation, in calling up old times and the many changes that have taken place within the past forty years. Sister Carey kindly gave me access to the papers of her late husband, Rev. Peter Jones, and I listened with great interest to the account of his last hours and death, for he seemed very near and dear to me, and everything pertaining to him was of interest to me. The beautiful and touching account of the closing scenes of his life and his character, from the gifted pen of sister Carey, I subjoin here, as being more appropriate than anything I might say :

"TUESDAY, MAY 20th, 1856.—My dear husband, accompanied by myself and Dr. Griffin, left home for Toronto, not without much previous prayer and consultation whether it was advisable to venture such a journey, with one whose strength was so greatly prostrated. We reached the hospitable dwelling of our old and tried friend, Br. Ryerson, about 5 P. M., where we had been invited, and as usual received a kind welcome, with subdued feelings of mingled pain and pleasure.

"WEDNESDAY, 21st.—Dr. Bovell came early with Dr. G. and after careful examination, confirmed all Drs. M. and

G., of St. Catharines, had said; but also discovered a disease of long standing, in the region of the heart. The Dr. informed me after we left the room, that disease had made great progress, and that his continuance here any length of time, was very uncertain; he said my dear husband was falling a sacrifice to his former exertions for others.

"FRIDAY, 23d.—My dear husband is evidently worse and not able to rise at all to-day. The Revs. E. Wood and Gemley, and sister Taylor called, prayed most fervently, and conversed most sweetly about the things of God, and his wise and loving dealings with his own children. He responded to all, saying: 'All is well, I feel resigned to the will of my heavenly Father who will do all that is right and best.'

"THURSDAY, 29th.—The Rev. James Richardson kindly called.

"MONDAY, JUNE 1st.—Little better; sickness somewhat abated. Dr. Hannah, Revs. Jobson and Gemley came to dinner, after which, at my dear husband's request, Dr. Hannah administered the Lord's Supper. It was a very solemn time, when feelings, such as words cannot express, filled our hearts. We knew that he would never again drink of the fruit of the vine, till he drank it in his Father's house above.

"WEDNESDAY, 3d.—This morning, Dr. Bovell brought Dr. Hodder with him. Sister Taylor came and sweetly prayed and talked with him. He told her he found it difficult to collect his thoughts, or keep his mind for any length of time upon one subject. 'Oh, yes, Br. Jones,' she replied, 'but a look of faith, a desire is enough; Jesus knows all your wants, and will supply them, without words to tell him. When you wish water, or anything else, without speaking, sister Jones knows by your look or sign, what is needed, and is ready to supply your wants; how much more the Savior, who is touched with pity, and sympathizes in all your sufferings!'

"TUESDAY, 10th.—Very, very low, apparently worse than any day before. My soul so cast down, groans and tears were my only relief.

"WEDNESDAY, 11th.—What alternations of hope and fear; this morning favorable symptoms appeared.

"THURSDAY, 12th.—Dr. Ryerson returned from Conference. He prayed with him, and told him the Conference news, to which he listened with deep interest, making special enquiries about the Indian Missions, and appointments to them.

"SATURDAY, 15th.—He was quite cheered with the thought of seeing his dear children, and happy home again.

"MONDAY, 17th.—Dr. Ryerson kindly aided me in preparations for our homeward journey. The Dr. then went to the railroad office and made arrangements for his comfort as far as possible, to Paris.

"TUESDAY, 12th.—In the evening Dr. Ryerson prayed for the last time by the dying bed of his dear friend and brother. Seeing me much affected, he took my hand, and with a heavenly smile on his countenance, said, 'We have lived most happily together for many years, and it is hard to part; do not weep, dear; Christ will take care of you and the dear children; he will give you grace, supporting, strengthening grace; in a little time we shall meet again, and spend eternity together with Jesus.'

"WEDNESDAY, 18th.—In extreme weakness he awoke

this morning. After a day of travel, and of great fatigue and excitement, he felt almost overwhelmed with gratitude, as he laid down again on his own couch alive, and he said several times, 'Bless the Lord! bless the Lord! What shall we render unto the Lord for all his benefits towards us?'

"THURSDAY, 19th.—My dear husband very low this morning. Many called to see him. To his friend, Rev. H. Biggar, he said, 'I am resting on the atonement.'

"SATURDAY, 21st.—My husband passed a very restless night. The Rev. J. Ryerson and wife came, and during prayer he felt very happy. He presented sister Lincoln, who, with her excellent husband, came to see him, with a book, as a dying gift, saying, 'The religion of Jesus is enough for a dying hour.'

"SUNDAY, 22d.—Through mercy my dear husband passed a quiet night, but in the morning threw up a quantity of clotted blood. Our kind friend, Mrs. Nelles, spent the day with us. He gave our servant a book this day, telling her to serve God faithfully to the end of her life. Being too ill to hear much reading or talking, a little from the best Book, and some from 'Thoughts in Affliction,' was all he could endure. It was excessively hot, and he slept much.

"MONDAY, 23d.—Spent a very restless night. A great many friends called to see him, who will remember how kindly and thankfully he enquired after the welfare of their families, and often said, 'Has so and so been to see me? tell them I wish to shake hands with them before I go home.' He gave books to several as dying gifts, and when able, signed his name, dictating a few words to be written. A number of Indians from the New Credit came to-day.　It was affecting to witness their deep sorrow as they gazed on the emaciated form of their long-tried, faithful friend.　He said to Br. Carey, 'Tell the Indians at Muncey, if I had my life to live over again, I would wish to live as I have in the service of God.'

"TUESDAY, 24th.—The dear afflicted Indians met several times during the day for singing and prayer.　He exhorted them all to meet him in a better world.　They 'all wept sore, fell on his neck and kissed him, sorrowing most of all for the words which he spake, that they should see his face no more.'

"WEDNESDAY, 25th.—The Rev. C. Byrne and wife came ; neither saw any hope of his recovery.　Br. Byrne prayed most fervently.　As our dear Charles had not arrived after two telegraphic messages, Mr. Strobridge kindly sent his son to Simcoe to fetch him.　Our good friend, Mr. Nelles, was in daily attendance, and administered much consolation.

"THURSDAY, 26th.—Many called to take a farewell to-day.　To one taking both hands in his, he said, 'I am going home, going to my Father's house above ; all is well.'　After taking a little ice jelly, it was too evident that the silken cords which had bound him to earth, were soon to be loosened ; and as his family were now all together, they were summoned around his dying bed, that they might, for the last time, receive his blessing, and listen to the faint, yet touching relation to prepare to meet their God.　His beaming look, his expressive smile as he commended each separately, with patriarchal dignity, to the care of his covenant-keeping God, can never be forgotten.　Placing his hand on the head of dear Charles, giving him one of his Bibles and his dressing case, he said, "Be a good, obedient, loving son to your mother, and as much as possible fill my place." He then exhorted him to give his heart to God. He then put his hand on dear Frederick's head, giving him another of his Bibles, telling him he hoped that blessed book would be his guide to heaven; that he would read it, and meet him in a better world; he also gave him his gun, saying, 'God bless you, son; be a good son to your mother, and loving to your brothers.' Then to Peter Edmund he said, also placing his hand on his head, 'God bless the lad; take this watch which I have used so many years, and keep it for your dying father's sake; give your heart to God, and we shall meet again. Take this Testament, read it, and may it guide you through life to glory.' Then, to dear George Dunlot, who sobbed aloud, and clung to him, he said, 'Be a good boy, love God, obey your mother, love your brothers; here is my hymn-book; I have used it a long time; keep it, and use it for my sake; here are two volumes for you to keep in remembrance of me.' He then put his hand on his head, and said, 'God bless you, my sweet child.' He then took my hand, and kissing me said, 'I commend these dear boys to the care of their Heavenly Father and you. Train them up for heaven. God bless you, dear. I pray we may be an unbroken family above.' Shortly after this, turning to his kind and constant friend, Rev. A. Nelles, he put in his hands three volumes of Chalmer's Works, saying, 'I give you these as a parting memorial of your dying friend. I thank you for all your kindness; I hope we shall meet above.' After this, he slept for a long time. The Rev. Mr. Alexander came in the evening; he responded during his prayer, saying, 'Amen,

amen.' When Mr. Burwell asked him how he felt, he replied, 'Sinking, sinking;' I said, 'Yes, dear, into the arms of Jesus.' He replied, 'O, yes.' He gave his sister, Mrs. Brant, three books, saying, 'I give you these as tokens of remembrance of the brother who was convert-ed at the same time you were. May God bless you and your family, and may we all meet again in a better world!' From this time his eye-sight failed, so that he could scarce-ly see at all, but he heard distinctly, and always seemed conscious. If I was out of the room for a few moments, friends would come and say, Mr. Jones is asking for you. Dear creature, he seemed to want me by his side all the time.

"Friday, 27th.—My dear husband slept most of the night. In the morning he asked to see Abraham, our hired man, and taking his hand, said, 'I shall soon be gone, and want you to be faithful in taking care of every-thing, just as if I were here; try and love and serve God; there is nothing like a preparation for death; God bless you and your partner; look well after the interests of my family. God bless Abraham.' Rev. W. Sutton and many other friends called. To all he addressed a few parting words. To the doctor, who had attended him faithfully and skillfully, he said, taking his hand, 'I thank you for all your kind attention; you have done all you could, but it is the will of God to take me home. I hope you will give God all your heart, and meet me in a bet-ter world.' Hearing him say, 'Blessed Redeemer,' I said, 'you can say, "I know that my Redeemer liveth."' He said, "I can say that all the time." This afternoon the Rev. J. B. Howard and his wife came. They only returned home to-day from a long visit, or would have been often by his side. They sang sweetly (which he seemed fully to enjoy) the beautiful hymn:

    " 'We speak of the realms of the blest.'

"SUNDAY, 28th.—My precious one was too low to speak or see, but he showed consciousness by just saying, 'Yes,' when spoken to, and evidently knew his friends by their voices. It was on the morning of this day, that he took hold of my hand with a most affectionate and indescribable look, and said, 'I have something, dear, I wish to say to you, and I may as well mention it now: You must try not to be alarmed, or too much grieved, when you see me die; perhaps I may have to struggle with the last enemy.' Dear creature! what an example of kind consideration, even in death. I said to him, 'How can I do without you, love?' He replied, 'Jesus will take care of you." As this never-to-be-forgotten night drew on, the actual approach of death was too evident. The friends who watched with me till midnight, were Mrs. Brett, Mrs. Johns, daughter of old Capt. Brant, Mr. and Mrs. Beamer, Mr. C. Welles and Mr. G. Johnson, Mohawk. About 10 P. M., he said, and these were his last words, 'God bless you, dear.' After this, I said, 'If you have given the last token of love, and spoken the last word, do, dear, show you are conscious, by pressing my hand, and assuring me that you die in the full prospect of a blessed immortality.' He did so, feebly, but with all the remaining strength he had, twice. From this time he laid perfectly quiet; whether conscious or not, we could not discover. About half past one there was a decided change; I saw the long dreaded event was near. I desired the dear boys and his mother and sister might be called. We were all soon around his dy-

ing bed. Every breath was watched, as nearer and yet
nearer the last enemy approached, and an union was to
be dissolved from which had been derived so much happiness. It seemed to me that the flesh and the spirit had
a long and a hard struggle. Oh, the agony of that hour!
Oh, such a scene! bleeding hearts that have witnessed
can understand, but no words can describe. Fainter and
yet fainter still, the last quiver of the lip told all was
over; the warfare was accomplished, and the spirit had
taken its everlasting flight. As I tried to trace its progress, methought I heard shouts of victory resound
through the vaults of the New Jerusalem, as the redeemed Indian bands hailed with a fresh song of triumph
the benefactor of their race, the friend of suffering hu-
manity, and the adorable Savior who had prepared for
him a seat in glory, purchased with his own precious
blood, bid him welcome, with the plaudit, 'Well done,
good and faithful servant, enter thou into the joy of thy
Lord.'

CHARACTER.

"As a husband, he literally obeyed the command of
the great apostle, contained in the fifth chapter of Ephe-
sians, from the twenty-fifth verse. In him I found combined everything that was amiable, tender, confiding,
faithful and judicious. I think it is Newton says, 'A
friend is worth all hazards we can run.' I knew this
when I united my destiny with his, notwithstanding the
fearful forebodings, and the cruel things that were written and said. I knew that he was a man of God, a man
of faith and prayer, a friend in whom I could trust, and
I looked with pity on those who, from ignorance and
prejudice, viewed the alliance with contempt, deeming

them not worthy to tread in the shadow of my honored husband.   Never, from the day of the happy espousals, had I cause to lament that our destinies were united Would that all who marry white men possessed in them the same lovely christian graces that rendered my home with my noble Indian such an abode of peace and love. But he is gone ! gone to his reward ; and he who 'turned many to righteousness, now shines as the stars forever and ever.'   Daily I need the present promise, 'My grace is sufficient for thee ; my strength is made perfect in weakness.'

"As a father, he ruled by love; perhaps too much like Eli, a little firmer rein might have been occasionally for the advantage of his sons; but in him his boys found a friend ever ready to give them advice, a father who joined in their amusements, instructing and helping them in every way that would promote their happiness or improvement.   His children both loved and feared him, for lenient as he was, I never knew him pass over sin without severely punishing the guilty one.   With filial confidence his boys trusted to his judgment, and reposed in his tender love.   For hours have I seen them listen with delighted attention to the fund of anecdotes he had treasured up in his memory, particularly Indian stories. The loss of such a father is irreparable.   May his mantle fall on each of them, and may 'God bless the lads !'

"As a master, he was mild and persuasive.   Often have I marvelled at the patient forbearance he has displayed when greatly provoked to anger ; but religion had wrought that change in his heart which enabled him to 'endure all things.'   He was 'slow to anger ;' he knew how to 'rule his spirit,' and many times has his 'soft answer turned away wrath.'   Those who served him faithfully, always found in him a friend and kind adviser ; but when he met with imposition or ingratitude, he faithfully warned, and if that failed to produce the desired effect, they parted.

"As the priest of his family, he always made it a rule to be short in reading and prayer, so as never to weary the children or servants.   His prayers were very simple and devotional, offered up in strong faith.   He often mentioned individuals by name, as their circumstances required particular notice.   The poor and the needy, the sick and the dying, the widow and the fatherless, were seldom omitted in his supplications at the throne of the heavenly grace ; and I have often thought, since his departure from our midst, how much of our present comfort we owe, through Jesus Christ, to his intercessions at the mercy seat.   I believe no sincere prayer is ever unanswered, although it may not be in accordance with our short-sighted desires, consequently how many needful blessings may his widow and fatherless boys expect to descend on them.

"As a friend he was firm in his attachments ; he was a man whose friendship and society needed to be sought ; he never courted the favor of any, and I often told him he lost the intimacy of many who would have proved valuable friends, by his backwardness to intrude unsolicited into any society.   His amiable and gentle manners rendered him a favorite with all who knew how to appreciate real worth.   He was faithful in giving advice and reproof, but it was always done in so mild a manner, it was impossible to take offence.   His Indian brethren can bear testimony that 'faithful were the wounds' of their friend, Peter Jones. He never saw sin in them without pointing out the evils resulting from it, and ever encouraged industry and virtuous deeds. They all looked up to him with respect, and consulted him as their *best friend.* May the Lord raise up another to fill his place!

"His course of reading and study was desultory. His was a mind that gained more from the study of men and things, than from books, although, whenever he got interested in a work, it was difficult to divert his attention from it. As his early education had not encouraged application or deep study, neither had formed a taste for mental culture, it could not be expected that in his later years, with the cares of a family, very poor health, and a vast amount of business to transact for his tribe, that he should be able to devote much time to reading. He never took much interest in biography, and when I expressed my surprise, he would say, 'Persons are extolled too much. Bible biography is honest.' And I am certain nothing would have grieved him more than that his character should be set forth to the world as blameless. He was well informed on all the great events of the day.

"As a correspondent, he was punctual and explicit, his style varying according to the subject and parties he addressed. He could be solemn, touching and comforting, or humorous and loving. He never wrote (except purely on business matters,) without saying something of the Savior. I believe those friends who have his letters, will keep them for his sake.

"In preparing his sermons, the Bible and prayer, with the teachings of the Holy Spirit, were his principal aids. Having several Commentaries, he made use of them when he needed light thrown on any difficult passage. His notes were rather concise, depending more on the teachings of the Holy Spirit than any preparations for the pulpit. He often said he could never preach, however much time he took to prepare a sermon, unless the Lord helped him. In summing up my dear husband's character, I should say his actions, words and looks were governed by a principle of uniform consistency, humility and moderation. Amidst popular applause, to which in the old country he was no stranger, he kept on his steady course, and never seemed the least inflated, even by the notice of monarchs, and the great and noble of the earth. He was remarkable for integrity in all his dealings with his fellow creatures, never taking advantage of ignorance. This was one excellence that raised him so in the estimation of the Indians; they placed implicit confidence in all he said, and trusted the management of their temporal affairs in his hands. Not only was he chief over the tribe to which he belonged, but the Muncey town and Moravian Indians made him chief in their tribes, and urged him to do their business for them. In one instance, he paid, I think, £200, which no law could have obliged him to do, but a sense of honor made him spurn the temptation to take advantage on that account. I think the circumstance of his rising so superior to the generality of his countrymen should be noticed. Although he was evidently chosen by God to do a great work, and prepared by his Spirit for the accomplishment of the same; still the remarkable way by which he was guided through the wilderness, his preservation from the temptations so fatal to youth, and especially Indians; his never having the least desire for the accursed fire-water; the marked blessing that rested on all his lawful temporal undertakings, so that he rose by industry, honesty and piety, to a respectable and honorable station in society ; these and many other circumstances demand remark, not only to his own credit, but for the glory of that God who made him by his grace what he was.

"ELIZA JONES."

"Brantford, C. W."

This account of the death of my old friend and fellow-laborer affected me deeply, and as I read over the labors of his life, I do not wonder at the respect with which he was viewed by every one who knew him.

Br. and sister Carey now drove with me to the New Credit Mission, where we found many of the Indians still living, who were the first fruits of the Grand River Mission. I found Peter Jones' mother yet alive, although in very feeble health. [I have since received intelligence of her death ; she died in the Lord.] I prayed with them, and the tears streamed down their eyes as they thought of the time when they first listened to the prayers of the Missionary. These Indians have a Reservation of twelve miles square, divided into farms which compare favorably with any I had seen among the whites ; good houses, good fences and barns, everything in as good order as their white brethren. I was told that one Indian during the past summer had raised from a farm worked by himself, over one thousand bushels of grain. They have a good church and parsonage, and are under the entire control of the Wesleyans, who appoint their minister from year to year.

After taking leave of these good people, I went on and called upon Br. Wm. Ryerson, who lives on the spot where, thirty-two years before, I worshiped with the Indians for the last time. The Indians here have sold out to the whites, and now all through this part of the country appear fine farms and splendid houses, giving token of the thrift and energy of Canadian farmers. Br. William has purchased him a small farm, and being in comfortable circumstances he purposes spending the evening of his days in this quiet spot. He has been one of the most popular and successful preachers in the Wesleyan Canadian Conference, but now holds a superannuated relation. He was raised, converted, and commenced his itinerant life upon the first circuit I travelled in Upper Canada. May his last days be peace.

How changed the face of the country. Everywhere I go nothing seems natural. Where once was nothing but woods and foot-paths through the forests, now are seen handsome farms, good roads, large villages, flourishing manufactories, and everything denoting the presence of man.

At Muncey town, where, thirty-seven years ago the forest hid the wigwams of the savage—where the deer bounded along in perfect liberty—where naught was seen but the form of the Indian—as he followed the chase through the windings of the forest, or strolled along the banks of the river in pursuit of fish—where the only music heard was the death chant of some unfortunate prisoner, or the unearthly yell of the war dance, as those fierce, untutored sons of the forests circled round the warpole, or listened to the magic incantations of some celebrated pow-wow as he delivered to them the will of the Great Spirit—where I had stood alone as the representative of Christianity and civilization, facing the flashing eyes and frowning countenances of that hostile band of warriors who thirsted for my blood because I wished to turn them from their old customs and their idolatry—where, as I held up to their sight the Book of books, and told them that it contained the will of the Great Spirit to them, their flashing eyes grew dim, their countenances changed to smiles and looks of friendship, and their purpose, once so strong in the faith of their forefathers, now changed to seek and know the will of the Great Spirit as revealed to them through the Bible,—there at that place is the beautiful and flourishing model farm of the Mount Elgin Industrial High School for the benefit of those Indians who wish to advance still more in the knowledge of civilization and the arts, and instead of a waste and howling wilderness, well well cultivated farms, with all the improvements of modern husbandry, are spread out to the view, presenting a change as strange and wondrous as that wrought by the magician's art. But that the reader may be able to comprehend the extent of the change produced in that country, I will insert an extract from the Jubilee Sermon of Rev. Wm. Case, which although lengthy, will give as concise an account of the state of affairs as any that can be offered, and for Scriptural doctrine and choice Methodistic reminiscences, it is unsurpassed by any production of the kind. The sermon was delivered before, and at the request of the Wesleyan Canada Conference, assembled at London, Canada West, June 6th, 1855 :

"In the visit of those brethren, Torry and Jones, are some of the most interesting communications with the Indians that I have known. The prejudices of the chiefs were strong and determined, arising out of the abuses and injuries their people had received from the white man, who had 'ruined them by whisky, and dispossessed them of their lands;' and they dwelt much and strongly on the *cold-blooded* massacre of the Moravian Indians, at Muskingum. The controversy continued for hours, and with such discretion on the part of our missionaries, that when the council closed, it was found that much of the prejudice of the opposing chiefs was subdued, and they ceased to object, by saying, 'we will think more upon the subject.' At this interview, and others that followed, the foundation was laid for the conversion of the three tribes.

"The accounts which are given of these councils need only to be read to be admired, for the wisdom, patience and discretion of Torry and Jones, in answering objections, and urging the claims of the Gospel. I will notice one, as a specimen of the wisdom in which the whole controversy was conducted:

"On our saying that the Great Good Spirit had sent us to tell them the good and right way, they replied that the Great Spirit had sent *them* prophets who told them they must live as their fathers had done, and keep up their ancient customs. We then said, 'But the Good Spirit has given us the good Book; that this book informed us that the good Spirit made all men ; told us to love and do each other good ; the same good Book told us the right way to worship, and informed us of the Savior of sinners. Now the Great Spirit has not given *you* any such book, but he has given it to *us* and told us to hand it to our red brothers. If you obey this good Book, it will make you wise and happy, and direct you most safely to a happier life to come. Now, brothers, we come to hand you this good Book, and to teach your children to read it, that they may be wise and good.' This discourse seemed to have effect. They paused and seemed thoughtful, and at last said that they would not oppose those who wished to hear the word, and to send their children to the school.

" On our next visit, we found our affairs more prosperous; the school had become popular with the Indians. There were eighteen children, and a prospect of more. With the like discretion were the objections of the chiefs answered and explained in regard to the murders at Muskingum, and the use of ardent spirits. They did not, however, attempt to justify the wrongs they had suffered. Some stern, some truthful pen may record them.

"It was previous to the good work on the Grand River, that the people of God became unusually fervent in praying for the Indians, several of whom offered pecuniary assistance for the support of a missionary among them. In like manner, when the Christians of Bay of Quinte heard of the conversion of the Indians in the west, (for we spoke of it at all the quarterly meetings) a like fervent spirit was manifest for the conversion of the Indians of Bay of Quinte and Kiugston.

"In the meantime, Peter Jones and others, from the Credit Mission, accompanied me to Bellville, where the gospel was preached to the Ojibwas of that vicinity, aud where similar changes were wrought by the power of God. The conversions commenced in the spring of 1826. From a state of drunkenness, poverty and degradation, not to be described, these Indians, too, became a sober, praying people, and immediately entered upon a settled, industrious course of life.

"The journal of the Grape Island Mission contains not a few remarkable events of providence and grace; as those of the divine care and guidance, powerful conversions, fervency of devotion, piety of the children, patience in sufferings, triumphant deaths, the faithful labors of missionaries and teachers, the influence of the mission on the white inhabitants, both in the vicinity and elsewhere;

the schools, as the day, the Sabbath, the infant and industrial schools. It is also to be noticed that a number of the converts have been useful in extending the truths of religion to other tribes. The names of Sunday, Beaver, Moses, Paul, Frasier, Chechang, Crawford, Steinham, Salt, Blaker, are on the list of laborers; several of whom have carried religious instruction to the tribes of Lake Huron, Lake Michigan, Lake Superior, and Hudson's Bay, to the extent of two thousand miles in the north. Many of these events we have on record, others are remembered by the missionaries and teachers, and may yet be given to the public. This people remained on Grape Island, near Bellville, eleven years, where they were employed in gardening, farming, house-building, and some of the trades, as that of smithing, shoe-making, &c.

"The Indians of the Grape Island Mission having been fitted for a more enlarged sphere of labor in civilized life, they were, in the spring of 1837, removed to the township of Alnwick, near Rice Lake, on lands assigned them by Sir John Colborne. Here they are provided with comfortable dwelling houses, barns, cattle, farming-tools, saw-mill, &c.; chapel, school-house, missionary and school teacher. The buildings, cattle and mill were paid for out of the Indians' annuitant funds. The cost of the chapel, in part, the parsonage, and the missionaries and teachers have been at the expense of the society. Before their conversion, they were in habits of great irregularity. In scenes of drunkenness and revelry, they would, in a few weeks, waste their annuities, return to their hunting grounds in the wilderness, too bare of clothing to endure the severities of winter. Since their conversion, their annuities and presents from the Government have made them comfortable for clothing and bedding throughout the year.

"These Indians now, (1837,) numbered 212, having increased twelve in the eleven years since their conversion. In eleven years previous to their conversion, they had diminished about fifty.   Here at Alnwick too, extensive brick buildings have been erected for the education of the children of this and neighboring bands, the expenses of which have been defrayed by a voluntary subscription of one fourth of their annuities.   They have also set apart for school purposes, two hundred acres of land, as a farm for improving the scholars in the business of agriculture. They bear the expense also of clothing and board of fifty children in the Industrial School, the missionary and teachers being paid by the Missionary Society.

"RICE LAKE.—The introduction of Christianity among the Ojibwas, of Rice Lake, is kindly furnished by our Indian friend, Rev. Peter Jones, as follows :—During the Methodist Conference, at Hamilton, near Coburg, in Sept., 1827, several of the converted Indians from Grape Island, and others of us from River Credit, met at the Conference by direction of father Case.   The Indians pitched their wigwams in a grove.   Here religious services were held.   During this time, chief Sawyer, Big Jacob, and others, were sent to Rice Lake to invite the Indians to come down to our encampment.   Next morning they returned, accompanied by Capt. Paudaush and Peter Rice Lake, the two chiefs, and thirty or forty others.   After refreshment, we commenced religious talk.   We told them what great things the Great Spirit had done for us at the Credit and Grape Island, to which they all paid great attention, and seemed much impressed. During the same day, Bishop Hedding, father Case, Dr. Bangs, and other ministers, visited and addressed the Indians; prayer and religious instruction were continued till towards evening, the Indians becoming more and more deeply impressed. At length the Spirit of the Lord was poured out in great power upon the minds of the Indians, and many cried aloud, 'What shall I do to be saved?' That we might have more convenience for giving them instruction, an altar was formed by placing a pole against two trees. To this place the mourning penitents were invited to come and kneel, for instruction and prayer, and instruction was given them as their several cases seemed to require.

"It was not long when chiefs Rice Lake and Paudaush arose and expressed their joyful feelings, saying they had found peace to their souls, and they gave glory to God for his mercy. Then another and another gave the same testimony, and ere the meeting closed, every adult Indian was made happy in the pardoning love of God. O, what a joyful time! The wilderness resounded with the voice of joy and gladness! At the Sabbath services which followed at the Conference, the Indians saw for the first time, a body of about thirty ministers, heard the preaching of the Bishop, Dr. Bangs, and others, witnessed the impressive ceremony of ordinations, the sweet melody of song, by the whole congregation, with all which they were much impressed, and greatly edified. On the return of the Rice Lake converts to their home, Capt. Beaver and others from Grape Island were requested to accompany them, for the purpose of further instruction and edification in the christian faith.

"The following occurrence will show the nature of the temptations the Indians had now to encounter, the device of the *white pagans* to ensnare them, and the firm resistance they showed against their two great enemies, the *Drunkard* and *Rum*. One of the disciples of whisky was 'sure he could induce the Indians again to drink,' and providing himself with ardent spirits, he moved in his canoe over to the island where the Indians were encamped. Leaving all at the shore, he went up to the camp, and inviting the Indians down, brought forth his bottle. 'Come,' said he, 'we always good friends; we once more take a good drink in friendship.' 'No,' said Capt. Paudaush, 'we drink no more of the fire-waters.' 'O, but you will drink with me; we always good friends.' But while this son of Belial was urging them to drink, the Indians struck up in the tune of *Walsal*, the new hymn they had lately learned to sing—

> " Oah pa kish-ke cheen go twauk
> Keye e ne she nah baig."
> "O for a thousand tongues to sing
> The great Redeemer's praise ;"

and while the Indians were singing, Bacchanalian, defeated in his wicked device, and looking like a *fool*, paddled away from the island, leaving the Indians to their temperance and their religious devotions.

"In the records of this work are incidents of very lively interest; as their ready reception of the Gospel, their firm resistance of temptation,—the industry of the women for the support of the children while at school; as also the useful labors of Peter Jones, H. Biggar, Miss Barnes, and others. The results are, improvements in morals, temporal comforts, and religious duties; and besides, several of this tribe have been usefully employed in extending the gospel to other bands, both in Canada and Michigan.

"'LAKE SIMCOE.—The following is also from the pen of Mr. Jones. In 1827, John Lunday and myself, accompanied Rev. Egerton Ryerson to Newmarket, where we found some Ojibway families of Lake Simcoe, among whom was Chief Perahbick. To these families we spoke on the subject of Christianity. They listened with attention, and expressed a willingness to be taught the white man's religion. This, I believe, was the first attempt to introduce the Gospel to the Lake Simcoe Indians.'

"During the summer of this year, native exhorters were sent from Grape Island, who visited them in their wigwams and sang and prayed with them. A conviction for sin was soon apparent, and they began to pray. At length the whole tribe of six hundred was brought under religious influence. On one occasion, with the efficient assistance of Mr. Jones, we held religious services among these Indians for five days successively, during which they were instructed in the commandments, the Lord's prayer, the apostle's creed, the office and influence of the Holy Spirit, as also the nature of the ordinances of baptism and the Lord's Supper. At the conclusion of the services we baptized one hundred and twenty-two of the adult converts! Such a day of power and blessing was seldom witnessed among the Indians. To a deep and humbling conviction of their sinfulness, which constrained them to cry aloud for mercy, was succeeded a joyful assurance of the Savior's pardoning love. Their feelings were expressed by weeping, and by shouts of praise and glory to God for his salvation.   On some occasions, they were so overpowered as to be unable to stand, and were borne away from the services to the wigwam in the arms of their friends.   This was in June, 1828.

" The converts were now united in Society, with native leaders, each leader having twelve or fifteen in his class. From this body have been raised np some of sterling worth, among whom were Thomas Briggs, of about sixteen, and Henry Steinhaur of about ten years.   Of the former, when the leaders were to be appointed, Thomas was proposed by the Indians.   To this we objected, on account of his youth, but the Indians urged, saying, 'Though he is young, he prays and speaks like an old man.'   This pious and lovely youth of sixteen was then appointed the leader of about twelve persons, some of whom were of the age of fifty or more.

" Of the latter, then ten years old, was Henry Steinhaur, whom, with the consent of his widowed mother, we took to Grape Island, where, after a few years in the mission school, he was entered at the Cazenovia Seminary, and instructed in the higher branches, including the Latin and Greek.   He was afterwards employed for several years as teacher in the mission schools ; then, finishing his education at Victoria College, was, in the spring of 1840, appointed with Rev. James Evans, to the Hudson's Bay Mission, where he has labored fourteen years as school-teacher, preacher of the Gospel, translator, and in the printing of the Scriptures.

"We would proceed in these details, but the limits of a single discourse do not permit.   We have, however, to add, that as we have referred with delight to some of the labors of the Church in fulfillment of her covenant engagements, and have seen the ways of the Lord to be mercy and truth, we would with equal pleasure refer to the conversion of the natives of Saugany, St. Clair, Fort Malden, Michigan, Mackinaw, Kewawenoug, Lake Superior, Garden River, and the several stations in the Hudson's Bay territory. In all those bodies of Indians similar awakenings, conversions and happy changes have been the result of our ministry.

"Of the Hudson's Bay Mission you have the deeply interesting tour by our deputation, the Rev. John Ryerson, giving account of that country, its trade and commerce, the state of missions, both of ours and other Churches; a work ably written, and which we cordially recommend to the friends of missions. It has one fault: it should have contemplated the advance of Christianity among the numerous Indian tribes of the Thousand Miles Plains, then over the Rocky Mountains, to Vancouver's Island, where, on the shores of the Pacific Ocean, we anticipate meeting with the missionaries on the Oregon, to recount in songs of gratitude the toils, and crosses, and triumphs of the gospel among the pagan tribes of a wilderness of three thousand miles.

"Well, then, brethren, we are already on the way. Two missionaries, the Rev. Messrs. Wolsey and Steinhaur, will leave this Conference in a few days. They go by railroad to Galena, thence to St. Pauls, four hundred miles on the Mississippi, (distant from its mouth two thousand miles) and near the centre of North America; thence by ox-cart to Red River, four hundred miles; thence to Edmonton, the 'Rocky Mountain House,' one thousand miles west. At this new mission, a British trading post, our brethren are appointed to labor among the pagan Indians of the Rocky Mountains, where they expect to arrive in the month of November next.

"We may here remark that during the thirty years of our missionary labors among the wild men of our forests, fourteen bands of wandering pagans have been converted; people degraded in ignorance, and besotted by strong drink, without either houses or domestic animals. These have been instructed in the christian religion, gathered into villages, provided with dwellings of comfort, and taught the duties of domestic life. They now possess oxen, cows, horses, and other domestic animals, with farming implements. Both day and Sabbath schools have been in operation in all these villages, from the commencement, where their children have had opportunity for education.

"We may further remark, that the several bodies are still under the pastoral care of faithful ministers and teachers; that the voice of prayer and praise is heard in their families and public assemblies; that native laborers, among whom are able ministers of the gospel, have been educated and trained for the Indian work; that the work is still in progress, both north and west, the Divine blessing attending the word for the conversion of souls, and the edification of the Indian Church. Two noble institutions, too, have been erected, and are now in operation, the one in Alnwick, near Coburg, the other at Mount Elgin, near London, on the River Thames.

"At these institutions the Indian youths are taught the common branches of an English education, as well as agriculture, on the farms attached to those institutions. At each of those establishments, provision is made for the board and clothing of fifty Indian youths. If the

Indians have not availed themselves of the advantages of the schools, as they might have done, it is no fault of the Church. She has provided for their education efficiently, and she enjoys the pleasure of knowing that her labor is not in vain in the Lord!

"We have made reference to the conversion of Indians in Michigan, and the south shore of Lake Superior. On the subject of missions to the Indian tribes, the Methodist Episcopal Church in the United States, and the Wesleyan Methodist Church in Canada, have known no political boundaries, each assisting the other with men and means. The former *commenced*, and for many years contributed largely for the support of the 'Canada missions.' We in return commenced *their* missions in Michigan, and we are happy still to afford them native laborers in their Indian mission work. We remember with grateful emotions, the liberal donations and fervent prayers of christian friends, as well of other Churches as of the Methodist, in the United States. We are happy to learn that the early and constant friend of the 'Canada missions,' the Rev. Dr. Bangs, is still living, at an advanced age, to witness the permanent and increasing progress of christian missions, both in Canada, the United States, and elsewhere.

"During the same period of thirty years, more than one hundred townships, newly surveyed and settled, have been visited and religiously instructed, and Sabbath-schools established. Our Church has now in the mission field, twenty-one missionaries to the Indians, seventy-nine ministers to the domestic missions, sixteen day school-teachers, fifteen day schools, two of which are large industrial institutions, 10,624 members; 1,142 of that number are Indians. She is still acting on the plan, that in the new settlements, 'dwelling-houses and chapels should rise up together;' and with the sound of the falling forest, the voice of salvation should be heard.

"After the Canada Conference was, by mutual consent, separated from the Conference in the United States, and an union formed with the British Conference, the missions were committed to the general oversight of the Wesleyan Missionary Society in England. In these arrangements, the religious interests of the Indians and new settlers continue to be provided for; and such are the grounds of confidence in the management and success of these missions, that ample funds are raised in the country, by voluntary subscriptions, without foreign aid. The collections for the year now closing, are about thirty-six thousand dollars. Thus far has the Church kept the 'covenant and statutes of the Lord.'

"That other and further duties are included in the divine covenant, is most evident; but those are permanent. At the same time it is not to be forgotten that the Church has been early and constant in the circulation of the Holy Scriptures. She has also established at Toronto, a Book Room, and printing office, which has afforded a large amount of religious reading to the people of Canada, during the past twenty years. It is still accomplishing its high mission by the 'spread of scriptural holiness throughout the land.' During the past year, more than twenty thousand volumes of a sound religious literature, in addition to four thousand of our valuable weekly periodicals, have been issued from the Book Room. We have much reason to be pleased with the establishment, as a means for diffusing religious instruction, second only to the preaching of the word, by multiplying and scattering abroad a sanctified literature, a blessing to the Church and to the land. Her voice, too, has been heard in high and loud denunciations against the drunkenness and revelry of the times, against gambling, whether by cards, or by lotteries, by dice, or other 'games of chance.' By gambling few have been gainers! thousands ruined. The obligations of the holy Sabbath, too, have been urged, and its violaters warned.

"In conclusion, I suppose it is expected that I say something of the divine dealings with myself, having arrived at the advanced age of nearly seventy-five, and been engaged as a minister of the gospel for fifty years. My birth was in the town of Swansea, on the seaboard of Massachusetts, on the 27th of August, 1780. After years of religious impressions, and a sinful course, I was converted in February, 1803. In June, 1805, I was admitted as an itinerant preacher in the New York Conference, then in session at Ashgrove; and having volunteered for Canada, I was appointed with Henry Ryan, to the Bay of Quinte circuit. I have much reason to believe that my appointment to this country was in the order of Providence, and divinely directed. A field thus distant was the more suitable, to wean me from a numerous circle of friends; and a new country was best adapted to my youth and inexperience. I have every cause to be satisfied with my choice, and abundant reason to be grateful to my christian brethren, and the inhabitants of Canada generally, for their generous and marked hospitality which has everywhere been shown me in every part of the Province.

"In connection with this subject, I beg to relate an incident which occurred in my journey to this country. It was while travelling through the forests of Black River. As I was drawing near to the field of my future labor, I felt more and more deeply impressed with the importance of my mission, and my insufficiency to preach to a people already instructed. As yet, but a boy, only about two years since my conversion; devoid of ministerial talents as I was of a beard, I feared, on account of my incompetency, that I should not be received in a strange land. So strong were the emotions of my heart, that I dismounted my horse and sat down, and wept and prayed. While thus weeping, these words were spoken to me in a voice that I could not misunderstand, 'I will go before thee—will prepare the hearts of the people to receive thee; and thou shalt have fathers and mothers, and children in that land.' This promise I have seen fulfilled to the letter; and I hereby give glory to God for this and a hundred promises more, which have by his blessed word and his Holy Spirit, been impressed on my heart. It is proper here to say that, of the fifty years of my ministry, six of them were spent in the labors of the New York Conference, from whence I first came; i. e., one year on the Ulster circuit, and five years on the Cayuga and Oneida districts. And happy years they were. The piety and hospitality of the people—the zeal and devotion of the ministers with whom I was happily associated—the mighty outpourings of the Spirit, and the revivals of religion which everywhere in the limits prevailed, made the country a hill of Zion, a real 'Mount Pleasant.' A few only of those excellent ministers are still living. I have them in my eye, they live in my heart, and I hope to meet them

> " 'Where all our toils are o'er,
>   Our suffering and our pain ;
> Who meet on that eternal shore,
>   Shall never part again.' "

"The ways of the Lord I have seen to be 'mercy and truth,' in numerous instances of exposure and danger. Five times have I been laid low with fevers, bilious and typhus ; and although with no home of my own, I was provided for among strangers, who watched at my bed-side for weeks together, nursing me with christian solicitude, and faithfully administering to my recovery. The Lord reward them in that day! Sometimes in those afflictions, but more afterwards, I found they 'yielded the peaceable fruits of righteousness,' and then how sweetly could I sing,

> " 'Oft from the margin of the grave,
>   Thou, Lord, hast lifted up my head ;
> Sudden I found thee near to save,
>   The fever owned thy touch, and fled.'

"In my labors it has been my lot to be much on the waters, both in summer and in winter. While travelling the Catskill mountains, on the Ulster circuit, in 1807, my route took me across about twenty streams, which, in heavy rains, swelled to the overflowing of the banks ; but I suffered no injury, and never missed my appointments. I was, indeed, once in that year overwhelmed with my horse in the Delaware river, but I escaped in safety, my horse reaching one shore and I the other. Once was I shipwrecked on Lake Ontario. Five times have I been through the ice with my horse, on the bays, rivers and lakes of Canada. Through all these dangers, the Lord in his providence delivered me; and then I have sung with delight :

> " 'Oft hath the sea confessed thy power,
> And given me back at thy command,
> It could not, Lord, my life devour,—
> Safe in the hollow of thy hand.'

"The christian minister, in any perplexity, has abundant sources for relief, as that of the Church, his experience, the Bible, and his God. If the first fail him, he is sure of relief from the last. 'In all thy ways acknowledge God, and he shall direct thy paths.'—Prov. iii. 6. For the encouragement of my young brethren, allow me to make allusion to a few cases out of many, very many more.

"In 1806, I lost my health by hard toils in the swamps of Canada, and for three months my strength was wasting away by fever and ague. I now thought I should receive an appointment suited to my feeble state; but contrary to my expectations, my appointment was to the mountains of the Ulster circuit. I felt it as a disappointment, and thought I could never ascend those lofty summits, nor endure the toils of a circuit of three hundred and thirty miles around. But, submitting all to God, I went forward, and I have reason to believe it was the very circuit the best suited to my febrile state, for such was the purity of the water and the salubrity of the atmosphere, that I immediately began to recover. My health was again established, so that at the next Conference I again offered myself for Canada.

" Again, as I sat at the foot of the mountain, feeble in strength, unable as I thought, to perform the labors of that circuit, I opened my Bible to read, when, without forethought, my eyes fell upon Isaiah xli. 14, 15. And so it came to pass: I regained my strength, the mountains were easily overcome—myself and colleague, Robert Hibbard, were greatly aided by the Spirit; we could 'thresh the mountains'—revivals in religion prevailed, and one hundred were that year added to the societies. (See the Minutes.)

"Again, in 1808, on my arrival at Black Rock, the embargo prohibited the transport of property across the line. At first I was perplexed, and knew not what to do, so I went to the hay-loft and fell on my face in prayer. I asked the Lord, as I was engaged in his work, to open my way to fulfill my mission in Canada. Having committed all to God, I returned to my lodgings at the inn, when a stranger smilingly said, 'I should not wonder if the missionary should jump into the boat, take his horse by the bridle, and swim round the embargo.' I did so, swam the Niagara river, and landed safely in Canada.

"Having seen so many years, I can scarely expect to continue much longer, though yet, as you perceive, my voice is strong and clear, and I am full of life and spirit; and yet, my mind recoils at care. Sensible of this infirmity, I still desire to be free from a burden which has pressed so heavily in the numerous and weighty charges of the past fifty years. Not only a voice, but a heart to feel! I love the assemblies of the saints, and the fireside where conversation is free with children's children, on the piety of those who have passed away — their acts of faith and their triumphs in death—as well as of the glorious work of God in by-gone days! These visits to the scenes of my former labors, have been seasons of great delight, and I hope if I live, to enjoy them still in days to come.

"To my brethren in the ministry, I am happy to say that there appears at present little to interrupt the peace ful prosecution of the work. Free from agitations which occasion pain, but produce no good—the work of revivals in happy progress—in friendly alliance with other Protestant branches of the christian Church,— with them engaged in the cause of the Bible, of education, and of christian benevolence, we proceed in the joyful work of offering salvation to the lost, and of feeding the flock of God which he has purchased with his own blood.

"We cannot, however, forbear to remind you of the prevailing sin of the age,—*the love of gain*. As yet, most of you have disregarded the rise of property, and the wealth of cities. Your temporal interests have been forgotten in the care and welfare of your flocks. This is right ; and the promise of the Savior, in Matthew, vi. 33, is being fulfilled by the Church in the increasing comforts for yourselves, and supplies for your families.

"We are reminded, too, of the onerous duties devolving on the worthy President of the Conference, to whom is committed the general oversight of the Church ; and to afford him that support which his arduous labors require. Connected with his extensive charge, is the oversight of the numerous missions, both domestic and Indian, which, extending daily as they do, must induce increasing solicitude and labor ! Although laborious, their success and prosperity renders the duty a delightful one. It calls, too, for grateful acknowledgments to the Parent Society in England, from whom both valuable men and generous means have been willingly afforded, to maintain and extend the influence of our agency among the Aborigines.

"During various periods of our history, they have not hesitated to give assistance to our *domestic missions*, from a consciousness that they were yielding to the just claims of the necessitous and destitute of their own race, some of whom were among the brightest ornaments of their own pastorate at home. Appeals to them on behalf of the Indians of America, always met a prompt and benevolent response; and we rejoice in our relationship to a Society whose successful missions are found throughout the world, verifying the almost prophetic saying of our common founder—'The world is my parish.'

"To parents and Christians generally! We call aloud, in the language of the Savior, 'Pray ye the Lord of the harvest, to send more laborers into the harvest!' Too many are favorable to worldly professions for their sons, apart from the interests of the Church. Mothers! Devote your sons from their birth, to the service of God and his Church! As encouragements, remember Hannah and her Samuel! that already two hundred young men have been converted in Canada, and engaged in the ministry. Hundreds more will be wanted, as the harvest fields are enlarged. Who has not heard of the piety of the venerated Mrs. Wesley; of the faith of mother Kent, of New England; of mother Covel, of the Catskill mountains; of mother Ryerson, of Canada; and many other mothers in Israel, and of their sons in the ministry. In 1807 I came to my appointment in a small log cottage in a gorge of the mountains of the Ulster circuit, where I met with two itinerant ministers, twin sons of a pious mother. After the sermon by one of them, I met the 'class,' when I congratulated the mother on having two sons in the ministry; the reference was sufficient, it kindled anew the ardent flame in her heart, and she broke out in expressions like these: 'Yes, glory to God, I know how they became ministers! On my conversion to God, my soul was so blest, and I felt such love for my Savior, and for the souls he had redeemed by his blood, that I wanted to tell it to the whole world. I went to the cradle where my boys were asleep, and kneeling over them, I wept and prayed, and devoted them to the service of God, and the ministry of the Church. Now, here they are, ministers of the gospel! Glory to God; glory to God in the highest!' This was 'mother Covel.'

"To my lay christian brethren: May I be allowed to call your attention to the case of your enfeebled and worn-out preachers. There is scarcely a subject for sympathy more touching than that of a minister in the decline of life, after having worn away his palmy days in the service of the Church, brought to the necessity of asking alms for himself and family! I have known such and may witness it again.

" 'There comes,' says one, looking out from a comfortable dwelling, 'There comes, now, old Mr. ——; he can't preach any more, and he will stay with us a fortnight, I suppose, or want something for his wife and children.' Facts worse than this; read it in ' *Western Methodism*,' by J. B. Finley, p. 411, as follows:

" 'In 1815, Russell Bigelow commenced his itinerant labors in the Ohio Conference, and for twenty years labored in that and other Conferences in the western settlements. Faithful and unwearied in his labors, and everywhere successful, too, he was beloved and respected by all. While he was able to preach, all was well. Bright faces and open hands greeted him in all his walks; but, alas! when disease preyed upon his system, and he was no longer able to preach the gospel, faces were hidden and hands were turned away! Unable to labor more, he rigged up a jumper, and under deep depression of spirit, he returned to his destitute family, a wife and seven children, with them to linger in poverty for a time, and then to die! In about 1814, I saw young Bigelow. He was with me in the pulpit in Albany, and a lovely youth he was. He was then on his way from New England to Ohio. When I read of his sufferings and death, I sat down and wept aloud.'

"Brethren, you who have accumulated wealth, and have your families provided for, think of your worn-out preachers, and leave to the Conference a few hundreds for their support.

"On the peace and prosperity of the Church, I offer my christian gratulations. From the experience of the past, I am persuaded her members will ponder well before they allow themselves to be drawn into questions of controversy, the influence of which may divert their minds from the work of God in the growth of grace, and the advancement of pure and undefiled religion throughout the land. Amen."

Shortly after the delivery of this sermon, while at the Wesleyan Indian Mission at Alnwick, he fell from his horse, and died soon after, from the effects of the fall, at the honored age of seventy-five. His departure was mourned by many, both in the States and Canadas, and many tributes of respect were paid to his memory. Dr. Bangs, of New York, on the reception of the news of his death, preached a funeral sermon in honor of his former friend and fellow laborer, and from

the obituary notice in the Canada Conference Minutes,
I extract a few additional particulars :

"The eventful period when he assumed the christian
profession, is thus briefly stated by him : 'After years of
religious impressions, and a sinful course, I was converted
in February, 1803.'   At no time was there evidence that
the peace he possessed was fluctuating, and that the light
of his Heavenly Father's countenance had become dim.
In his exhibition of the graces of the Holy Spirit, there
was neither uncertainty nor extravagance ; and even to
old age, there was in his disposition and demeanor a
childlike simplicity, affection and uniformity, which elic-
ited the willing testimony, 'This is a man of God.'

"His body was never robust, and his habits were
always temperate. His presence was dignified and pre-
possessing.   His mind, though never trained scholasti-
cally, was vigorous, searching and tenacious, and by much
reading, observation and experience, it became enriched
with a knowledge as practical as it was adapted for all
the purposes which his diversified positions in the Methodist Church required. His acquaintance with Wesleyan
doctrine, discipline and usages was correct and compre-
hensive ; his publication of those doctrines judicious,
experimental, persuasive — often pathetic ; his enforce-
ment of that discipline in its integrity, while there was
no lack of fidelity to our incomparable system, was invariably marked with moderation and caution ; his pastoral assiduities for adults and youth, parents and children, were spiritual, fatherly, and unremitting.

"A divine hand led him into the ministry, and his
hallowed charity prompted him to volunteer his services
for Canada ; after which, some remarkable answers to

prayer, and much success, confirmed him in his choice of this magnificent and favored Colony of the British Empire.   And his selection of Canada at that time was expressive of a heroic intention, and a burning zeal; for the recesses of the wilderness had been little explored, and ruggedness, privation and peril awaited his footsteps, while the scattered settlers were for the most part without stated Gospel ordinances, and the aboriginal tribes were pagan and degraded; but he entered upon, and discharged with inflexibility of purpose, his arduous duties, won the esteem of the people everywhere, and brought many souls to Sinai, and then to Calvary.

"In 1805, he was received on trial by the New York Conference of the M. E. Church, a commanding and beloved branch of the great Wesleyan family; in 1807, was received into full connection, and ordained Deacon ; and the following year he was ordained Elder, when the apostolic Asbury was a Bishop of that Church, and had the widespread States of the American Union, and Canada, for the field of his evangelical and most effective superintendency.   The Rev. Mr. Case commenced his itinerancy on the Bay of Quinte, and his first six years were spent under the direction of that Conference.

"In 1810, he was appointed a Presiding Elder, and for eighteen years he had charge of important Districts—the Cayuga, the Oneida, Chenango, Lower Canada, Upper Canada, and Bay of Quinte.   In 1828, he was made Superintendent of Indian Missions and Schools.   In 1830, and the two following years, he was General Superintendent, *pro tem*, of the Methodist Societies in Canada.   For several years he was a missionary to the Indians, and Superintendent of Indian translations.   In 1837, and for fourteen years continuously, he was Principal of the Wesleyan Native Industrial Institution at Alnwick, until ably succeeded by the Rev. James Musgrove.

"In 1852 he was permitted by the Conference to visit different parts of the work, as his health enabled him; and without being superannuated, it was his wish—and his fine social spirit made it a pleasure—to pursue this course, until his Master should bid his servant rest. As an early pioneer and untiring laborer of our Missionary Society, he was highly respected by his brethren, and by none more so than by the honored President of the Conference, the Rev. Enoch Wood, under whose very able general superintendency of the missions for the last eight years, he was a faithful missionary.

"In the language of our Missionary Notices, we record the opinion of our lamented friend, that 'However once to be valued in the offices he once filled, and among his brothers and sons in Conference assembled, when he would rise with coolness and decision, and by his deliberate and prudent counsels, carry many with him, it is thought he was best known as our Apostle to the Indians; and for them he lived and died. Here we want space to set forth his early and manly dedication of himself to their interests; his acquaintanceship with their condition; the adaptation of his powers, and acquisitions, and means, to their necessities; his influence over them; his sympathy, his vigilance, his shrewdness, his tenderness, his authoritativeness, his travels, labors, indefatigableness, success. The efficiency of a native agency was his prayer. He witnessed the conversion of a native with exultation. Many Indians from the wilds of North America, once ready to perish, will be his glory and joy forever.

"He had many friends in Canada, and elsewhere on this continent, and his unsullied reputation had extended to other lands. The Wesleyan Societies of Canada cannot forget his person and his tender courtesies. They cannot forget his mature christian excellencies, his intelligence, sound judgment, and salutary counsels. They cannot forget his patriotism, his pure philanthropy and attractive catholicity. They cannot forget his works of faith, and abundant labors of love for half a century.

"His Wesleyan survivors would emulate his great virtues, and follow in his path of distinguished usefulness, rejoicing exceedingly that the same adorable Being who gave a Swartz to India, an Eliot to America, and a Barnabas Shaw to Africa, gave also a William Case to this country, whose name will ever be associated with the past progress, the perpetuity, and the glorious future of Methodism in Canada."

CHAPTER XVII.

From the extracts I have given, it will be seen that the mission which commenced thirty-eight years ago upon Grand River, by the conversion of two young natives, has continued to spread until its members are numbered by the thousand, and from every part of the northwest, through all that vast territory around Hudson's Bay and west to the Rocky Mountains, and even beyond, the call for help is continually increasing. "The aboriginal population is variously estimated, at from 200,000 to 500,000 souls, all very generally free from the vice of intemperance and favorably disposed towards the religion of the white man."[*] This number the reader will remember are those that have not as yet received the gospel, but are anxiously expecting it. There were in 1855 twenty-one mission stations, where one or more missionaries were sent, each having

---

[*] "Narrative of Rev. John Ryerson's tour to the Wesleyan and other Mission Stations, in the Hudson's Bay Territory."

a society of converted Indians to take charge of. The reports of these missionaries are very interesting, as showing the toils and privation endured by them for the sake of those poor benighted people, and the spread of the gospel among them in spite of opposition, ignorance and superstition. Rev. Wm. Herkimer, an Indian, writing from Rice Lake, says :

"You have, dear brother, been at Rice Lake, our beautiful Mission, and as I have heard, you have spoken well of it. Could you visit us now, or by-and-by when the crops are ripening, you would still admire our little village, with its green slopes down to the water, which, beneath a cloudless May sky, and as far as the Islands, is dotted all over with points of fire from the little waves dancing in the sunlight. The white man puts everything under him. The waves of our Lake, free since the Great Spirit made them, are free no more. Iron bands bind them from shore to shore. The white man's fingers are strong fingers. Iron bands in his hands become as pliable as the sinews of the deer in woman's hand, when she is beading a moccasin. God has been good to us Indians, in letting us see these times. Glory be to his name ! I am in good spirits. Last Sabbath was the best quarterly meeting we have had on the mission. God was with us. To him be the praise. Often have I been here, but it appears to me that this spring there is more light and life on the Lake, in the field, and in the sunlight, than there used to be. Ah, here it is. We have good meetings. God is with us. The people are all busy on their farms. Soul and body are being cared for, and our good

God has not waited for us to go half way to meet him, but has, glory be to his name! come right here, to our own homes, and is blessing us."

From G. M. McDougall, at Garden River, we have the following:

"The Indian is no theorist; his case demands *present help*. Give him Christ as a present Savior, and then—to use the words of chief Payahpetahsung,—'with nothing but the big house which Murceda has built us for a shelter, and a few rabbit skins for our clothing, we are rich.'

"During the past year, several have died in the Lord. Among these were two Roman Catholic women, who were savingly converted while living among our people. One of these, (whose disease was consumption,) we visited a short time before her death. For several days she had not spoken intelligibly. We endeavored to point her to the Savior, and then commenced to sing the hymn,

'Jesus my all to heaven is gone,' &c.,

in the native tongue, when, to the astonishment of all present, she began shouting, 'Praise Jesus, I love Jesus, I shall soon be forever with Jesus.' She continued in this happy state of mind till the next evening, when her happy spirit took its flight to mansions on high.'"

The missionary from Pic River writes:

"This new mission is established at the mouth of the Pic River, on the north shore of Lake Superior, near the Hudson's Bay Company's Tent. When I received my appointment to this remote field of missionary toil, it was with considerable reluctance and trembling I entered upon it. But I came, hoping it was my providential path. Trusting in the Lord, I determined to do all I could to advance the good cause, and for this I have labored day and night in my weak way. During the year, I have visited the Indian in his wigwam. Last ,winter I spent four or five weeks in search of the poor benighted pagan on his hunting ground, in the interior of this cold country, and have laid night after night on the top of the snow, without shelter; sometimes I have found a foot of snow on top of me in the morning. We may not always reap an abundant harvest from our toil. Yet when there is some good effected, it is cause of much gratitude to Him who condescends to employ such feeble instruments in improving the condition of those who sit in darkness. At this mission we have a few that enjoy the comforts of religion, and meet in class regularly. In all, nineteen have renounced paganism, given up their images, and are striving to serve the true God. One who was converted last fall, continued faithful during the winter, and this spring, while on a hunting excursion, he died in the triumphs of faith.

"Three families have promised to build houses at the Pic, and remain, which, we hope, will induce others to do the same. My first effort was to build a house with my own hands, 14 feet square with a cellar, which I com·pleted in September last. I had no shingles, so I made the roof of timbers, laid close together, then plastered and covered it with cedar bark. The Hudson's Bay Company kindly furnished me with plank for the floor, and several other materials without charge.

"All the Indians I have met with in this remote country, give the utmost attention to the Word of Life, and often they come to me and enquire what they must do to be saved. 'The harvest is great but the laborers are few.'   GEO. BLAKER."

From the Missionary at Norway House, Rossville, June 14th, 1855:

" I am happy to inform you that we still are in the enjoyment of peace and prosperity. On Christmas eve, we held a missionary meeting,— the first, probably, ever held in the place. All the donations to the mission cause from all sources, amount to something over £12 sterling. About a week ago, we equipped two brethren, and sent them on an evangelical tour of two months to Nelson River. In building new houses, making new fields, and enlarging old ones, and making roads through the village, there has probably been more done this spring than in ten years previously, and it has required but little prompting to do it.

"We have inclosed and brought into cultivation, about one and three-quarters of an acre, and it has been rather a heavy job; but as it lay immediately joining the mission premises, I was apprehensive we might lose it if we waited much longer, as our Indians have manifested quite a spirit of improvement, and land in our immediate vicinity is being prized. We have now a little over three acres in all, belonging to the mission. We have, however, not planted our new ground, as we have nothing to put into it as yet.

"On our arrival here, I commenced the study of the syllabic character, and the Cree language. In two months I was able to read the morning service in Cree, written in this character. For three or four months I have been praying publicly in this language, and as we have a large number of Indians around us, I have occasion to converse with them from twenty to fifty times a day. I feel that, under these circumstances, to be compelled to use an interpreter would be an intolerable burden. It has taken much of my time to oversee the work we have done. In consequence of the kind of material we had to work with, I have found it necessary to be almost constantly present, and then I would not only tell how it should be done, but take hold and help. Thus I have worked at plowing, planting, fencing, ditching, grubbing up stumps and roots. We have a pretty good garden, and I have attended to that mainly myself. Early this spring I made, nearly all alone, two small boats that we needed for the mission, &c.

"I expect to visit Berrin River soon. This will take me from home about two weeks. I am happy to say we are all in usual health. Mrs. H. has not suffered from the effects of this climate, as she did from that of Lake Superior. We have additions to our number from time to time. A short time since, Adam Moody came and wished to join us. This man had got some knowledge of Christianity from the Church missionaries at Red River, and when Br. Rundle arrived here in 1840, he found Adam exhorting the Indians to be Christians. He is decidedly a man of talent, but some years ago stopped short in religion. He wishes to try again. One of the Company's servants, an intelligent watchman, and an Indian, have joined us within the last week or so.

"I have just returned from a visit to Berrin's River. The distance we travelled is about 260 miles. We spent three days with a company of most wretchedly degraded savages. We learned many particulars concerning them, and our prospects of doing them good.   I baptized two children of a member of ours residing at the place, and a few of the Indians expressed a desire to become Christians, and promised to visit me at this place soon.   I saw some of those Indians last summer, and promised them a visit this season.   Br. Ryerson also advised me to visit them.   I need not remind you how necessary it is for us to be particular in keeping any engagements we make with the Indians.   We used our own small boat;   two good brethren accompanied me, to whom I paid one pound each for the trip, besides furnishing them.   At the present time our men are away in the Company's service, taking furs to, and bringing from, York Factory, so that our congregations are smaller than usual.

"We have done what we could in the way of gardening, and raising our supplies, but an army of caterpillars has destroyed everything in all this region of country, except potatoes, and them very much.   I had one and three-quarters of an acre of barley, with turnips, one thousand fine cabbages, &c., but not one spire of barley, or a cabbage, is to be seen;   all, all is gone.   The like was never heard of here.   We are not anxious in regard to the amount of salary, but I am urgent that the Committee should fix the amount on some uniform scale. We are expected to abound in works of charity;   for instance, on our arrival, we found eighteen pounds of tea among the groceries furnished by the Company.   We have not used a particle of it except for the male teacher, and yet it is all gone.   We have a large population around us, so this old woman and that would send for *upesees*, it did them so much good.

"We should be furnished with some simple medicines,

for we are constantly applied to for them. I am anxious to save the Society from certain expenses as soon as it can be done with safety. I feel perfectly content with the appropriations made for our salaries. It is as near equal as earthly things can well be made. It will, however, require close economy for us to make the year's end meet with it. The customs and circumstances of the country render it necessary for us to have more servant's hire than in Canada. I think it very necessary that all our missionaries in this country should be strict temperance men. We are in usual health and spirits.

"July 26.—I write to acknowledge the receipt of your letter by the hands of Br. Woolsey, who arrived, with Br. Steinhaur, safely this evening, and will leave in a day or two for their appointed field of labor. It is easier to come from Canada to this place, than to go from here to Edmonton.   THOMAS HURLBURT."

We add two more letters illustrative of Missionary life in those high northern latitudes:

"OXFORD HOUSE, JACKSON'S BAY,
June 7th, 1855.

"You will have been aware by this time, that we arrived here on the 21st of August of last year, and at that time we only found one family on the mission; the rest had dispersed abroad on different parts of the Lake and other places, to catch fish and game. The general aspect of affairs was far from pleasing. The house was barely habitable, even at that period of the year, and the church scarely fit to perform Divine service in. Very little had been done to improve the general aspect of the place. The potatoes that Mr. Steinhaur had planted, in consequence of his removal to 'Norway House,' had been greatly neglected, the consequence was, that where we ought to have had one hundred bushels, we did not get near half that quantity, and these had not ripened when we had to dig them to secure them from the frost. The place, however, is 'beautiful for situation,' and with some labor and a little expense, can be made all that is desirable in these hyperborean regions. Since my arrival, I have been excedingly busy in fitting up the interior of the house, and in making several articles of furniture.

"The house, which is built with logs, and filled in with clay, was penetrated by every shower of rain, and the clay washed down on the floors, and everything else that happened to be in the way; added to which, it was literally swarming with mice, so that both our little daughter and the girl were bitten by them while asleep, and during my absence to York factory, Mrs. B. was obliged to keep candles burning in order to get any sleep. Not being able to procure a carpenter, I had to purchase a few tools and set to work in good earnest, and I can say most conscientiously, I never worked harder in my life; but I have done it cheerfully, knowing by experience that the Indians are more apt to learn by example than by precept. The house is now comfortable, as far as the small size of it will allow, and the extremely severe winter has been passed in comparative comfort as far as the cold was concerned.

The place, as I have already stated to you, was exceedingly bare of furniture, but I have made during the winter, two very good beds, one sofa, a good sideboard, a chest of drawers, a table, and several other useful articles. Besides which, with the assistance of the men I have hired, and the school-master, I have got a good fish house erected, 18 by 16, for which we have had to get out all the timber. I have also got about one thousand boards of various sorts sawed and brought on to the premises, also the frame timber for a school-master's house 26 by 18 ; the same for another building, which we require as a store-house ; ice-house and dairy, 24 by 13 ; also, enough for the addition of two wings to the dwelling house, each 16 by 14, and an excellent light clench work-boat 16 feet long, very nearly fit to launch, and which could not be purchased in Canada, exclusive of the sails, for less than £16. This, also, I have entirely built myself.

"On my arrival from York factory, I found that several Indians had returned, and from that time until the hunting season arrived, we had about twenty-five families on the mission. Two new houses have since then been built, and other Indians are preparing to build this season. Their attendance on the means of grace was good, scarcely one remaining away on these occasions.

"We have not been able to commence a school as yet, partly from the want of suitable and necessary books, of which, indeed, we have none; but principally from the fact, that the fishing was a complete failure, so that the Indians were under the necessity of taking away their wives and children, to prevent them from starving. Indeed, so extreme were the wants of many of them, that we have seen them cook the entrails of fish and rabbits, and other disgusting garbage, to keep body and soul together.

I am thankful, however, that no other evil consequences of the scarcity have come to our knowledge. I find that we shall have no difficulties in establishing a mission here. In this country, in consequence of its norther latitude, and long winters, (the lake is now, June 7th, partly covered with ice,) the Indians must be principally dependent upon their hunting for their subsistence, as nothing but a few vegetables can be raised. The consequence is, that they are necessarily absent from the mission nearly seven months of the year, with the exception of occasional visits.

"At Norway House they have an annual examination of the School, when considerable sums are collected from the gentlemen of the company, which are laid out in suitable clothing for the children ; but here, in consequence of our isolated position, being quite out of the line of travel, we have no such resources, and unless we can procure articles of clothing suitable for children of both sexes from three to ten years of age, we shall never be able to keep anything like a school in operation. But if we had these little aids, we should soon have a good School, as I think we could easily collect from sixty to seventy scholars.

"In conclusion, let me say, that we never more fully felt the need of the prayers of the faithful than now ; and I feel confident that if our case be fully brought before the Church, that we shall not fail in securing the sympathy and prayers of its members. Here we have no christian communion, no one to converse with or consult, whatever difficulties may arise, and in case of dangerous illness, no medical aid to be obtained within two hundred miles. But our trust is in God whose mercy and aid never fail.

"R. BROOKING."

"Lac-La-Pline, Fort Frances,
July 4th, 1855.

"As Sir George Simpson will pass here, I write a few lines beforehand, in order to fulfill my promise, which I mentioned last winter in my letter. Early in the spring I visited the River Indians, and held a consultation with them in reference to establishing a mission at the Munido Rapids. Some of them were willing, but those who appeared to have the most influence opposed the object.

"The Indians from different parts have been tenting near this fort for several days, and performed their customs of metaisms, dancing with a human scalp, war-whoop, the pretended intercourse with the spirits of animals, and gambling. They are aware of the service which I am kindly allowed to hold every Sabbath in one of the largest rooms in the fort, but they do not attend. The only course I pursue is to speak to them one by one; and I perceive that several would embrace Christianity if they were not intimidated by the principal metas, who get clothing from their 'fellow Indians by initiating them into the customs, and telling pretended revelations successively. I learn that they do these things every year in the month of June; hence their combination against receiving instruction from missionaries.

"I know not the number of Indians that have been tenting here, the greater part of whom have left for the American territory, to receive their first payment for the lands which they have surrendered. The chief of this band was the one who threatened me not to speak to his young men last year, but he was quite low this summer, for he is under the displeasure of his band, on account of their lands in the American territory. Though they know my sayings against their deceptive and barbarous customs, yet they have not acted rudely towards me, as I expected, when so many were tenting on the Portage. On one occasion several of them came into the yard of the fort naked, variously daubed with vermillion, oxide of iron, and clay, with guns and tomahawks, and half drums. I asked one of the party what they were going to do. 'To perform one of our customs,' said he. It was the war-dance, war-whoop, &c. They performed this three several times this summer. It is a begging custom, but I do not favor it. ALLEN SALT."

The rapidity with which the news of the great work of God among the Six Nations, spread to the west and north-west among the Indians of that country is surprising, when we take into account the fact that they have no regular methods of conveying intelligence from one nation to another; but to Indians, religious news, or anything concerning the will of the Great Spirit towards them, is of great importance in their estimation, and when couched in the language generally used to describe such events, it acquired great interest in their eyes, and was among the items of news of greatest importance, when they met around their camp-fires or mingled with each other in their councils. In this way, the news of what the Great Spirit was doing for Indians in Canada, soon traversed the vast plains of the West, crossed the Rocky Mountains and reached the Flathead Indians upon the coast of the Pacific.

Of such importance was this intelligence to them, that they immediately called a general council of their nation, and after mature deliberation they appointed four of their most distinguished chiefs, renowned for their wisdom and prudence, to make a journey to St. Louis, where lived Col. Clarke, a man who had been among them, and by his honorable conduct had won their esteem and confidence. They started upon their long and toilsome journey of three thousand miles and over, through swamps and over mountains, crossing trackless plains and journeying through hostile countries, until they reached the place of their destination. Here they found their friend, Col. Clarke, who welcomed them to his house and hospitable board, and treated them with the attention due to their rank. They told him the object of their journey, how they had heard that the Great Good Spirit had sent a Book by the hands of the white man, to their brethren towards the rising of the sun, that this Book told them of the will of the Great Spirit in regard to their manner of living and worshiping, that their brethren who had received it, had now become very wise and happy, and they concluded by requesting Col. Clarke to send them a white man with this great

Book, that they too might listen to the words of the Great Spirit and become wise and happy.

The Colonel assured them that he would use all his influence to obtain what they so anxiously desired, and invited them to stay with him several weeks, until they should recover from the fatigues of their journey. They did so, but two of them were taken ill while at his house and died.   The Colonel, according to his promise, published a call to the Churches of the United States, shortly after my return from Canada, stating the particulars of his interview with the Flat-head chiefs, and asking them to furnish what was so loudly called for.   This went the rounds of the press in the States, and though thousands of ministers, commissioned from on high to preach the Gospel to all nations, read the appeal, and saw before them the door opened wide for the introduction of the Gospel and the evangelization of thousands of a benighted race of fellow mortals, yet but one of all that host of God's elect, felt constrained to leave his home and friends and brave the perils of a wilderness, to carry the tidings of a crucified Savior to those waiting thou-sands.

The Rev. Jason Lee, of one of the eastern Confer-ences of the M. E. Church, felt constrained to take his life in his hand, and to go to that distant land to carry the tidings of mercy and salvation to those who, through the order of Providence, had so ardently desired it. With a travelling companion he started across the continent, and after a long and toilsome journey, reached the nation of Flatheads, where his labors were abundantly blessed. This was the commencement, not only of that extensive mission of the Pacific, but also of the republic of Oregon.

In the year 1819, in consequence of a grant made by government, of one hundred acres of land to any one who would move into the new country back of the old settlements in the Canadas, and commence a farm by building and planting, there was a great emigration from the European countries and the older settlements of the Canadas. These formed the new townships where I travelled the first years of my stay in Canada. The oak plains along the rivers were soon taken up, and crops were easily put into the ground, as they had only to girdle the trees that were scattered thinly over the country, and thus cause them to die, when they could fell them at their leisure.

Rough shanties, or small log houses, were put up to screen them from the inclemency of the weather, and then they awaited the ripening of their crops with contentment. Among these I labored, often tying my horse to a tree as I dispensed the Word of Life to those who, while in their native land, listened to the regular preaching of a well settled country, but who now were deprived of all means of grace, and, like sheep without a shepherd, wandered unwatched and uncared for.

Where the city of London now stands, and in the surrounding country, I travelled much, and had the pleasure of forming the first societies ever established in those parts. Hundreds of persons who had grown up to manhood within sound of the gospel, and had remained unconcerned about their soul's welfare, though the children of many prayers, now greeted the appearance of a minister with tears of joy, and listened with attention to his words.

CHAPTER XVIII.

On my return from Canada, I attended a camp-meeting near Geneva—found the people encamped in the grove, but not as devotional as formerly on such occasions. However, some good was done. I returned by the head of Seneca Lake and stopped at Mr. Mathews, where I was taken sick, the fatigues of my long journey to Canada being too much for my broken down constitution. I was detained with this kind family several days. May the Lord reward them a hundred fold in this life, and in the world to come, with life everlasting. On the following Sunday I preached in the Pokeville church. Thirty-two years had rolled away since I had preached in this place. Then we had no church, but preached in a school house.

Two brothers, Caleb and Chauncy Smith, have resided in this society forty or fifty years, and have been leading members of the Church. The two years I travelled Ulysses circuit, Br. Caleb was the leading circuit steward, and Br. Chauncy was class-leader. I always called them "Caleb and Joshua," for, like them of old, they were always leading on the sacramental host of God's elect to victory. May they finish their course with joy, cross the Jordan of Death triumphantly, and enter into the rest above, where I hope to greet them, and all the good brothers and sisters of Hector.

Between Cayuga and Seneca Lakes, I still find many old friends who are now among the most able and influential of the land. Many whose homes formed a resting place for me while cultivating Immanuel's land, are still living, surrounded by children who have joined in the way their fathers trod, and many who have passed on before, have left to their children the legacy of a good example, and an unwavering trust in God. May they profit by their parents' example, and so live while on earth, as to meet with them above.

I reached home after an absence of two months; found my family comfortably well. My eldest son had been better during my absence, than for two years previous.

After a short rest, I attended a camp-meeting held at Lebanon, the home of my boyhood. Many associations connected with this part of the country, render it peculiarly interesting to me. But a few miles from this camp-ground, is the place where, more than fifty years ago, the venerable Eben White presided at a similar meeting. I was but a small boy at that time ; my father and mother were there, and I well remember the manner in which the Lord manifested himself to his people·in all his fullness, and where the slain of the Lord were in the camp. I never think of that meeting without a thrill of emotion. Many times since then, while passing that consecrated spot, have I hitched my horse, and walked over the ground, hallowed by so many associations, and as I wiped the falling tear from my eyes, I have lifted up my heart in prayer to God, asking for a more full return of those early scenes in our meetings at the present day. Here also repose the remains of my honored father, my eldest brother, his wife and only daughter, all of whom, I hope and trust, have made heaven their home.

In this neighborhood lived my first class-leader, J. Hitchcock, who, for deep piety and sound judgment, was unsurpassed by any around him. Br. H. was among the first to open his doors to Methodist preaching, and the weary itinerant always found a welcome at his table. Years have rolled by since these veterans left the Church militant for their home above. And may all their children—children of many prayers, see to it that they fail not in meeting their honored parents in heaven.

October 28th, our dear but much afflicted son, passed away from earth to join the ransomed host above. He was a child of great promise, learning easily and rapidly anything that was taught him. He was religiously inclined from his infancy, and when he first mingled with other children at common schools, he acted the part of a little missionary, so shocked was he at their wickedness, and so anxious was he to reform them. At the age of sixteen he experienced religion, and from that time forward lived a devoted life. He had many trials, temptations, and conflicts to endure, and from the peculiar nature of his disease, was debarred from many of the privileges commonly enjoyed by Christians, but his trust was in the Lord, and to him he went with all his troubles, his griefs and fears. His sufferings were great at times, seeming almost beyond physical endurance. For a few years before his death, his mental faculties much of the time were shrouded in the gloom of night, but at times the clouds would break away, and the flashing eye, and animated countenance, told that reason did but slumber. At such times much of his conversation was his love to God, and of the unutterable love that filled his soul. The Lord was merciful to him, and during his last days, suffered not the tempter to come nigh unto him. During his last moments, he was unconscious of the approach of death, but we know the Lord took him to himself, and that now he reigns in an eternity of joy.

> Rest, gentle sleeper, rest
> From all thy pain and anguish deep;
> For thou art now among the blest,
> No more by sin or grief oppressed,
> But hushed in quiet sleep.

In surveying my past life, I see many instances where I have failed to accomplish for God what I most earnestly desired to. I see I lacked that faith the ancients had, who "subdued kingdoms, wrought right-eousness, obtained promises, stopped the mouths of lions, quenched the violence of fire, escaped the edge of the sword, out of weakness were made strong, waxed valiant in fight, turned to flight the armies of the aliens." Had I been more fully imbued with the spirit of the blessed Jesus, how much more good I might have done to my dying fellow men, with whom I have been associated during the past forty-five years of my ministry. How much better I could have braved the storms and ills of life, and ascended higher in the kingdom of grace, to inhale the breezes coming fresh from the throne of God and the Lamb. My daily prayer to God is, that he will pardon all my sins, both of omission and commission, and blot them for-ever from the book of his remembrance ; that he will accept of me as his adopted son forever.

My trust is in him ; I feel that my faith rests on the atonement ; and I believe that the blood of Jesus Christ is sufficient to make a full and complete atonement for all sin, and to cleanse from all unrighteousness. Its healing power I have felt for fifty years, and I know that his precious blood avails for me at the mercy seat of God on high. I know I have entrance into the holy of holies by faith and humble prayer, and I can now say, "One thing have I desired of the Lord, and that will I seek after, that I may dwell in the house of the Lord all the days of my life, to behold the beauty of the Lord, and to enquire in his temple. In the time of trouble he shall hide me in his pavilion : in the secret of his tabernacle shall he hide me ; he shall set me upon a rock. And now shall my head be lifted up above mine enemies round about me : therefore will I offer in his tabernacle sacrifices of joy : I will sing, yea, I will sing praises unto the Lord. For I know the law of the Lord is perfect, converting the soul : the testimony of the Lord is sure, making wise the simple. The statutes of the Lord are right, rejoicing the heart. The commandment of the Lord is pure, enlightening the eyes. The fear of the Lord is clean, enduring forever : the judgments of the Lord are true, and righteous altogether. More to be desired are they than gold : yea, than much fine gold ; sweeter also than honey, and the honey-comb. Moreover, by them is thy servant warned : and in keeping of them is great reward."

And now, dear reader, I must close. In writing these incidents of my life, I have selected such as I thought were most marked with the special providence God, in showing how the Lord has blessed my feeble labors in trying to bring souls to Christ. I cannot expect to stay many years more with the Church militant, for already the frosts of sixty-five winters have passed over my head, and my weather-beaten bark is nearing the heavenly port. After braving a few more of the storms and ills of this life, if I hold on to the Holy Bible as my compass and chart, with an undying grasp, and keep Christ Jesus at the helm, amid the roaring tempest and the foaming billows as they roll darkly over me, I shall escape the rocks and quick-sands, and safely moor my bark in the harbor above, for my anchor already is dropped within the vail, and the light of the celestial city breaks in upon my vision. Until my Lord says, "come," I will stay on board the old ship Zion, for she is sure of the harbor, and I soon shall join in the song of the ransomed, 'mid the bright mansions where immortal friendship blooms in perfection. In the following beautiful lines, from one of our poets, the reader has the language of my heart :

"I love thy kingdom, Lord,
  The house of thine abode,
The Church our blessed Redeemer saved,
  With his own precious blood.

"I love thy Church, O God!
  Her walls before thee stand,
Dear as the apple of thine eye,
  And graven on thy hand.

"For her my tears shall fall;
  For her my prayers ascend;
To her my toils and cares be given,
  Till toils and cares shall end.

"Beyond my highest joy,
  I prize her heavenly ways;
Her sweet communion, solemn vows,
  Her hymns of love and praise.

"Sure as thy truth shall last,
  To Zion shall be given,
The brighter glories earth can yield,
  And brighter bliss of heaven."

9 783337 123505